# A LEGATE'S PLEDGE

## ROMAN HEARTS SERIES BOOK THREE

TANYA BIRD

*For Bec*

*Let no one escape sheer destruction, no one our hands, not even the babe in the womb of the mother, if it be male; let it nevertheless not escape sheer destruction.*

*- Cassius Dio*

# CHAPTER 1

October 210 AD

They rose from the earth and fell from the trees. Shadows and ghosts—yet he knew they could bleed. There were not just men but also women, painted and fierce, as skilled as their counterparts. There were no open plains with neat rows of soldiers. No structure or order. Only an invisible enemy hidden by jagged rocks and low-hanging clouds.

Nerva Papias had never killed a woman. The mere thought of driving his sword through a delicate female ribcage made his stomach turn. He could not help but picture his sisters when he conjured the image. Now he was leading the third Britannia legion through the highlands of Caledonia with orders to kill all in their path. Severus was no longer interested in taking prisoners.

Marcus Furnia rode at his side, eyes on the trees either side of them. 'What do you think?' The tribune's voice was haunting amid the shuffle of feet.

The fog was as thick as the air was thin, and the rising sun cast eerie light around them. Nerva looked up at the branches reaching out above. Where were all the birds? 'It is too quiet. Still no word from the scouts we sent ahead?'

'Not yet.'

Nerva looked over his shoulder. 'Check on the rear, would you?'

Marcus swung his horse and cantered off.

The thick terrain north of Antonine's Wall forced them to travel in single file, which meant the tribes hunting them could pick them off one at a time. Another disadvantage. The men were already tiring, and they had not even reached Longforgan yet. If Nerva had learned anything over the previous two years, it was that their enemy were not the simple-minded barbarians that Romans would have everyone believe.

His gaze swept the branches overhead, the muscles in his body growing rigid. He could feel them. Every shadow was beginning to look like a face.

Paulus Cordius trotted up beside him, his horse falling into step with Nerva's. 'Where is Furnia scurrying off to?'

His second in command was not a fan of the lower-ranked tribune, probably because Nerva preferred Marcus's company—far less ego to manage, and he carried out orders without questioning everything.

'What do you hear, Commander?' Nerva asked.

Paulus listened a moment. 'I do not hear a thing.'

Nerva nodded. 'Exactly.' A frog croaked, the sound too loud. His horse sidestepped. 'I do not like this gully. It puts us at a disadvantage. We should move to higher ground.'

'The forest is too dense. You can barely squeeze a shield between two trunks.' Paulus glanced up at the steep hill to his left. 'Better we pick up speed.'

Nerva did not mind input from his men, but Paulus made it a habit to disagree with everything that came out of his mouth. 'The men will tire too quickly.' He was about to give the order when the thick trunk of a rowan tree appeared through the mist, blocking their path. 'Halt.' He raised his hand.

'Halt,' repeated the centurion behind them.

The order echoed down the line. Feet stilled, eyes darting nervously—with good reason. Nerva was aware of the change in his heart rate, and he prayed the feeling in his gut was wrong. 'Check the base of the trunk,' he ordered Paulus.

The commander frowned at him. 'You want *me* to check it?'

*Here we go*. The man was above every order Nerva gave him. 'I want to know if its roots are intact or if it has been cut.'

Paulus's jaw ticked, but then he nodded. 'Very well.' He dug his heels into the side of his mare and trotted away, dissolving into the light.

The sound of a horse approaching at a gallop made Nerva turn. He could hear the rider shouting something but could not make out the words. The centurion closest to him glanced in his direction, his bottom lip clamped between his teeth. The horse emerged from the fog.

'It's a trap!' Marcus shouted.

Nerva immediately swung his gelding around. 'Horses to the rear!'

'Form ranks!' the centurion shouted, his men scurrying into rows facing east and west.

The sound of battle rang out along the gully. Somewhere in the distance, men were already fighting. Paulus returned to the group then, his sword already drawn.

'They have caged us in.' The soldiers parted to let him through. 'The tree was cut.'

'Easy now,' called the centurion to his men as he paced behind them. 'Hold the line.'

Nerva drew his own sword, every hair on his body standing on end. A horn sounded, long and deep. The noise shifted the air, disorienting them. Soldiers looked to the low-hanging branches above, then to the horizon.

'Shields!' Nerva shouted. Shields hit the ground in a unified thud, forming a protective wall. He glanced at Marcus, whose horse was stirring, absorbing the fear of the men.

The centurion continued to pace, a deep scowl etched into his brow. Everything was still for a moment. There was not even a breeze to shift the leaves. Nerva tightened his grip on his sword, his gaze sweeping the hill, pausing at every tree and rock. The ground began to rumble, a low vibration growing louder. It travelled up the legs of his horse, through the saddle, until it hummed through his body.

'Hold that line!' the centurion shouted, his tone growing urgent.

Nerva's eyes widened when he spotted a giant rock the size of a horse rolling down the hill towards them. 'Incoming!' There was no way the men could hold the line against a rock that size. 'Split your men,' he called to the centurion. 'Let it through.'

'Let it through!' the centurion shouted.

The men separated. Nerva turned to see another boulder coming behind them. He could hear more farther along and cursed knowing that the other cohorts would try to hold the line, because they were soldiers of Rome and had been trained not to run from stones. The distant sound of rock smashing through shields was accompanied by the screams of the men holding them. Nerva watched one roll past his horse, climb halfway up the hill on the other side, and then come back at them. The moment it stopped rolling, the centurion shouted, 'Form ranks—'

Before the line closed, an arrow pierced his neck.

Nerva knew there was no such thing as one arrow. A moment later they were raining from the sky. He saw them then, the Maeatae, appearing from thin air. No armour, helmets, or fancy crests. Only flesh and muscle covered in little more than fur and leather. Their skin was painted the colours of the mountains they possessed, enabling them to blend in with their surroundings. They descended the hill on foot, swords and axes in hand, impossibly fast. No fear or hesitation. Not only could they fight, Nerva knew from experience that they could *win*.

Steel screeched and shields clashed with axes. Their enemy broke through the line within minutes, seeping through the gaps, slaying soldiers left and right. A large man covered in scars advanced towards Nerva. A legate was the ultimate prize in the game of war. Soldiers were upon him before he had a chance to move. Another warrior came at Nerva, teeth bared. The legate fought atop his horse, eventually driving his sword through the man's chest. Just as he withdrew his weapon, someone dropped from the branches above him, knocking him off his horse. The two of them landed with a thud on the ground.

Nerva struggled to draw breath as he got quickly to his feet, sword raised. His weapon fell a few inches when he saw a young woman with liquid gold eyes blazing up at him. A tangled mess of chestnut hair covered one side of her face. She sprang to her feet, weapon pointed at him. He had always known the time would come when he would be forced to fight a woman, to *kill* a woman. Lifting his sword, he blocked her strike and shoved her back.

The campaign was supposed to be finished. The year before, he had believed the war over. They had retreated, withdrawing south to Eboracum before the onset of winter.

Then came the revolt.

'Finish them off,' Severus had said, his health and pride in tatters. 'Kill them all.'

Those words repeated in Nerva's mind as he stared at the woman with no idea how to proceed. She must have sensed his hesitation, because for a moment she just stared back at him. His gaze fell to the spray of blood across her collarbone and shoulder. She had already killed someone. No, not someone—one of *his* men. She growled, a noise that reminded him of when he used to spar with Mila. His sister too had growled, always towards the end of their match when her frustration had boiled over.

The warrior came at him with her sword. He blocked it again but did not strike back. She was surprisingly strong given her size, but his build was an advantage. When she came at him again, he shoved her back harder this time, willing her to turn and run. He would not give chase. But she did not run; she responded with a foot to his chest, sending him crashing back into his horse. He was forced to roll beneath the animal to avoid the weapon chasing him. She was good, but that was not the only reason he preferred the horse between them. His insides were in knots at the thought of what was to come. He began doubting his ability to see it through. It seemed a shame to break a perfect track record by killing her during his final campaign.

And it *was* his final campaign.

A feeling made Nerva glance over his shoulder, and there he found a bearded warrior ready to take his head off with an axe. He ducked and slashed the man's leg. The warrior collapsed to the ground, holding in a scream. Nerva did not have time to stand there watching him bleed out. He cut his throat and turned back just as the woman reached him. The sword was a hand's width from his neck when he caught her arm.

'Drop it,' he said in Brittonic.

Most of the tribes understood the common language. Two years of negotiations and interrogations had forced him to learn how to communicate with their enemy.

Her eyes widened slightly before narrowing on him once more. 'You first.'

She brought her knee up, but he was ready for that, lifting his leg just in time to protect his vulnerable area. 'Drop it,' he repeated, his grip on her tightening.

She tried to pull free, and the moment she realised she was outmuscled, she brought her face closer to his. 'So brave in your armour.'

Now it was his turn to be surprised—she had spoken Latin. He did not let it show on his face though. 'Very clever. Now drop the sword.' He twisted her arm until it fell from her hand.

A body slammed into his back, knocking them both to the ground. He let go of her arm, fearing it would snap in his firm grasp. She rolled out of his reach. If he stood a chance at fighting off the bare-chested man sprawled on top of him, he would need two hands anyway. But the man was not fighting—or moving, for that matter. When Nerva turned his head, he found a spear lodged in the warrior's neck. With a great heave, he pushed the dead man off. Sword still in hand, Nerva got to his feet, turning in circles, ready for her. But she was not there. Nor was his horse.

*Shit.*

A horn sounded, a deep moan cutting through the frosty air. Nerva blinked and looked around, unable to see farther than ten feet in any direction in that moment, only flashes of painted skin and armour. Then everything fell still, the only sound the groans of dying men. Walking forwards, his knuckles white around the hilt of his sword, he found only bloodied and dazed soldiers staggering in circles.

Their enemy was gone.

## CHAPTER 2

Brei stood with her sister and nephew, staring at the tall horse. She marvelled at the gelding's smooth coat and elaborate saddle. When she stepped forwards to rub the silky mane, the horse snorted and sidestepped.

'Oh, the Roman horse hates you,' Alane said, holding her eager son by the shoulders. 'What a surprise.'

'I can't believe you *stole* the general's horse,' Drust said.

Brei stepped back in line with them. 'I needed a fast exit.' She let out a noisy breath and glanced behind them to the huts where the wounded were being tended to.

'Does Father know you went after the general?' Alane asked, brushing her fair hair back from her face.

'If he doesn't, the horse might clue him in.'

Seisyll had remained behind after the battle to ensure they were not followed. He would be mad that she disobeyed him. As one of the chief's daughters, she was supposed to set an example.

'Can I ride him?' Drust asked, looking up at her with a hopeful expression.

She ruffled his hair. 'Absolutely not, but you can *lead* him to the stream for a drink.'

'And then ride him?'

Alane patted the boy's shoulder. 'Off you go.'

Drust stepped up to the gelding and took hold of the reins. The horse's front feet lifted off the ground for a moment. 'It's all right. I won't hurt you.'

Brei smiled to herself. 'Unfortunately, he doesn't speak our language yet.' At seven her nephew was already as fearless as the warriors who mentored him.

The women watched as the horse was led away. A gritted-teeth cry drifted down to them from one of the huts, and they both turned to look.

'I should go check on Reagan,' Alane said. Her husband had been injured during the battle, and a healer was cauterising his arm wound.

Brei turned back to the horse. Lavena had run down from the huts to join Drust. The two had been born on the same day and become fast friends since they took their first steps together. The events of the previous few days were playing in Brei's head as she watched the two of them conspiring.

Alane leaned in to her sister's ear. 'I can almost hear you thinking.'

Brei glanced sideways at her sister. 'Sorry, what?'

Alane's gaze went to the horse, then returned to Brei. 'It was ambitious going after the general. You were supposed to cover the men from the trees.'

'I ran out of arrows.'

Alane rolled her eyes. 'You're lucky he didn't kill you.'

'He could have.'

Her sister frowned. 'What do you mean?'

'The general.' Brei stretched her neck from side to side, trying to loosen the muscles. 'I think he could've if he wanted to.'

Alane's brow relaxed. 'Oh, please. A Roman with a beating heart is nothing more than a myth. More likely you were a stronger fighter and he knew it.'

'He told me to drop my sword.'

'So he could kill you.'

Brei shook her head. 'He didn't need me to drop my sword for that.'

'Well, you know what they do to the women they capture. He probably would've had his way with you first, *then* killed you.'

Brei cast a doubtful glance. 'Yes, I'm sure that was top of his mind as his men were crushed by rocks around him.' Things had been different since the revolt. The Romans no longer seemed interested in taking prisoners. They were killing all the Caledonii and Maeatae tribes they came across—even children.

'I'm surprised you left before killing *him*,' Alane said. 'You've been waiting for the opportunity ever since…'

Not an easy sentence to finish. 'I dropped my sword.'

Her sister looked down at the dagger strapped to Brei's thigh. 'But not your knife.' Before Brei could reply, Drust returned with the gelding. Alane went to speak again, but something caught her attention, and she reached for Drust's arm instead. 'Time to go.'

'But I want to stay with the horse,' Drust whined.

Alane began dragging him, looking past Brei again as she backed away. 'Later.'

A feeling of dread settled in Brei's stomach. 'Father's walking up behind me, isn't he?'

Alane's answer came in the form of a sympathetic look before she fled to safety with her child.

'I'll remember this,' Brei called after her. She turned then to watch her father striding across the grass towards her. He was still covered in enemy blood, and she wondered if he had left it there specifically for their conversation.

'You were supposed to cover us from the trees,' Seisyll said before he had even reached her.

His expression made her take a small step back. Annoyed at appearing intimidated, she tried to make herself a little taller while acutely aware of the tall shadow he cast over her. 'I ran out of arrows, and I saw an opportunity.'

'To *die?*'

She swallowed. 'To kill the *legatus legionis*.'

He crossed his arms and they grew in size. 'And did you?'

She looked away. 'No, but... at least he's on foot now.'

Seisyll turned to the gelding tethered a few feet away. 'Two hundred Maeatae dead and another hundred wounded, and this is what you're proud of?'

Her stomach fell. 'Two hundred dead?'

Seisyll's expression did not change. 'That number might've been less if you'd done as you were told and covered us from the trees.'

She bit down on her lip. 'How many Roman soldiers dead?'

'Around four hundred or so.'

While that might have seemed like an impressive number, she knew that one legion was made up of around five thousand men. The Maeatae did not have the endless resources their enemy seemed to have. 'That proves we're better fighters.'

'That proves no such thing. Anyway, it won't count for much when our people are all gone.'

She drew a breath. 'You're always saying that to kill an adder, you should cut off its head.'

His expression softened a little. 'And we have enough men for that. You're a good fighter, but you lack the experience and strength to go up against soldiers who've been fighting most of their lives.'

She lifted her chin. 'But not the skill.' Her eyes went to the huts once more. 'I'm a better fighter than most of the men up there and you know it.'

'So was your mother.'

That silenced her for a moment. 'Well, I don't recall her hiding up trees.'

'You weren't hiding. You had a job.'

'I had an opportunity.'

He sighed and placed an enormous hand on her shoulder. 'How will our people ever come back from this if all the fertile women are dead?'

Had it really come to that? 'Alane could have a few more on my behalf.'

Seisyll could not stop the laugh that erupted from him. 'Put that useless horse to pasture and come help the healers with their work.' He looked over his shoulder. 'There are more wounds than hands to mend them, and I'm leaving in the morning.'

'Let someone else track the legion's progress. You're exhausted.'

He shook his head and brought a hand up to touch the cut above his eye. Another battle marked on him. 'I'm not following them. I'm going east.'

Brei swallowed. There had been talk of Roman ships anchored offshore. They were being caged in. 'I'll come with you.'

'No.'

'You cannot fight an entire fleet with a handful of men.'

He rubbed at his beard, looking far more tired with every passing moment. 'And I cannot leave the village unprotected.' He looked past her to where their sheep were grazing. 'I want you and Alane to take half the flock northwest. Leave them somewhere they'll be easily found.'

'By who?'

'The soldiers.'

She understood then. There were not enough of them to fight every threat. Putting food in their path might prevent them from venturing off to go looking for it. 'You want me to move some sheep?'

'Get ahead of the legion, and then get out.' He brushed a finger under her chin and turned away.

Brei watched him leave before walking over to the gelding. If she had managed to kill the legate, that conversation would have gone very differently. She recalled the thrill of knocking him from his horse, then the moment he had laid eyes on her for the first time. His hard-set face had softened, and his sword had wavered. She was no fool. He had let her live—and she had let the fact trip her.

Taking hold of the gelding's bridle, she looked him in the eye. 'Next time, I'll save one arrow just for him. If he doesn't want to fight me up close, he can die from afar.' The horse remained wary as she rubbed his muzzle before taking the reins. 'Come. You better not be afraid of sheep.'

CHAPTER 3

Seven hundred and forty-six. That was the number of men he had lost in one attack. The part that hit Nerva the hardest was that they had been out-slaughtered four to one. Their enemy was dictating the terms of the fight. Their land, their rules, apparently.

The legion had made it to Longforgan without further incident, making camp in the dark and spending the evening tallying their losses. The next morning, they rose early and prepared to start again.

'The men are ready to depart,' Marcus said, striding alongside Nerva.

'Good.' Nerva looked around at the rows of men, packs loaded on their backs awaiting marching orders. 'I want some of the cavalry to ride ahead.'

'I sent twenty men ahead of us this morning. They reported back just a short while ago.'

Nerva stopped walking and turned to his friend with a concerned look. Marcus stopped also, a wry smile on his face.

'If it was bad news, I would've said something sooner.'

Nerva crossed his arms. 'You understand my reaction.

We have not had much good news thus far. What did they find?'

'Sheep.'

Nerva's eyebrows rose. 'Sheep?'

'Fifty head or so.'

Nerva looked back at his men as he thought. 'And no village in the vicinity?'

'Not unless it's underground.'

Nerva resumed walking. 'Would not put it past them. Do you not find it odd?'

'Of course I do.'

'And it is not the first time.'

Marcus looked across at him. 'You think they're leaving breadcrumbs?'

'Yes.' Nerva came to a stop in front of his horse—his *new* horse. 'They are trying to keep us on route.'

'So they can lay traps?'

Nerva mounted and gathered the reins, then waited for Marcus to do the same. 'Maybe. Or perhaps to keep us away from their villages.'

'So, we change route.'

Nerva thought for a moment. 'Or we stay on route, keep them happy, then send some men on a detour.' He kicked his horse into a trot. 'Let us take a look at these sheep.'

The flock was five miles north-east of the camp, grazing out in the open. Nerva sent soldiers in all directions to ensure no one was waiting for them; then, once he had established the area was safe, he gave the instruction for the flock to be slaughtered for food. Dismounting, he bent and studied the hoof prints in the grass, running a finger over them before looking in the direction they trailed off.

Paulus Cordius rode up with his usual scowl and stopped his horse next to Nerva's. 'Horses?'

'Looks that way.'

'Unusual.' The commander looked around. 'They usually travel on foot so we cannot track them.'

Nerva rose. 'Perhaps they needed to get in and out fast.'

Marcus rode up, and Paulus stiffened in the saddle as he approached.

'What is it?' Marcus asked, pulling up his horse and jumping down to join Nerva.

'You are the horse breeder,' Paulus said. 'What does it look like?'

Nerva looked up at the commander, then down at the ground. While Marcus did not like Paulus, he was outranked by the man and always behaved accordingly.

'Well, one is a highlander pony, the other is not.'

Paulus's smug expression fell just a little. 'Are you seriously trying to pretend you can tell that from a hoof print?'

'Yes.' Marcus looked up at him.

Nerva kept his eyes on the ground so Paulus would not see how much he was enjoying the moment.

'Different weight, size, but more obviously, different *gait*.'

Paulus looked away. 'So what? Perhaps they were moving at different speeds.'

'It's possible.'

Nerva squinted across at him. 'Is it also possible that it is one of ours?' If it was *his*, even better. Not only did he want his gelding back, he wanted to teach the woman who stole him a lesson.

Paulus's gaze was steady on him. 'Exactly how many soldiers had their horses stolen by women during yesterday's battle?'

'Watch yourself,' Nerva replied, staring at him until he looked away. The one time Nerva had ordered Paulus be disciplined for insubordination, Caracalla had come to the commander's aid. The fact that the two had been friends since childhood made him somewhat untouchable. 'I am going to take one century east, see where these lead.'

Paulus all but rolled his eyes. 'That is not a lot of men if you run into trouble.'

Nerva mounted his horse once more. 'I do not want to draw attention. I trust you can lead the rest of the men in my absence.'

Paulus gave a firm nod. 'Of course.'

'Good. Furnia, you are with me. Gather the men we need.'

Paulus levelled Marcus with a look before swinging his horse around and riding off.

'I think you hurt his feelings,' Marcus said as he mounted.

Nerva looked after the commander. 'He has no interest in accompanying me anywhere. The man cannot wait for me to die so that he can replace me. He will be thrilled to have me out of the way for the day.'

'I'd like to disagree, but I'm afraid you're right. Best watch your back.'

Nerva's mouth lifted slightly. 'That is what I have you for.'

Soon after, the men gathered eighty soldiers and marched east. The tracks led them back into the forest, where they rode beneath alder and willow trees, silent and watchful. A few hours later, they came across a stream, and the tracks disappeared into the water.

Nerva raised a hand as he came to a stop.

'Halt,' called the centurion behind him. The men stopped marching.

'Can't see where they left the stream,' Marcus said, looking around the bank on the other side. He glanced both ways. 'Which way?'

Nerva walked his mare into the water and looked both ways. He should not have been surprised that their enemy had found a way to make horses disappear. 'Upstream. If their village was south, I doubt they would have gone to all that effort.' He looked back in the direction they had come. 'How fresh would you say those tracks are?'

'Overnight. I don't think we missed them by much.'

Nerva nodded, then walked his horse up onto the bank on the other side. 'I am going to ride ahead and see if I pick up their tracks. You continue with the men and meet me farther up.'

'You're going alone?'

'They will hear a group of us a mile away.'

Marcus glanced about. 'Well, don't get too far ahead. If you run into trouble, we need to be able to hear your dying screams.'

Nerva smiled to himself and kicked his horse into a slow canter.

CHAPTER 4

The gelding was fast, and Brei pushed him faster still, ducking beneath branches as she wove between thick alder trunks. The wind dried the smile on her face. The horse might not have been as sure-footed as their highland ponies, but he was a lot more fun.

'Slow down!' Alane whispered behind her. 'We're supposed to stay together and not attract attention. In case you've forgotten, we're at war—and a long way from home.'

Brei slowed the gelding to a walk. 'That's why we have bows.'

Alane laughed. 'One bow and a handful of arrows each. Is that supposed to make me feel better?'

'You'd be surprised what I can do with a handful of arrows.'

Alane cast a disapproving glance at Brei as she came up beside her. 'We should let the horses drink at the stream before we leave it behind. It will be their last chance for some time.'

They had travelled south to cover their tracks before leaving the water and heading north beneath the cover of the trees. It was only a precaution. The Romans would be busily slaughtering their fat sheep and dreaming up dinner recipes before moving on.

Brei listened to the calls of dippers and wagtails in the trees around them. 'We should hunt on our way home now that half our flock is gone.'

Alane looked around. 'If there's anything left to hunt. By the time the Romans leave, these mountains will be nothing but barren hills.' She swung her horse in the direction of the stream. 'If they leave at all.'

Brei looked across at her sister. 'They won't have a choice. We'll make them leave.'

The women fell silent, listening for the sound of running water. A gentle decline led down to the small stream they had been following. It held water most of the year. When it came into sight, Brei stopped her horse and held her hand up. Alane pulled up her mare and looked about. There were no birds singing anymore. She looked to Brei as though waiting for an explanation, but all she had to offer was a feeling, a feeling that had been right plenty of times in the past.

The sound of a horse approaching made them both turn. Brei signalled to her sister to take cover, and they moved behind the trees, holding their breath as a soldier cantered by. If the man had bothered checking his surroundings, he might have spotted the horses, but he was too busy searching for hoof prints he would never find.

'I thought you said they wouldn't follow us,' Alane whispered once he had passed.

Brei stared after him. 'It's just one man, and he's not tracking us because Romans have no idea how to track properly.'

'Forget the water. Let's go.'

Brei shook her head. 'No, we should follow him.'

'Why?'

'To make sure he leaves.' She pushed her horse into a trot.

'Are you *crazy*? We need to go before he sees us.'

Brei did not slow down. 'Father left me in charge, and we're going to follow him.'

Alane made an exasperated noise before pushing her horse forwards.

The women trailed after him at a safe distance, until the soldier came to a stop. He removed his helmet and looked around with a confused and frustrated expression. Brei could not hear his thoughts, but she recognised defeat on his face.

'*Now* can we go?' Alane whispered, her voice so quiet it barely carried the three feet between them.

Brei narrowed her eyes on the man. There was something familiar about him that made all the hairs on her body stand on end. When he looked in their direction, her breath caught.

'What?' Alane asked.

Brei blinked. 'It's the general.'

'*The* general?'

The man dismounted, laid down his shield, and bent to scoop up some water with his hands. He drank, then splashed some over his face. Brei took in his neatly cut hair and clean-shaven face, his polished armour and his leather boots where woollen socks poked out of the top. Her gaze drifted to the crested helmet tucked under his arm. It was him all right.

'What's he doing out here alone?' Alane whispered.

Brei had been wondering the same thing, but she was not going to let an opportunity slip through her fingers while she pondered the matter. 'Stay here,' she whispered, pushing her horse into a walk.

Alane shook her head, eyes pleading. 'Don't you dare.'

Brei was already reaching for her bow. An unguarded

legate was an opportunity that would never come again. She could not just hide in the trees while he drank and washed in water belonging to her people. Kill him now or on the battlefield later.

'Brei' came a final plea from her sister.

The running water made enough noise to prevent them from being heard. The Maeatae could move soundlessly through the forest if they needed to, something the Romans knew nothing about. Their approach could be heard a mile away.

Drawing an arrow, Brei loaded her bow and took aim. Just as the string went taut, his head snapped up and he looked straight at her. The string slackened in her hand. His gaze fell to the horse she sat on, and his jaw tightened. She pulled the string tight once more and let go. Too late. He dropped to the ground, flattening himself against the mud. The arrow passed over the water, lodging in a tree on the other side of the stream. As she reached for another, he snatched up a shield and leapt to his feet. He ran *towards* her instead of away. She might not have been able to penetrate his shield, but she would have no problem taking out one of his knees.

As she took aim, he called out in Brittonic, 'Give me the horse, and I will let you live.'

She stilled once more. Who on earth was he talking to? Surely not her. She released the second arrow just as he dropped his shield to the ground, predicting her target. He cursed in Latin and continued forwards while pulling a dagger from a sheath belted to his waist. He tossed it up in the air and caught it by the blade, preparing to throw it. 'My aim is much better than yours. One way or another, I am leaving with my horse.'

She shot the arrow at his head, but he raised his shield in time. He stopped running then, lowering it a few inches to look at her. Her bow was reloaded and aimed at him once more. His dagger was still in hand.

'Give me the horse and your weapons, and I will let you walk away.'

She laughed. 'How about I keep the horse and kill you?'

Neither of them moved.

'What is it you Romans say?' Brei said, keeping a trained eye on the dagger. 'The spoils of war are for the victor.'

His shield fell a little. 'Well, the war is not over yet.'

'And yet I'm the one seated on your horse.'

Something resembling amusement flashed in his eyes. 'Only once I am dead can you lay claim to him.' He shifted slightly to the right, as though trying to see something, then frowned. 'Where is my saddle?'

Brei released another arrow. It struck the ground beside his foot. He surprised her by not moving a muscle, instead returning his dagger to its sheath. She reloaded her bow and aimed it at his face. Their encounter was not a friendly one.

'I do not want to kill you,' he said, 'so what am I supposed to do here?'

'You had no problem killing my mother.' The moment the words left her mouth, she wished she could snatch them back.

Pity flashed on his face, but before he had a chance to speak, Alane emerged from behind a tree, aiming another arrow at him. She was not a warrior in any sense of the word, but she could kill to protect her family if it were necessary.

The man turned his head to look at her. 'You really are like ghosts.'

'Better ghosts than monsters,' Brei replied.

The legate's gaze returned to her, and he let out a tired breath. 'You need to go before my men show up.'

Did he think her stupid? 'I let you live once. I won't make that mistake again.' She could have sworn she saw amusement flash in his eyes.

'You let *me* live?'

The snap of a stick breaking underfoot made her head whip around. At least a dozen Roman soldiers stood in a line behind her, swords drawn. She spun back to look at the legate just as her sister let an arrow fly. He ducked left and it passed over his right shoulder before skirting along the forest floor.

'Release another arrow and you will both die,' he said, his tone firm but calm.

If they were going to die, then Brei was taking him down first, and his men could watch. But when she took aim, she felt a familiar hesitation.

'What are your orders?' called one of the soldiers.

Her hands grew damp as she waited for his reply.

He looked straight at her. 'These women are going to drop their weapons on the ground, dismount, and walk calmly away.'

The soldier cleared his throat. 'But Caracalla's orders—'

'Stand down.' The legate's tone was firmer this time.

She could tell from his expression that he did not want their deaths on his hands.

Looking across at her sister, she noticed a sheen of sweat on her face. Alane knew they could not win this fight. If Brei had been alone, she might have fought anyway, but her nephew was at home waiting for his mother to return with dinner. Turning back to the legate, she asked, 'How do I know you won't kill us both the moment I drop this bow?'

He blinked. 'You do not.'

The only sound was a low whinny. Slowly, she lowered her bow, never taking her eyes from the man who was asking so much of her. She hesitated before dropping it onto the ground, along with her quiver of arrows.

'And the dagger,' he said.

He knew he was not the only one with hidden weapons. Reluctantly, she unsheathed her dagger and dropped it on the ground also. She felt completely exposed.

'Good,' the legate said. 'Now dismount and tell your companion to do the same.'

'That horse is *ours*,' Brei said, anger rising.

'Not anymore.'

She could have sworn his lips twitched. 'Do as he says,' she called to her sister before swinging her leg over the gelding's rump and dropping down.

Only once they were both on the ground did he approach her. She stiffened as he drew near, watching as he collected the weapons. 'Arms up,' he said when he straightened.

Her eyebrows came together. 'What?'

'You heard me. Arms up.'

She looked over her shoulder at the soldiers who had not moved, then lifted her arms. He stepped up and began patting her down.

'What are you doing?' she asked, flinching every time one of his hands clapped on her.

He went all the way down to her feet before rising. 'Checking you do not have another bow hidden beneath all that fur. Off you go.'

She remained where she was, scowling at him. 'You're really just going to let us walk away?'

'This time. If we meet again, I will not be so nice.'

She regarded him a moment. 'I would've shot you in the back, you know.'

His expression did not change. 'I know.'

'Brei,' Alane called.

She looked at her sister, who was getting more and

more anxious. The legate turned away and went to his horse. The gelding let out another low whinny and sniffed him in greeting. He patted the gelding's neck, his hand coming to rest upon a braided section of mane.

'Did you do this?' he asked, pointing to it.

She did not reply, instead gesturing for her sister to come to her. Alane walked nervously towards them.

'Enjoy the walk,' the legate said, his eyes practically laughing at her.

Brei crossed her arms. 'If you think you're going to follow us, you'll be most disappointed.'

His grey eyes shone at her. 'You cannot follow a ghost.'

Brei looked again at the other men, who watched them with suspicion. She gestured for her sister to go ahead of her, and she did something she could never have imagined doing: she turned her back to him, held her breath, and headed in the opposite direction of their village.

'Why did he let us go?' Alane whispered when they were some distance from the men. Her hands were still trembling at her sides.

Brei snuck a look over her shoulder, but no one was there. 'Perhaps there's such a thing as a Roman with a beating heart after all.'

CHAPTER 5

It had been four weeks since they passed through Antonine's Wall. Four weeks of damp, freezing temperatures, foot rot, and various illnesses that ravaged the camp.

Four weeks of mindless killing.

Caracalla was leading his army north-east along the Highland Boundary Fault. If all went well, they would meet at Balmakewan, sealing off the Midland Valley.

He could not remember the last time he felt warm. At least he had his horse back, even if the circumstances had caused some problems for him. He should never have let the two women leave, especially not the warrior who would have killed him without a second thought, but he needed to be able to sleep at night in order to survive. *Brei*, the other woman had called her. Now he just had to pray he would never see her again.

'Halt,' he said, pulling back on the reins. He raised a hand, and the men marching behind him stopped also. Marcus rode down the wet slope towards him, a group of soldiers following behind him. The horses' hocks dragged through the mud as they struggled to keep upright, despite there being no rain that day.

'What did you find?' Nerva asked as the tribune pulled up his horse. The others came to a stop behind him.

'A village three miles east of here. Small, but there are horses and other livestock. Fairly quiet. Given the location, I suspect their warriors are busy elsewhere.'

'They cannot be everywhere at once.'

'Lucky for us.' Marcus glanced over his shoulder at Paulus, who was approaching. 'What do you want to do?'

He wanted to pretend the village did not exist, but Severus's words rang in his mind. *No man left alive.* His stomach turned to stone. 'Are there children?' There were always children, but he asked the question anyway.

A nod from Marcus, whose dismal expression mirrored his own. Before he could say anything further, Paulus reached them, practically barging between them.

'What did you find?'

No one spoke for a moment. It was Nerva's decision as to whether he shared the discovery with the commander. If he did, they would raid the village. While he did not think much of the commander, he had to respect his commitment to the campaign—a commitment he himself lacked at that point in time. He also had to factor in his men. They needed to be fed, and there was not enough wildlife in the forest to sustain an army that size. They needed the grain and could do with the horses.

'A small village on the other side of the hill,' Nerva said finally. 'We will lose half a day if we go there.'

'The men will just have to move faster.'

Nerva stared at him. 'They need to be able to fight.'

Paulus swung his horse around. 'Then I will take one cohort and meet you in Kirkbuddo.'

Nerva drew a breath. 'That is not your decision to make, Commander.'

Paulus looked genuinely taken aback. 'We cannot just stroll by.'

He was right, of course, which only worsened Nerva's mood. 'Two centuries.' The words seemed to stick in his throat. He looked at Marcus. 'Good fighters.' The tribune nodded, swung his horse, and left at a canter. Nerva turned back to Paulus. 'One goes in. Furnia will take the other south and wait at the foot of the hill in case any try to escape.'

A nod from Paulus. 'We will meet you in Kirkbuddo?'

There was no need for him to go, but he felt a strange need to witness the atrocities he was ordering. At least that way he would never forget what Rome's leaders were capable of. 'No. I am coming with you.'

∽

NERVA WALKED his horse through the village, his gaze landing on a woman lying dead on the ground. His insides clenched. That was what the Roman army had become, what he represented, men who killed women in front of their children.

Dismounting, he looked around at the dead, some not even armed. The few men protecting them had never stood a chance against his highly trained soldiers. Now those men were lining up the survivors. What was he supposed to do with a handful of women and children who had tried to flee and been caught by Paulus? The eager commander was preparing for their execution.

Shouting from a nearby hut made Nerva turn. He could hear one soldier swearing, and another sounded as though he were laughing. As he moved towards the hut, something caught his eye. He stopped, his eyes meeting those of a young girl hiding behind a pile of tools. They stared at one another for a moment, and he saw that she was shaking.

He brought a finger to his lips before continuing on his way.

'What is going on here?' he asked, stepping inside.

Two soldiers snapped to attention. One was bleeding from the nose.

'This one is very feisty, sir,' the bloodied one said.

The other soldier stifled a laugh.

It took a moment for Nerva's eyes to adjust to the dark space, but then he spotted her across the dying fire in the middle of the hut. It was the woman from the river. *Brei*. He let out a tired breath.

'You,' she hissed, those golden eyes of hers like two burning suns. 'I should've killed you when I had the chance.'

'When did you have the chance?'

Her eyes narrowed on him. 'You followed us.' She snatched up a small clay pot and hurled it at his head so hard and fast he barely had time to raise his weapon. The pot burst apart on impact, sending shards flying in all directions.

'Calm down.'

'*Calm down*? You dare come to my village, slaughter my people, and then tell me to calm down.' She clutched a sword in one hand while the other felt around for things to throw.

When he took a step forwards, he saw one of his men lying dead at her feet with a dagger protruding from one eye. 'I gather that is your handiwork?'

The other men shuffled forwards to look, and all laughter ceased. Brei's answer came in the form of a hard wooden object. It struck Nerva's head, and he winced. He watched as a large spoon rattled to a stop at his feet.

'Really? We are fighting with spoons now?'

'I'll fight with only the stumps of my arms if that's all I have left.'

'It can be arranged.'

Somehow, she had gotten hold of a bowl, and it went hurtling towards him. This time he managed to duck, and it hit the soldier behind him. The man collapsed on the floor. The other soldier drew his weapon.

'Stop,' Nerva said to him, despite not having a better idea. *No prisoners.* He looked back at Brei. 'Put the sword down.'

She spat in his direction. '*Falbh dairich fhein.*'

He did not recognise the phrase. 'I do not understand.'

The soldier to his right cleared his throat. 'I might be paraphrasing, sir, but I believe she just told you to go have *relations* with yourself.'

Nerva's eyebrows rose. 'Charming.'

'Look around at what you've done.' Her voice quivered, the venom in her tone faltering.

They watched one another for a moment before he felt the need to look away. 'If you do not put down your sword, I will have no choice but to order my men to kill you.' He took a few steps towards her, and she raised her weapon. 'If you cooperate, perhaps I can find a way to spare your life.'

'I've seen what you do to the women you keep alive.' The hate had returned to her voice.

He took another step towards her.

'Don't come any closer.'

Her feet remained anchored to that one spot. Now that he thought about it, her feet had not moved the entire time. He looked down at the floor and saw that she stood on wooden panels. When his eyes travelled back up to meet hers, he saw her swallow. It was a door. She was guarding something, or more likely someone.

Nerva really should have killed her at that very moment, then dragged her bleeding body aside to retrieve whatever was hidden beneath her feet, but the only people hiding would be women, children, or the elderly. Able-bodied men would not hide underground.

'Your name is Brei, is it not?' he asked her.

She hesitated before nodding.

'Brei, this is what is going to happen. You are going to put down your weapon, and I give you my word that you will not be killed.'

The soldier behind him cleared his throat. Brei searched his face, no doubt trying to figure out his next move.

'You won't let me go.'

He shook his head. 'No.' A pause. 'The sooner you surrender, the sooner we will *leave*.' He glanced down at her feet, hoping she would comprehend what he was offering. He would say nothing of the people she was protecting if she cooperated.

Her sword fell a few inches, the creases on her brow softening. 'I put this down and we leave?' She was understandably sceptical.

He nodded. 'Yes.' She had little choice but to trust him —again.

The tension in the moments that followed was palpable. Brei opened her hand and the sword clattered to the floor.

'Take her outside with the others,' Nerva instructed the soldier with the bleeding nose. The other one was groaning on the ground. 'Then return for your companion.'

Brei stiffened as he approached but did not fight when he took her by the arm and led her out of the hut. She glanced over her shoulder at Nerva before disappearing from sight. Another soldier replaced them in the doorway, looking around. 'Shall I search the place, sir?'

They would take anything edible or of value. As much as Romans liked to pretend the Maeatae were simple barbarians, their craftsmanship suggested otherwise. Some of the pieces confiscated over the previous two years had even inspired goldsmiths back home.

'I will search the hut myself,' Nerva said. 'I want another set of eyes on the woman who just left here. She is stronger than she looks.'

The soldier saluted before leaving.

Nerva looked over to ensure the guard on the ground was still out of it before going to the spot where Brei had stood. He ran two fingers along the groove in the wood until he found a nook that fit one finger. Slowly, he lifted the panel and peered inside. At first, he did not see anything and thought perhaps it was just grain storage, but then seven faces came into view. Five children, an elderly woman, and the woman who had been with Brei when they ran into each other at the stream. Both her hands were clamped firmly over the mouths of the two youngest children. She clearly did not trust them to keep quiet. She froze at the sight of him, waiting to see what he would do. He brought a finger to his lips before replacing the panel.

'Any grain, sir?' came a voice from the door.

Nerva turned to see the soldier from earlier returning for his friend. 'It is spoiled.'

Marcus entered the hut behind him, a small cut above his eye had left a trail of blood down his face. It seemed some people had tried to escape after all—and failed. He stepped aside to let the two soldiers pass. When they were gone, Nerva joined Marcus at the door. They stood together taking in the aftermath.

'Why does every victory feel like a defeat?' Nerva asked.

Marcus switched his helmet to his other hand. 'I hate this place. Even if we do take the North, what sane man would want to live here?'

Nerva's mouth twitched. 'Men ordered to.'

'My next campaign better be somewhere warm.'

'You are assuming you are going to survive the cold.'

The women and children were lined up between the huts, down on their knees with their hands tied behind their backs. The young girl Nerva had spotted behind the tools earlier was now among them. Paulus was striding along the line looking painfully smug.

'Everything you had now belongs to Rome!'

Marcus exhaled through his nose. 'I'm so tired of his speeches. Why he feels the need to lecture them prior to killing them I've no idea. In a moment they won't remember a word he said.'

'Do not let them see your fear,' Brei called out, though she looked at the young girl trembling beside her when she said it.

Nerva brought a hand to his forehead, picturing his sister Dulcia at the same age. She had been so timid and afraid of the world. 'We should take them with us. They might be of use, as they know the land better than we do.'

Marcus's eyebrows rose. 'Caracalla won't be happy if you show up with prisoners.'

'Can you honestly stand here and watch them die?'

'If you order me to, I can.'

Nerva shook his head. 'Well, I cannot.' Stepping down onto the dirt, he called out, 'Get them on their feet. We are taking them with us.'

Paulus turned sharply to look at Nerva, a hand resting on the hilt of his sword. Judging by the tight set of his lips, he was not in agreement. 'Caracalla said no prisoners.'

'Caracalla is not here,' Nerva replied. 'And your orders come from me.'

Paulus sniffed and continued along the line. 'Very well. Let them witness the extinction of their tribes.'

Brei raised her chin as he passed, and he stopped in front of her, hooking a finger under her chin and examining her face.

'Oh, Caracalla will love you.'

Brei pulled back from his hand. 'Why? Does he have a death wish?'

'That is quite enough, Commander,' Nerva called out. 'All of you, on your feet.'

Paulus pulled Brei up and held her much too close. 'Are you ready to watch the rest of your people die?'

She held his gaze and said in Latin, 'You can level the mountains and fill the swamps, but you can't erase us.'

Paulus drew his knife and pressed the blade to her throat. 'I can. One barbarian at a time if I have to.'

'You have your orders, Commander,' Nerva called out. 'Follow them.'

Paulus shoved her away.

'What sort of man cuts the throat of a child?' Brei said, spitting at Paulus.

Nerva tried not to listen as he mounted his horse. That mouth of hers was going to get her into trouble. His gaze went to the young girl who stood with her. Her eyes were closed, her teeth chattering. There was a pool of urine where she had been kneeling. Nudging his horse forwards, Nerva went to her and said in Brittonic, 'You cannot march with your eyes closed.' His tone was gentle.

She opened them, and a look of recognition passed over her face. Being so young, he had hoped she would remain hidden. He was not sure how she would go over the long distance. But there were no longer any safe havens.

Brei looked over her shoulder at him, distrust in her eyes. He slipped his helmet on and continued past them. Paulus had mounted also and trotted to catch up to him.

'General—'

'Let us go while we still have some light, Commander.'

'You heard our general,' Marcus shouted, striding towards his own mount. 'Move out.'

It was possible Nerva had sentenced those prisoners to a fate worse than death. He could not watch over them forever, could not protect them from the hardships ahead. All he could give them was a few extra moments. There was every chance they would later wish their throats had been cut, their bodies left to the land.

'Burn everything,' Paulus said, his horse pivoting.

Nerva glanced once in Brei's direction, saw the panic on her face. 'Burn nothing. It will only give away our location.'

As they resumed their march, he could feel Paulus's gaze burning holes in his back of his helmet.

CHAPTER 6

*I*f they were waiting for Brei to fall, complain, beg for water, or show signs of tiring, they would be sorely disappointed. No one complained, not even Lavena, who was only seven years old. She had not made it into the hut in time. At least she had her mother with her.

Brei closed her eyes for a moment, grateful her sister and nephew had been spared the long march to… Her eyes opened. Where would it end? She knew the direction they travelled but had only a vague idea of what awaited them. If only the other warriors had been there, they might have stood a chance. But her father had gone east, believing a few sheep thrown in the path of the legion would spare them. He had told her to remain behind under the pretence of protecting the village, and she had felt annoyed and excluded.

Then she had failed him.

A realisation hit her at that moment: she would never see him again. Nor would she see Alane and Drust, or her grandfather, or any of the others. The only people she had left were tethered behind her like animals. She turned to check on them. They followed in single file, paling with every mile. As the chief's daughter, she was responsible for keeping them alive. The problem was, she knew there were far worse things than death.

Brei looked over her shoulder, checking on everyone. Her gaze fell to Lavena, who followed directly behind her. Dark circles enclosed her green eyes. They had been marching for a day and a half, then forced to stand while the soldiers made camp, to watch while they ate, and freeze while they warmed themselves in front of fires. Sleep was fleeting, and for Lavena, it was the first time she had slept away from their village.

'Tired?' Brei asked.

Lavena nodded.

Brei looked up at the sun to gauge the time. They would probably continue for another few hours. Not a problem for her, but for a young girl like Lavena, it was the difference between collapsing and not. 'Not too much longer.' She attempted a smile that she hoped was reassuring.

Another nod, and then the girl's gaze returned to her feet.

The soldiers may have been fit, but the terrain was tough on them, even harder with those large packs on their backs. Each one weighed as much as her. Their feet slipped constantly on the lichen-covered surfaces, and their frozen hands struggled to keep hold of their weapons. It would be the perfect time to attack as fatigue gripped them, but no one came.

Lavena collapsed. Brei heard the air leave her lungs as she hit the rocky slope. Turning, she grabbed hold of the girl's arm. 'Up. Quickly now.'

'I can't,' the girl replied, and her feet slipped out from under her again.

Brei managed to keep her upright this time, but her

head was slumped so far forwards that her chin was almost resting on her breastbone.

'Walk,' the girl's mother, Morna, whispered behind her, giving her a shove. 'They're coming.'

Brei carried her along as best she could with bound hands.

'Halt,' called the approaching centurion. The other soldiers stopped marching in unison. 'What the hell is going on here?'

'She tripped,' Brei said in Latin. 'I'm just helping her up.'

It was clear by the centurion's expression that whatever patience he had left would not stretch far. 'Get her walking, then.'

'Come on,' Brei whispered. 'Just a bit farther.'

Lavena nodded and took a few steps before collapsing once more.

'If she can't march, she stays here,' the centurion said, taking a step towards her.

'No!' Morna cried.

Brei looked around, pulse racing. There was nothing for miles. She would die where they left her. 'I'll carry her.' Brei crouched and gestured for Lavena to climb onto her back.

The centurion laughed. 'You won't make it to the top of the hill.'

'I'll make it all the way to camp.'

Lavena collapsed against her, and Brei rose, taking hold of one of her legs while the other hung limp. She looked the centurion straight in the eye. 'We're ready.'

He shook his head and signalled to one of his men. 'Cut the girl loose.'

Brei's grip tightened on the girl's leg. 'I told you, I can carry her.'

The sound of a horse approaching at a canter made the

centurion turn his head. He stood to attention as the legate approached.

'What is the hold-up here?' the legate called to them, looking from the centurion to Brei.

After two days marching with his legion, she had finally learned his name. Nerva looked every bit the pompous Roman in his ridiculous armour.

'Nothing for you to worry about, sir, just removing some dead weight so we can reach our destination before dark.'

Nerva pulled up his horse and looked at Lavena. 'Dead weight?'

'The girl cannot stand, sir,' replied the centurion. To prove his point, he stepped up and kicked Lavena's leg, which hung limply.

Brei could not stop her reaction. Raising a knee, she shoved him back with it. The centurion's face reddened as he drew his dagger.

'You want to die with the girl, is that it?' he said, moving towards her.

'Enough,' Nerva said.

'I told him I would carry her,' Brei said, looking up at him.

Nerva's expression did not change. 'Carry her? Through mountain terrain with your hands tied?'

'Yes.'

The centurion shook his head. 'She'll slow us down.'

Nerva turned to him tiredly. 'If she does, then do what you must. Until then, get your men moving.' He swung his horse around. 'The only person slowing us down right now is you.'

'Can you untie my hands?' Brei asked Nerva.

Nerva turned his horse and cantered away.

'Let's move!' the centurion ordered. He thrust a sharp finger at her. 'I expect you to keep time with my men.'

Everyone moved forwards once more.

'Thank you,' Morna whispered from behind.

Brei did not respond. She needed to reserve all her energy for the walk. One of the commanders, the one they called Marcus, rode back a few times to check on them. While he never spoke to her, he had kind eyes, and she suspected he was someone the legate trusted. She saved all of her glaring for the centurion in front of her, who kept looking over his shoulder to remind her he was watching.

It was almost dark when they reached Kinnel. While she did not keep time with the men, she did keep up, much to the centurion's disappointment.

'Halt!' came the order down the line.

Brei fell to her knees and licked the sweat from her dry lips. Morna rushed forwards to take her daughter. Brei rested her forehead on the backs of her hands and gritted her teeth against the pain in her back and shoulders. After a long moment, she turned to check on the girl, pleased to see her looking livelier than she had earlier.

'Thank you,' Morna said.

Brei only nodded, suddenly aware of her unbearable thirst. The men had deliberately not given them water, but her kind could go without food and water much longer than any spoiled soldier.

'On your feet,' shouted the centurion. 'You rest when we do. You can help the men make camp.'

Brei glared at him, then looked over at Lavena to see if she had it in her. The girl stood on legs resembling those of a filly just born, jutting her chin in a way that made Brei proud.

'If you expect to be fed, you'll *all* help,' barked the centurion, visibly annoyed by Lavena's renewed energy. He walked over to Brei and untied her wrists with a punishing tug. The coarse rope scratched against her already raw skin. 'Let's see how strong you barbarians really are.'

The other prisoners watched her with expressions of pity. They were not warriors but mothers, cooks, and healers. One of the women had watched her young son die at the hands of these men. All she could manage now was a vacant stare accompanied by long stretches of silence.

'She can raise the posts for the officers' tents,' the centurion said. 'By herself.'

The other soldiers exchanged smirks as Brei was ushered towards a ten-foot wooden pole being removed from a mule. A frown settled on her face as it was dropped at her feet by two slaves.

'Go on,' the centurion said, waving a hand. 'Our men need shelter.'

She walked along it, then bent, gripping one of the smooth ends as best she could, hoisting it to chest height with one enormous heave. She remained there for a moment, wondering how on earth she was going to get it the rest of the way without help. Meanwhile, the centurion retrieved his vine staff and slapped it against his hand.

'In case you get lazy,' he said.

She just watched him for a moment, imagining all the ways she could kill him. Preferably slowly, his mouth open in surprise as the life drained from his smug face. She would make sure she was the last thing he saw before he died.

'What are you looking at, *barbarian?*'

She really wanted to reply but said nothing. Repositioning her hands, she pushed with all her might to lift the pole above her head. Her arms shook beneath the weight, but she was determined to complete the task.

Lavena stepped forwards. 'I'll help you,' she said, holding on to the pole.

'No,' Brei said. The centurion had been very clear she was to do it alone. Before she managed to get another word out, the centurion lunged forwards and brought his rod down on the girl.

A squeak escaped Lavena as she staggered backwards, her hands going over her cheek and eye. Morna rushed forwards to remove her daughter. The pole wobbled in Brei's grip. She stepped aside to let it fall to the ground. It rolled, stopping at the centurion's feet.

'Pick it up,' he sneered, walking towards her with the vine staff raised.

She had wanted to pacify him as best she could so those unable to defend themselves would not need to. But she was more warrior than nurturer. So, when the rod came down, she caught it. The centurion's eyes widened as she tugged it from his grip. Maybe it was the thirst and hunger, the fatigue, or the events of the past few days that made her snap. When the centurion opened his mouth to speak, she leapt at him, pushing the vine staff into his throat with the force of ten men.

A soldier ran at her, but she swung a leg out, connecting with his chest and sending him crashing backwards. The centurion's face went from red to purple, the veins in his face bulging. He fumbled for his sword with one hand while the other tried to push her away, but she kept blocking him.

'You should've cut my throat when you had the chance,' she hissed, pushing harder still.

They came running from all directions then, tackling her to the ground and crushing her under their combined weight. There were at least four men piled on top of her. Her ribcage squeezed, and she waited for the snap of bone.

'What is going on here?'

Brei could not see who had spoken. Raspy coughing came from the centurion as he tried to draw breath. The weight on her eased as the men got to their feet, dragging her up with them. Next thing she knew, she was face to face with the commander who had given the speech about the extinction of her people. Yes, she would remember his name and face with those close-set eyes. Paulus Cordius.

'You again,' he said, glancing over at the centurion who was crouched on the ground holding his neck. He turned back to Brei. 'Your pretty face might have fooled the general, but nothing can save you from me now.'

'I'm not afraid of you.'

His mouth lifted in a smile. 'Not yet.' Turning away from her, he said to the men, 'String her up.'

CHAPTER 7

Nerva made a point of separating himself from the prisoners, leaving them in the charge of his capable men. He had spared their lives against his better judgement, going against direct orders. That was all he could do.

'The men are settled,' Marcus said, falling into stride with Nerva as he headed towards his tent.

'How are our food supplies?'

'Adequate grain, salt, and oil. Some rabbit. No one's complaining—yet.'

Nerva smiled as he strode between the cavalry tents in their neat rows. The smell of bread and meat cooking had taken over the air and was making him hungry. 'Are the prisoners settled?'

Marcus drew a breath and looked around. 'All but one.'

As soon as Nerva heard those words, he knew which one. He waited for Marcus to elaborate.

'I thought you didn't want to hear anything else about them.'

Nerva stopped walking. 'That was true until you threw me those breadcrumbs.'

The tribune hesitated before speaking. 'The chief's daughter. She tried to strangle a centurion. Cordius is dealing with her.'

It took him a moment to absorb those words. 'Dealing with her?' An image of her being crucified sprang to mind.

'She's alive for now, but you know what he's like. Wants to make an example of her.'

Nerva closed his eyes for a moment. He had known she would snap eventually, and of course he could not have her strangling his men. 'Where is she?'

'Let the men handle it.'

'Take me to her.'

The tribune shook his head. 'This way.'

He led Nerva past the officers' tents to where a crowd had gathered. The sound of leather slapping flesh reached them. It was the familiar sound of discipline that was carried out on a daily basis, only this time it was not one of his own men.

'Move aside,' Marcus called ahead of him.

The spectators turned to look, splitting down the middle to let them through. Nerva saw her then, arms raised above her head and secured with ropes. Her tunic was ripped to her waist, her back striped red and head slumped forwards. She was panting through gritted teeth.

Nerva's gaze met Paulus's as he passed him. The commander lowered his whip, seemingly annoyed by the interruption. Nerva went to stand in front of Brei, and she raised her head to look at him. She wore the same determined expression she always did whenever they met. This was not a woman who could be easily broken. He stared into her bloodshot eyes for a moment. 'I am beginning to regret my decision to spare your life. It seems you are causing my men some grief.' He spoke in Latin, knowing she could understand most of it.

'You protect your people, and I protect mine.' *She* spoke in Brittonic.

Paulus flicked the whip and frowned across at Nerva. 'What did she say?'

That man needed to learn when to keep silent. Ignoring him, Nerva looked down at her trembling legs. No longer a ghost but flesh and blood in that moment. 'Cut her down. Put her with the others.'

'I am not done,' Paulus said, his tone sharper than it should have been with his superior.

Bristling, Nerva turned to face him properly while Marcus cut her down. The fact that Paulus had chosen to carry out the task himself said so much about him. 'You are done if I say you are.' When he was sure the commander understood, he turned and walked away. He had to get out of there before he did something foolish, like pick her up off the ground. The Maeatae were not blameless, he reminded himself. The only reason he was stuck north was because they had revolted, forcing Severus's hand. There was no space for sympathy when his entire purpose for being there was to eradicate her people.

Marcus caught up with him just as he reached the tents. 'Don't let that pretty face fool you.' He looked behind them to ensure no one else could hear. 'I called in on the centurion she nearly killed, and I've no doubt she meant to finish the job.'

'She is a warrior. Of course she meant to finish the job.'

Marcus brushed a hand over his short hair. 'It's easy to become distracted when your enemy looks like a daughter of Jupiter.'

'I am a legatus legionis in the Roman army, not a boy reaching puberty. That woman could be ninety and covered with warts, and my reservations would be the same.'

Soldiers stepped aside to let them pass as they headed for the large tent at the end of the two rows.

'This doesn't fall on you,' Marcus said, his voice low. 'History will not speak of the atrocities of General Nerva Papias.'

Nerva pushed through the opening in the tent and finally came to a stop. 'But I must live with every order I carry out.'

Following him into the tent, Marcus looked around. 'When this is over, when you're back in Rome with a beautiful wife and grown sons, you'll barely think of this time or place again.'

'My beautiful wife?'

'Yes, the one your mother is hard at work selecting for you.'

Nerva felt himself relax. 'Oh, that one.'

The tribune moved to leave, then changed his mind. 'Before I go—'

'Gods, what now?'

Hands went up in mock surrender. 'I was just going to ask if you wanted me to send a medic to the girl.'

Nerva drew a breath and looked heavenward. Tending to her wounds would not sit well with his men after she had attempted to kill one of them. 'Be discreet.'

∽

The women lay Brei on her stomach in the dirt because there was nowhere else to put her. Despite there being a few healers among them, there were no herbs or medicines of any kind, only a ration of drinking water and widespread thirst.

'Drink it,' Brei said to the women, trying to keep the misery out of her voice and failing. 'Don't waste it.'

Looks were exchanged but no one objected. Lavena had

already emptied her cup and sat licking her cracked lips. Back home they had an ointment that would fix them, but home was twenty miles south.

'Will they give her something for the pain?' Lavena asked her mother.

'I don't think so.'

'What if the wounds fester?'

Morna sighed. 'They don't care.'

A rogue tear rolled down Brei's nose. She did not have the energy to brush it away. Alane would have known what to do at that moment; she was the sensible and nurturing one. Her father joked all the time that Brei was the son he never got. Instead of boys, four daughters, two living —for now.

'You can lie on my lap if you want,' Lavena whispered in the dark.

Brei blinked. 'I'm all right here. Get some rest. I won't be carrying you tomorrow.'

'I'll carry you instead.'

Brei almost managed a smile.

The flicker of torchlight made everyone else turn and look. Brei just closed her eyes. A moment later, light was cast over them.

'There she is.'

Brei slowly turned her head towards the familiar voice. It was Marcus, the one with the kind eyes. He held the torch out farther, illuminating her injuries. An older man stepped out from behind him and peered down at her.

'I see.' Stepping forwards, he crouched down for a closer look and placed a case at his feet.

Brei tried to move away from him.

'He's a *medici*,' Marcus said, as if that was supposed to put her mind at ease. Seeing her confusion, he added, 'A healer.'

That only increased her confusion. Why would they send a healer?

'Keep still,' the medic said. His tone suggested he had not volunteered for the role.

Brei did as she was told, because she needed to be well for the sake of the others. She lay still while he slapped a few ointments on her, smells she did not recognise. As quickly as he had arrived, he was on his feet again, the light deepening the crevices on his face.

'Keep the area clean and dry.' He turned away. 'Or not.'

'Something for the pain?' Marcus asked.

The medic squared his shoulders. 'Needed for our *own*, sir.'

Marcus stared at the man for a moment. 'Very well.' His gaze fell to Brei. 'Food is on its way.' He looked to the soldier who had been assigned the task of guarding them. 'Make sure she is tied up at all times.'

'Yes, sir.'

The guard dragged her up into a seated position and bound her wrists and ankles. The flickering light retreated, and the footsteps faded. The women sat huddled in the cold, staring into the dark. Brei expected the promise of food to be an empty one, but later, a man arrived with some barley bread, tossing it into the centre of their group like they were dogs. If the man delivering the food was hoping to witness a feeding frenzy, he left disappointed. The sleepy women stared at the bread as though it were a poisonous mushroom. Eventually, hunger got the better of them, and one of their healers picked it up, smelling it before tearing off a tiny piece and tasting it.

'I think it's safe.'

They divided the bread equally and ate in silence, aware of the guard watching their every move. The moment they finished eating, they fell asleep, despite the absence of blankets or a fire…

'Brei.'

She was dreaming.

'Wake up.'

Her lids were heavy and teeth chattering.

'Brei.'

No man in that camp knew her by name. And if they did, they would not bother using it.

'Brei.' Louder that time.

Her eyes snapped open, taking a moment to focus. She found Nerva crouched in front of her and immediately looked around in a panic, assuming something was wrong.

'It is all right,' he said. 'I have something for you.'

She carefully disentangled herself from Lavena and sat up, looking suspiciously at the cup in his hand. Steam rose from it. 'What's that?'

'Willow tea. For the pain.' He held it out to her.

She did not take it. 'Why are you giving it to me?'

Standing, he said, 'If you do not want it…'

'I do,' she said quickly. It was not the pain relief she wanted but the warmth.

He crouched down again and placed it between her bound hands. She had hoped he would leave so she could share it with the others, but seeing that he intended to watch her drink it, she brought the cup to her lips and smelled it before taking a tentative sip. The hot liquid made her shiver.

'Do you really think I would poison you?' Nerva asked. 'There are far easier ways to be rid of you that do not require waiting for water to boil. If I want you dead, it will be done.'

She regarded him over the rim of her cup as he rested an elbow on his knee and looked down at Lavena.

'Did she eat?'

Brei took another drink and closed her eyes as the liquid warmed her throat, chest, then belly. 'Yes.'

'Good.'

She opened her eyes. 'I can't figure you out. One moment you're tearing through villages, the next bringing your enemy medicine.' She watched as an emotion she could not quite identify passed over his face.

Standing, he held his hand out for the cup. She drew a breath and downed the remainder of the tea before handing it to him. 'I don't get to keep the cup?'

'So you can beat one of my men to death with it?'

'I don't need a cup for that.' She almost thanked him but caught herself. He was her enemy, and she his prisoner.

Nerva looked down at her for a moment as though about to say something. Then, shaking his head, he strode away without another word or glance in her direction.

## CHAPTER 8

Seven days later they reached Balmakewan. Caracalla's army was waiting there for them. They too had suffered losses, over twelve hundred men since passing through Antonine's Wall. Now Nerva stood inside the young emperor's tent, bringing him up to speed.

'They may be smarter than we initially thought,' Caracalla said.

Nerva struggled to keep his expression neutral. Of course they were. He waited for Caracalla to continue.

'Half the time the people were nowhere to be seen and their livestock unguarded.'

'A strategy to keep us on course, sir. If the food is available, we will not go looking for it.'

'Exactly what I said.' The emperor scratched at his wiry beard and studied Nerva for a moment. 'I hear you arrived with prisoners, despite orders to the contrary.'

Nerva suspected Paulus Cordius had personally delivered that news to Caracalla. Any opportunity to make him look incompetent. The scary thing was, he was next in line for the role when Nerva finally stepped aside. 'There were healers among them.'

'And children.' Caracalla added. 'I know you have a soft spot for them, but they will not be small forever.'

'No, sir.'

Caracalla waved a dismissive hand. 'I do not judge too harshly. I too have spared lives along the way. The women make for interesting bed companions.' He paused, a smile on his lips. 'Perhaps you figured that out for yourself.'

'I am here to fight and take care of the men, sir.' As if Nerva needed another reason to dislike the man. He tried to change the subject. 'How is your father, sir?'

Caracalla leaned back in his chair and let out a breath. 'He remains in Eboracum and has taken to his bed. The cold plagues him, but he refuses to leave.' It was said with a hint of disdain, as if the man's failing body were his own fault. It was no secret Caracalla wished his father gone. Severus's death would bring him one step closer to ruling alone.

'I am sorry to hear that, sir.'

Caracalla appeared unmoved. 'While sad, the sooner he is gone, the sooner we can leave this place.'

It was not the location Nerva despised so much as his reason for being there. Without the bloodshed, the sound of five thousand men marching behind him, and the constant threat of attack, he might have come to appreciate the raw beauty of Caledonia. 'We have made excellent progress, sir, despite the losses.'

Caracalla nodded. 'I agree. We should celebrate that progress.' He cleared his throat. 'Have the prisoners brought here tonight. You will join us, of course.'

Nerva was going to ask what for, but he realised he already knew the answer. 'You will be most disappointed with their condition, sir.'

'So have them cleaned up.'

A familiar feeling clawed his insides, the same feeling he used to get whenever his sisters had been mistreated growing up. Once again, he found himself in a position of power, yet unable to help in any meaningful way. 'Very well, sir, but you must forgive my absence. I need sleep.'

Caracalla regarded him with amusement. 'Have you not figured out yet that these mountains are without morals?'

Nerva blinked. 'I certainly have, sir.' Turning, he marched from the tent.

∼

Brei finished her bread and water and tried to ignore the smell of meat cooking. The scent made her mouth water. She looked down at Lavena, who was sitting beside her, taking greedy lungfuls of air.

'I can almost taste it,' the girl said. 'I'd kill for a piece of pork right now.'

Morna looked around. 'Don't let the guards hear you say such things.'

Brei smiled to herself. Everyone was in a good mood after having had their first proper wash in days. They had been given soap, towels, and clean clothes that were much too big, and far too Roman looking for their liking, but they did the job of keeping them dry and warm.

Brei's smile faded the moment she heard the sound of gravel crunching under heavy boots. The women all turned in that direction, holding their breath. Night had arrived, and all she could see were the outlines of five men. Every hair on her body stood on end.

Soldiers emerged into the torchlit area where the prisoners had been confined for the evening, looking between them as though searching for someone. Brei looked for Nerva's face among them, but he was not there.

'On your feet,' one of the soldiers shouted. There was not a familiar or friendly face among them.

Brei understood the instruction but did not move. The

others looked to her for a translation. But if it was the end of the road, Brei was not just going to stand and walk calmly to her death. First, she would kill as many of the soldiers as she could.

'You heard him. On your feet before I beat the lot of you,' another said.

Brei drew a breath and looked around at the worried faces. 'Stand up.' She pulled Lavena up with her and placed herself between the girl and the men. When they were all upright, one of the men walked among them, peering into their faces before looking down at their breasts, hips, legs. Brei moved herself even farther in front of the girl.

'More light,' the soldier said, gesturing to the man holding the torch. He stepped forwards until the flame lit up their faces. 'You,' said the soldier, pointing. 'You, and you two,' he finished, pointing at Brei and Lavena.

'General Nerva said no one with ailments and no children,' another said, nodding towards Lavena.

'Caracalla can decide that for himself,' replied the soldier, then gestured for the four of them to start moving.

'Mumma,' Lavena said, backing away.

Brei took her hand and smiled reassuringly. 'It's all right. I'll be with you.' These were not men they could say no to.

The soldier narrowed his eyes on Brei. 'And no funny business from you. I'll cut your throat if you so much as open your mouth.'

She just stared blankly at him.

'I know you understand me.'

Brei would behave—unless they gave her no choice. She looked back at the others and saw their fear. Morna began to cry as her daughter was led away. Brei realised at that moment that the men had not taken the strongest women, but the youngest, or rather the prettiest. She faced forwards, her grip tightening on Lavena's hand. The only way they were getting to that child was over her dead body.

'Move,' shouted one of the soldiers.

Brei pulled the girl closer to her as they walked, gesturing for the others to keep up. She studied the men around her, noting the number, position, and accessibility of their weapons. Then her gaze wandered to the tents either side. There was nowhere to run to.

The women were marched through the centre of the camp, past the cavalry towards the much larger tents at the end. No one paid them much notice. Many of the soldiers were either sleeping or gathered in groups drinking their wine rations. Brei's heart drummed a little faster as they approached the largest tent.

Just as they reached it, Nerva stepped out of a neighbouring tent. Dark circles enclosed his eyes, and he seemed distracted. When he looked up at them, he stopped walking, his gaze going from Brei to Lavena who was huddled at her side.

'Halt,' he barked at the men.

The soldiers stopped and turned to salute him. The women stopped behind them, all eyes on him.

'Where are these prisoners going?' Nerva asked.

'To the emperor, sir.'

Nerva took a step towards them. 'And the child?'

The men looked between one another before one said, 'She looks plenty old enough to me, sir.'

Nerva reached the man in a few strides, grabbing him by the tunic and turning him to look at the young girl. 'Does she really?' He released the man with a shove. 'Is that who we are now? When we are not killing children, we are raping them?'

The man did not have an answer.

When Nerva stepped back, Brei noted the tense set of

his jaw. He was a fish out of water, and she could not help but feel sorry for him.

'No children or women with ailments. Were the orders not clear?'

'They were clear, sir,' said the man who had objected the first time and been quickly overruled.

'Take those two back,' Nerva said, gesturing to Brei and the girl.

'Both?' the soldier asked, visibly confused.

Nerva's hands curled into fists. 'That one had skin torn from her back just a few days ago. Do you really want to present her to Caracalla?'

Brei looked over at the other women who would go in her place. 'Send me,' she blurted. 'Send only me.'

Nerva sighed. 'Noble of you, but you are in no condition—'

'It's just my back. The rest of me is fine.' She could handle men like Caracalla, and had done many times.

'The emperor chooses his own company,' one of the soldiers snapped, giving her a shove in the other direction.

Brei's gaze fell to his sword. In a few beats, she could have it pressed against his throat. Her fingers twitched.

'I will take them myself,' Nerva said, grabbing Brei by the arm and tugging her away from the group before she had a chance to act. Lavena scurried after them.

'My men can handle it, sir.'

'So far your men have proven incompetent' came Nerva's reply as he marched her away from the group.

Brei looked over her shoulder at the others, feeling as though she were betraying them. It was probably not the first time they had lain with a man against their will, but who knew what Roman men were capable of in bed. She only knew one woman who had been with a soldier, during the treaty, a transaction of sorts. 'You should've let me go instead,' she said, trying to turn to Nerva.

He kept a firm grip on her arm. 'You have a strange way of saying thank you.'

'I don't need your protection.'

He breathed out a laugh. 'Do not flatter yourself. It is not you I protect but Caracalla. If he dies at the hand of one of the prisoners I spared, how will that look?'

'A lot like justice.'

'For once, can you just close your mouth and walk.' He glanced down at Lavena, his expression softening. 'Try to keep up.'

She nodded.

'I could've handled that pig of a chief,' Brei added.

'He is not a chief. He is an emperor of Rome. Do you know what would happen if you tried any of your usual tricks on him?'

'Yes. There would be one less Roman in the world.'

His response came in the form of a shove, but she stopped walking, forcing him to do the same. Another sigh. 'Now what?'

'Let Lavena go. No one will even notice she's missing. Just let her go right now.'

Nerva shook his head. 'I cannot do that.'

'Please. She's just a child.' Seeing that her words were having the desired effect on him, she continued. 'There are other tribes nearby, people who will take her in.'

Nerva's expression hardened. 'And soon they will all be dead, Lavena with them if she managed to make it that far.' He lowered his voice. 'Your people broke the treaty. What did you think was going to happen?'

She stepped in front of Lavena. 'The Romans never left. You people with your ridiculous army and big walls. You're a stain on this land.'

'Your people forced our hand. Do you not get it? Nobody is leaving until you are all gone.'

Her scowl deepened. 'We're not the only losers here.

You arrived with what? Fifty thousand men? How many will you leave with?'

He gave her a shove to get her walking again. 'Your whining is going to wake up the whole camp.'

She watched him as they walked. 'If Lavena dies, her death will be on your hands.'

He did not argue the fact. 'Tomorrow we march to Kair House, where you will be put on a boat and taken downriver to our waiting fleet.' His voice was almost a whisper. 'Then you will be loaded onto a ship.'

She was silent a moment. 'Where is the ship going?'

'Rome.'

She shook her head as she absorbed what he was telling her. 'Rome? I can't go to Rome.'

'Believe it or not, it is the safest place for you right now.'

'My family is here.'

'Your family has nowhere to escape to. Our ships are all along the coast, and our troops have closed off the midland.'

Brei slowed, her legs no longer cooperating. 'They will fight their way out.'

'And they will lose.'

She searched his face, hoping to see lies but finding only truth. 'If they're going to die, I'm dying with them.'

A pained expression crossed his face. 'Young children often remain with their mothers. Lavena could end up in a wealthy household and have a good life.'

'She had a good life, right up until the moment your army arrived and slaughtered her brother in front of her. He was only thirteen.'

It was Nerva's turn to stop walking, her words pushing him back. 'I am trying to save your life, both of you.'

Brei opened her hands in front of her. 'You've destroyed everything.' Her voice was getting louder. 'We never had thousands of men to sacrifice in a display of power, nor would we.'

He moved closer and covered her mouth with his hand. Her first reaction was normally to throw a knee up, but she forced herself to be still.

'Enough,' he whispered, easing the pressure. 'You are going to have to stop fighting me every step of the way.' His hand fell away. 'Start walking.'

Brei never had trouble finding words. According to her father, her sharp tongue was her biggest downfall. But there was sincerity in Nerva's tone that silenced her. Or perhaps it was just the fatigue catching up.

Glancing down at a wide-eyed Lavena, she pulled herself together and started walking.

CHAPTER 9

The endless glances in his direction were not improving Nerva's bad mood. Fed up, he looked over at Marcus. 'Something you want to say?'

The tribune looked behind them to ensure no one was listening. 'Want to tell me why you've barely spoken three words all day?'

They were on horseback, just three miles from Kair House. 'Meeting with Caracalla has that effect.'

'I don't think this is about Caracalla.' He almost sounded amused. 'I think she's gotten to you.'

'Who?'

'Don't give me *who*. You know who. The pretty one who likes to strangle our men.'

Nerva faced forwards again. 'Do you think that is my type?'

'That's the thing, you've never really had a type. Roman women of all calibres throw themselves at you during dinner parties, and all they get in return are good manners and safe conversation.'

'It is called discretion.'

'So you do lie with them?'

Nerva just shook his head.

'All I'm saying is that you're not one to swoon over a pretty girl and let your feelings get the better of you.'

'Correct.'

Marcus leaned in. 'Until along came a little wild thing who fights better than you do.'

'She is not a better fighter than me.'

'She stole your horse from under your nose.'

'She is a better thief than me, I will give her that.'

Marcus continued to stare at him, apparently not done with the subject. 'You like them wild.'

'Shut up.'

'You do.'

It was partially true. Brei reminded him of another highly spirited woman in his life. 'She reminds me of Mila,' he finally admitted.

'Your sister?' Marcus mulled that over for a moment. 'I see it now. You're always bailing her out of trouble also.'

'An old habit, perhaps.' He looked out at the swamp to their left that seemed to stretch on forever. 'I do not like our position.'

The tribune glanced over at the stagnant water. 'We're almost—' An arrow flew past his head.

*Hiss. Hiss, hiss, hiss.*

A searing pain exploded in Nerva's side as an arrow struck the gap in his armour, just beneath his arm.

'Form ranks!' Marcus shouted, swinging his horse in the other direction. The men ran into position. 'Shields!'

Nerva gritted his teeth and snapped the shaft of the arrow. He would have to wait for a medic to remove the tip.

'Cover the general!' Marcus called, dismounting and snatching up a shield from an injured soldier. He cursed when more arrows rained down on them.

Slipping from the saddle, Nerva collected a shield also and ran to join the other men. 'Horses to the rear!'

A moment later, he was covered by a protective layer of shields, annoyed that he had left his men exposed and trapped. He held his breath as he drew his sword, trying to keep the shield steady above his head.

'Go to the back,' Marcus called to him as another round of arrows beat against their shields. 'You're no good to us injured.'

Nerva shook his head. 'If I can hold a weapon and remain upright, I can fight.'

'Right turn!' Marcus shouted.

The men shuffled into position, pilums protruding through tight gaps. After a long wait, the arrows stopped falling. The only sounds were panting and shuffling feet—and a woman crying in pain. Nerva could feel blood running down the inside of his tunic as he looked in the direction of the prisoners, trying to remember how far along the line they were. He had kept them close to ensure Brei did not get herself into trouble again. They would not be tucked under shields like the men.

Shaking his head and cursing, he broke away from the safety of the century and moved to the back, keeping low as he crept along the line of men. The prisoners were easy to spot as they were uncovered, some of them already dead, one writhing on the ground like a trampled snake. He stopped walking and searched for Brei among them, finally spotting her alive at the far end. She was laid over Lavena like a human shield. The girl's mother was also alive, huddled next to them. Brei raised her head, looking to the swamp while everyone else watched the hill on the other side.

'Steady, boys,' someone said as they waited for the Maeatae to emerge from the trees.

Something held Brei's attention in the water, and she

pushed herself up onto her hands and knees to get a better view. Amid the chaos, she had managed to cut herself free. He watched as she got slowly to her feet and crept towards the water's edge. She stopped, toes pressing into the mud as she leaned forwards, peering into the murky water. Looking at what? Nerva's heart slowed to a heavy thud as he read her expression. His gaze returned to the swamp, his unease growing. *Surely not.* Before he had a chance to act on his gut feeling, a creature burst from the water. The only indication that the creature was human was the outline of a blade in its hand.

'About-face!' Nerva shouted. 'They are in the water!'

Men turned in confusion, their shield wall faltering. The swamp creature threw his weapon, striking one of the soldiers in the face. A tortured scream rang out around them; then the water bubbled and shifted, and men rose like monsters in children's nightmares.

*Hiss, hiss. Hiss.*

More arrows came from the trees, accompanied this time by rocks the size of a child's head. Nerva took off at a run towards the water's edge, his shield raised over his head. In those clothes, Brei looked like a Roman woman. She was just as much a target as the soldiers in that moment.

Nerva reached her in a few strides, covering her with his shield as he dragged her back from the water's edge. Stones pounded down on them, sending pain up his arm and down his side.

'Hold the line!' someone shouted.

*Hiss, hiss, hiss.*

The moment Nerva reached Lavena, he threw Brei onto the ground. 'Stay down!' She immediately huddled with the girl and her mother. Laying the shield over the three of them, he turned and ran towards the water.

IT TOOK Brei a few moments to process what had happened. For the briefest period, she had foolishly thought herself *saved*. But the moment she looked the warrior in the eyes, she had known she was in trouble. The soldiers had stripped her of her identity. She looked like a Roman.

'What's happening?' Lavena asked, her body shaking violently. 'Are they here to save us?'

Brei blinked every time something hit the shield. It was the only thing between them and death. Peeking out of a gap, she watched as Nerva ran into the water, driving his sword through the stomach of a warrior.

'We need to make a run for it,' Morna said.

'No,' Brei said. 'Stay down.'

'And die? I have my daughter to think of.'

'No one will protect you.' Though Nerva had protected them.

Lavena squealed as a large rock cracked the shield.

'We'll head for the trees,' Morna said. 'Call to them in our tongue.'

'They won't hear you.' Brei glanced again at Nerva, who was fighting an endless stream of swampmen. 'You'll die before you reach them.'

*Hiss, hiss.*

'Look around you,' Morna said, her tone desperate. 'We're as good as dead if we stay here.'

*Hiss.*

'We stay,' Brei said firmly.

Shaking her head, Morna pushed the shield away and dragged Lavena to her feet. 'Come with us.'

'Get down!' Brei reached for Lavena, but just as her fingers wrapped the girl's arm, an arrow pierced her tiny shoulder. Morna screamed, and Brei dragged the girl beneath the shield. 'Down!' Brei yelled, but it was too late. A rock fell from the sky, and the screaming stopped. She covered Lavena's eyes as her mother collapsed on the ground beside them, eyes wide and blood running in all directions down her face.

Lavena sobbed violently. 'Mumma.'

Crying was a good sign, but they could not afford to draw attention. 'I need you to stay as still as possible and be very quiet. Can you do that?'

The girl was shaking uncontrollably, but she managed a nod. 'It hurts.'

'I know, but it will hurt a lot more if I try to pull it out.'

The arrows stopped the moment the Maeatae broke through the lines of soldiers, their battle cries oddly comforting. It was time for Brei to get up. She could not cower on the ground with the dead while her people fought to their deaths. Kissing Lavena's cheek, she said, 'Don't move. Understand?'

'Where are you going?' The girl's voice was laced with panic.

'I'll come back.' Brei slipped out from beneath the shield and pushed herself up onto her feet, preparing to fight alongside her people. Then she made the mistake of glancing at Nerva. He was thigh deep in the water and outnumbered. He would die in that swamp, and the thought sat like a stone in her belly.

Her eyes went to the dead soldier a few feet away who had kept hold of his sword, even in death. She bent and snatched the weapon from his hand, and when she straightened, she came face to face with a ghostly pale Nerva. He was panting, his skin glistening with sweat, his lips stained with blood. She could have killed him. She had never been more certain of anything in her life.

Nerva looked down, and she followed his line of sight to a deep gash that ran the length of his thigh. His leg and foot were soaked with blood. She had no idea how he was standing. Her sword fell a few inches, and she looked up at him again, the fight gone from her.

He opened his mouth to say something, then collapsed at her feet.

## CHAPTER 10

Nerva knew he was at sea before he had even opened his eyes. He felt the gentle lift and fall of the ship, heard the creaking wood, tasted the salty air. Gods, how long had he been out?

Forcing one eye open, he looked around for something familiar to mentally grab hold of, finding only barren walls, a table with a jug and cup on it, and a stool. With a groan, he pushed himself up onto his elbows. His side hurt, his leg throbbed, and his head felt like someone had hit him with a hammer. Lying back down, he tried to recall his last memory. He had been in the swamp, mud swallowing his feet and the water stained red around him.

*Brei.*

Nerva had told her to stay down, but when he looked over, he saw her standing alone with a sword in hand, turning in circles amid the violence. He had not realised the extent of his injury until he reached her. Lavena's mother lay dead nearby, and the girl was nowhere in sight. That was when he noticed the gaping wound on his leg. The icy water had numbed everything, a parting gift from the North.

Propping himself up onto his elbows, Nerva looked down at the fine Roman blanket covering his legs and breathed a sigh of relief when he counted two of them.

The cabin door creaked open, and Nerva looked over just as Marcus poked his head in. Seeing that he was awake, the tribune stepped inside.

'He lives.'

Nerva blinked against the light that followed him in. 'You sound surprised.'

'If you had seen yourself a few days ago, you would understand why.' He went to stand by the bed. 'How's the leg?'

'Difficult to tell when everything is sore. How bad is it?'

'It's still attached, so that's something. You'll be walking with a limp for a while and have one of those scars that children whisper about.' He pulled up the stool and took a seat. 'The physician will be by in a moment.'

Nerva pushed himself up into a seated position. 'How long have I been out?'

'Four days.'

'*Four days?*' He raised his arm to rub his forehead and winced.

'Did you forget about the arrow wound?'

'Evidently.' He carefully placed his arm back down. 'All right. Tell me everything.'

'You lost a lot of blood.'

'Not that. How many dead?' Nerva braced, knowing whatever the number, it would be too high.

Marcus leaned forwards and rested his elbows on his knees. 'Five hundred deceased. Another three hundred seriously injured. Around half of them auxiliaries.'

Nerva sat with those numbers for a moment.

'Caracalla arrived with his legion just in time.'

As much as Nerva despised the man, he was a soldier like his father. 'Thank the gods for that.'

A knock came at the door, and the physician stepped inside. 'Ah, he wakes,' the old man said, as though it were a joke of some kind. 'We'll have you up and about by the time we get to Rome.'

'Rome?'

Marcus clapped his hands together. 'Yes, we're going home. Cordius practically shoved me onto the ship with you.'

'He will be loving this entire thing.'

The physician pulled the blanket back and got to work. Nerva made a point of not looking, as his stomach was still adjusting to being at sea.

'Fluids,' the physician said to Marcus. 'He will need lots of them.'

Marcus walked over to the table and poured a cup of watered-down wine. When he handed it to Nerva, he said in a hushed voice, 'He's mad as a mule but did an excellent job piecing your leg back together.'

The physician hummed to himself as he unwrapped the leg and studied his handiwork. The smell of vinegar took over the air.

'Did any of the prisoners survive?' He could not hold the question in any longer.

Marcus crossed his arms, one corner of his mouth lifting. 'You want to know if the warrior survived, is that it?' He rocked on his heels. 'Brei. Is that what you call her?'

'That is her name, yes.'

The tribune nodded. 'She saved your life, you know.'

'What do you mean?'

'She tore clothes off a dead soldier to wrap your leg, then dragged you over to a pile of corpses to wait out the fighting.'

'You saw her?'

Marcus shrugged. 'Snippets. I was a little busy.'

He was thoughtful a moment. 'And the young girl?'

Marcus exhaled and shook his head. 'Brei is the only one from that group who boarded. That's all I know.'

'You were focused on the men, as you should have been.'

'They were going to execute her until I told them she saved your life.' He glanced over at the wound. 'Of course, that created a new set of problems.'

'I can imagine.'

'Everyone wants to know *why*.'

Nerva shook his head. 'I am certain Cordius will come up with some scandalous reason that will satisfy Caracalla.'

'The men will just assume you were sleeping with her.'

Nerva nodded. 'Better they think that than label me some sort of traitor.'

They both watched as the physician secured the fresh bandage, Nerva trying to ignore the growing pain.

'It's a good thing Severus worships the ground you walk on,' Marcus continued.

'For now. He will not be around forever.' Severus was the man who had seen the soldier in Nerva ten years earlier, the day he stepped into the arena to defend his sister.

'Geta likes you.'

'And Caracalla tolerates me.' Nerva looked at the physician. 'When you are finished, I would like to meet with the *trierarchus*.'

Marcus shook his head. 'You should eat something first.'

The physician stopped humming and turned to look at him. 'Some light exercise will do you good, but the tribune is right. You need to eat or you won't even make it to the door.' He guided Nerva back down onto the bed and lifted his arm. 'But first I need to check on this arrow wound.'

THE SMELL below deck made Nerva's stomach turn. Urine, faeces, and vomit blended with the odour of unwashed men. Most of the prisoners were Roman soldiers who had been caught doing the wrong thing. His hand went over his nose and mouth as he descended. While accustomed to the smells of war, this was something else. The sound of violent coughing stopped him. Gods only knew what diseases they had brought on board with them. One thing he knew for sure was that in those conditions, it would spread like fire.

He waited a moment for his eyes to adjust. She was not there.

'On your feet,' he called to the guard seated on a crate against the wall.

The man looked up, then stood to attention. 'General, sir.'

'At ease,' Nerva said, hobbling down the last few steps. He was already exhausted. 'I am looking for a prisoner. A native, actually.' There was no point giving a name. He was the only one foolish enough to have learned it. 'I cannot see her.'

The man looked around, thoughtful. 'All the prisoners are before you, sir.'

Nerva's gaze went to the three women seated in the far corner, none of them Brei. 'You are certain there are no other women aboard?'

The guard fell quiet again, and then his eyes widened as though recalling something. 'There was another, a Maeatae woman. Caused the men some grief, so we had her put in confinement.'

That was definitely her. 'Where is she?'

The guard hesitated. 'She's quite aggressive, sir.'

'I know.'

Looking confused, the soldier turned and marched off

in the other direction. Nerva did his best to keep up. The sound of retching followed them along the narrow passageway, all the way to the small door at the far end. Keys rattled in the guard's hand, and Nerva gestured for him to be quiet. He wanted to see her before she saw him. Stepping up to the tiny window, he peered inside, searching for her. It was too dark to see anything, so he moved closer, his nose brushing the iron grid.

*Bang.*

Nerva flinched as a fist landed against the door. Even the guard behind him jumped at the sudden noise. Golden eyes flashed, just inches from his. The brightness softened as Brei took him in, and she stepped back from the door.

'You.'

'Me.' He turned to the guard. 'Open the door.'

'Sir—'

'Now.'

The man reluctantly stepped forwards and unlocked the door. When he moved back from it, Nerva took the keys from his hands. 'You can leave us.'

'Yes, sir.' The guard frowned at the door, still ajar, before marching off in the direction from which they had come.

Nerva drew a breath, then pushed the door open. It whined in protest. He hesitated before entering, eyes moving over the shadows. Just because she had not killed him once before, that did not mean she would not try to kill him in the future. He waited for his eyes to adjust and spotted her leaning on the bulkhead in the far corner, watching him. 'What did you do to end up in here?'

She shrugged. 'I taught your men some much-needed manners.'

'I see.'

Brei's gaze fell to his bandaged leg. 'I'm surprised to see you alive.'

'I heard you saved my life.'

She looked away. 'It's not in my nature to kill an unconscious man.'

'Not even a Roman one?'

Her eyes returned to him with interest. 'I thought I'd let your injuries do the heavy lifting.' She watched him for a moment. 'Is that why you came here? To thank me?'

He limped over to hold the wall. 'I am sorry about the others, about Lavena.' He was quiet a moment. 'What happened?'

Her eyes clouded, then cleared. 'I left her behind.'

His eyebrows came together in a firm line. 'Because she died?'

'She was alive. Injured, but alive.'

He shook his head. 'I do not understand.'

Brei was silent a moment. 'I left her on the battlefield, amid the dead.' She blinked. 'The Romans were collecting the injured, men carrying men—hundreds of them. There was no one to tend the dead.'

'You planned it, then.'

She drew a breath. 'My people were watching from the trees. I could feel them. So, I told her to stay hidden until the Maeatae came for her.' Brei's voice cracked. 'I don't know if she made it. I only know that no Roman would have seen to her wounds while their own lay bleeding. And I have no idea how to remove an arrow.'

'So, you gave her a chance.'

'Maybe. Or maybe she died alone because of me.' She looked to the hull as if there were a window there instead of more darkness.

He struggled to find words. 'For what it is worth, I hope she made it.'

Brei looked back at him. 'Me too.'

Straightening, he took a moment to get his balance before limping back to the door.

'I was indebted to you,' Brei said, stopping him. 'That's why I saved your life.' He turned to look at her. 'And I feel sorry for you.'

His eyebrows rose. 'For *me*?'

'Your heart's not in this war.' She looked over at the door, which he had left open. 'Not smart, General. Even at your fittest, I could outrun you.'

'You will not get far. Unless you have fins I am unaware of.' He could have sworn he saw amusement flash in her eyes. She was certainly more relaxed around him than she had been in the past. 'Some of the other prisoners are sick. You might be better off staying in here for now.'

She regarded him for a moment. 'You don't need to worry about me, General. You're the one who looks ready to fall down.'

He reached out and took hold of the doorframe for a moment. 'How do you find the energy to talk back? I expected you to be a grieving mess.'

She tilted her head. 'Why? My family aren't dead.'

'Even if by some miracle they survive this war, you will never see them again.'

'Of course I'll see them again.' Her face hardened. 'Do you think this is how it ends for me? I drown in my own self-pity and just surrender to the Roman way of life?'

He stared at her. 'I think you are naive. Assuming you do not fall ill and die on this ship, you will disembark into a world you cannot even fathom. The noise, the stench, the chaos. The city you are headed to is a stark contrast to the clean air and green mountains you have known your entire life. You will be taken to a market, given a number, and sold like livestock.'

'Then I'll find a way home.'

Nerva exhaled. 'You fought well, but you lost.'

She swallowed, said nothing for the longest time. 'I'll see my family again, or I'll die trying.'

His finger tapped the edge of the door. 'If that belief gets you through, then hold on to it.' He limped through the door and pulled it shut behind him.

CHAPTER 11

The ship had hit bad weather, the type that nauseated even the strongest of stomachs and had men praying. Feeling useless, Nerva left his cabin and made his way slowly to the deck, where fifty or so men ran back and forth. Violent water sprayed them from each side. They shouted to one another, their words snatched away by the howling winds that carried them south. It was a good thing Nerva's bed and table were attached to the wall and floor, or they would have broken apart.

'Get below,' one of the crew shouted at Nerva as he ran past, unaware that he was speaking to a legate. It was not the time to pull him up on the fact.

Seeing that he would only be a hindrance in his condition, Nerva returned below, but instead of going to his cabin, he made his way down to the prisoners. He was thrown from wall to wall as he descended, his leg throbbing as he worked extra hard to remain upright.

The smell of sick hit him before he reached the bottom. Looking around for the guard, he found him perched on a stool with his head in a pail. Nerva walked closer, using the wall for balance. 'Keys,' he said, when he reached the guard.

The man looked up, and when he went to stand, Nerva put a hand on his shoulder. 'At ease.' He took the keys from the man's belt, then made his way down the narrow passageway. It took Nerva a moment to locate the lock and even longer to get the key in. He peered through the small hole in the door as he turned the key, ready for Brei's usual antics. But as he pushed the door open, he was met by the sound of retching. She was crouched in the corner with her back to him, one hand pressed to the wall for balance while the other gripped the pail.

'Are you all right?' he called to her.

He could tell by her expression when she turned around that she had not heard him enter. She collapsed against the wall, ghostly pale with an unnatural shine over her skin. 'Have you come to gloat?'

The ship leaned suddenly, forcing him forwards. 'Just wanted to check if you are still alive.'

'Barely.' She ran a hand down her face. 'What are my chances of getting off this ship?'

He sank down onto the floor beside her. 'Not very high, I am afraid.'

Brei pulled her legs up and rested her cheek on her knees, looking at him. 'I never get sick.'

He smiled and swallowed down his own rising nausea. 'They are not faring any better out there.'

'I can hardly breathe in here.'

They both closed their eyes as the ship rose once more.

'I might let you out if I could trust you not to assassinate the crew.' The sound of the side of the ship hitting the water made them both flinch. Brei grabbed hold of his arm for a moment, then quickly let go.

'You Romans have a god for everything. Isn't there a weather god you can pray to?'

He breathed out a laugh. 'That would be Tempestas, goddess of storms.'

She glanced across at him. 'A woman?'

He could hear the amusement in her voice. 'Of sorts.'

'She's angry.'

'It certainly seems that way.'

Brei drew a slow breath. 'I really need to get out of here.'

He looked up at the roof. 'I have enough on my plate without worrying about you being loose.'

Her eyebrows came together. 'What plate?'

'It is just an expression.'

'An expression of what?'

His gaze returned to her. 'To have a lot on one's plate means one has enough to worry about already.'

She flattened her shoulders against the wall as the ship rose again. 'It would be much easier if I could just kill you.'

'Why don't you?'

She was quiet a moment. 'You have saved my life too many times. It's a matter of honour.'

He rolled his head to look at her. 'Right now, you are desperate, and desperate people are capable of all kinds of dishonourable atrocities.'

'Atrocities?'

He exhaled as the ship fell once more. 'Terrible acts.'

'How fitting that you people have a special word for it.'

The ship rocked, and they were both silent again. It was surprisingly comfortable despite the circumstances, probably because he knew she was too sick to do anything foolish.

'Can I ask you something?' she said after a long silence.

'Yes.'

Her hands went to her stomach. 'Were you desperate when you committed all those *atrocities*?'

He did not bother to ask which ones she was referring to. Every action she had witnessed since the beginning of the war could be viewed that way. 'I was doing my job.'

She glanced sideways at him. 'That explains why Tempestas is so angry.'

Nerva noted the sincerity in her expression. 'Rome's gods are for Rome. Perhaps she is angry that you stole my horse on the battlefield.'

'You got him back.'

'You shot an arrow at my head.'

'You're surprisingly agile.' She rested her cheek on her knees again. 'If I had been quicker, I wouldn't be on this boat crippled by sickness.'

'If you had killed me, you would have died at Cordius's hand the day we arrived in your village.' He faced forwards again. 'He would have cut your throat. Though you are attractive enough, so he might have raped you first. They would have found the children hidden beneath the floor, and we both know what would have happened to them.'

Silence rang out between them as Brei digested the brutality of his words. 'I never thanked you for sparing their lives,' she finally said. 'My sister and nephew were among them.'

He was about to remind her that the entire Midland was under Roman control, then thought better of it. 'If you are still alive in the morning, I will get you out of here for a few hours.'

She closed her eyes. 'Thank you.'

'Do not make me regret it.'

## CHAPTER 12

Brei suspected Nerva was off somewhere having a good laugh as she cleaned fish on deck. She was not averse to the dirty work, but doing it beneath the watchful gaze of a Roman guard with her feet shackled was something else entirely. Where on earth did they think she was going to run to?

'You're slowing down,' the guard said, poking her with the toe of his boot.

She liked to pretend she could not understand him, watch his frustration grow and hear his voice get louder and louder, as though volume were the problem. But she really did not like him putting his feet on her. Rising from the crate, she regarded him for a moment. 'You want me to slow down?' She exaggerated her accent and fought back a smile when he rolled his eyes and let out an exasperated noise.

'Not slower, *faster*.' He gestured to the pile. 'Now pick up that fish before I beat you with it.'

She would have liked to see him try. Remembering the promise she had made to Nerva to behave, she sank back down onto the crate.

'Barbarians,' the guard mumbled as he leaned against the taffrail.

Brei shot up again, and the man straightened. Before she had a chance to retaliate, Nerva appeared. She took a step back from the guard when Nerva stopped beside her, looking between them.

'Is there a problem?'

The guard stood to attention, looking far less smug suddenly. 'No, sir, only that the girl can't understand me.'

Nerva's gaze drifted to Brei. There was amusement in his eyes. 'Oh, I think the girl can understand you just fine. Perhaps she would prefer to be back in her cell.'

'No,' Brei said. 'I would prefer to work.'

The guard eyed her suspiciously because her speech had suddenly improved.

'Leave us,' Nerva said, glancing back at the guard.

The man cast a filthy look in her direction before stepping away. Nerva waited until they were alone before reaching into one of his pockets and pulling out a rolled-up sheet of parchment. Opening it, he held it out to her.

'Can you read it?' he asked.

Brei took a step towards him. The clink of the heavy chain around her ankles drew Nerva's eye, but he said nothing of it. He had likely requested them. She took a moment to study the marks on the page. 'No.' She knew she smelled of fish guts and felt oddly self-conscious being that close to him. 'What does it say?'

He rolled it back up and returned it to his pocket. 'It is a letter. I wondered if you knew how to read.'

'I can read, just not Latin. You Romans are always assuming we're stupid. Perhaps to make yourselves feel better about killing us and stealing our land.' She nodded towards his pocket. 'What does it say?'

'It does not matter. I wondered, is all. If you could read,

it would greatly improve your prospects when we arrive in Rome.'

'My prospects?'

'Your value. The higher the value, the better the household.'

She looked down at her hands, wishing she could wash them. 'They are just marks right now, but if I studied them for long enough, I could probably find meaning.'

He looked out at the water. 'Perhaps I could teach you. You are smart, and I suspect you learn fast.'

She searched his face until his grey eyes returned to her. Then it was her turn to look away. 'What do you care if I can read or not?' she asked in Brittonic.

'You should speak in Latin from now on. Practice is important.'

He had managed to avoid answering her question. 'Can all of your slaves read?'

Nerva shifted his weight from one foot to another. 'Some in my father's household. Not all.'

'What about *your* household?'

'When I am not sleeping at the barracks, I stay with my family. I have no need for my own *domus*. When I marry, perhaps.'

She cleared her throat. 'All right. Teach me to read if you think it will help.'

Nerva nodded. 'Get cleaned up, and then I will send for you.'

Her eyebrows rose. 'I'm to go to your cabin?'

'Yes.'

'Where you sleep?'

'Yes.' He crossed his arms and waited.

She searched his face for a hint of anything untoward. 'I won't lie with you.'

His eyes creased at the corners, like he was laughing at her. 'You have a rather high opinion of yourself.'

'Not really, just a very low opinion of Roman men.' She stood a little taller. 'You are the one who said that I was pretty.'

'It was an observation, not a proposition.' He moved as if to leave. 'If you are not interested in learning, then just say, *"No, thank you"*. Now is also the time to brush up on your manners.'

Her cheeks flushed. 'I just wanted you to know where I stand.'

His gaze fell to her feet. 'Ankle deep in fish guts.'

She looked down also. 'It masks the smell of the crew. They sweat wine.'

He laughed, then covered it with a cough. It was the first time she had heard him laugh, and she felt oddly proud of being the cause of it. He gave her arm a pat, like one does a child.

'I am rather fussy about the women I invite to my bed. You are quite safe.'

The colour in her cheeks deepened.

Grinning, Nerva added, 'You know, you do not smell so great yourself.' With that, he turned and limped off in the other direction.

~

'WHAT DO YOU MEAN, you're going to teach her to read?' Marcus said, a smile tugging at his mouth.

Nerva was lying on the bed with his leg elevated in hope of reducing the throbbing. 'It will improve her value, and valuable slaves are treated better by their masters.'

Marcus shook his head and sat on the edge of the table. 'I thank you for that brief lesson on the workings of slavery. If you don't mind me saying so—'

'I do.'

'This seems like a rather complicated path to wherever it is you two are heading.'

Nerva closed his eyes, feeling hot suddenly. 'We are not headed anywhere.'

'Pfft.' The tribune picked up one of the letters on the desk and began reading it. 'You did not tell me Dulcia had another baby.'

Nerva turned his head and looked. 'They are private letters.'

'Another girl.'

Nerva gestured for the letters to be brought to him. Just as Marcus dropped them into his hand, there was a knock at the door. He went to open the door on Nerva's behalf. Brei stood with a guard either side her.

Marcus turned to look at him. 'I shall leave you to your *lesson*.'

Nerva would have thrown something at him if he had the energy and reflexes necessary, but the tribune stepped around Brei and disappeared. Nerva's head pulsed as he sat up, even more so when he noticed one of the guards had a blood-crusted nose.

'Come in,' he said tiredly.

That same guard shoved her forwards. Given her size, she held her ground well. He would have a word with the man later, but not in front of her. Could not have her getting any more ideas.

'Remove the irons and leave us.'

The guards looked at one another. 'Best leave them on, sir,' one said. 'Even in irons, she's trouble.'

Nerva went to stand, then changed his mind. His head felt dizzy. 'Yes, I am well aware of the fact. Do as I have asked, soldier.'

The man stepped forwards, giving Brei a stern look as he uncuffed her wrists before crouching down to remove the shackles. When he was done, he turned to salute Nerva and exited the cabin behind the other soldier. Brei rubbed her wrists and looked around the room. If he did not know her better, he might have thought her nervous.

'Bring that stack of letters and the stool.' Nerva turned his body so he could lift his bad leg back onto the bed, wincing as he did so.

Brei looked him over before going to the table. 'You have been walking too much.' She snatched up the papers and pushed the stool across the floor with her foot.

'Probably.'

She stopped halfway between him and the table and sat down. Even at that distance, he could smell the soap he had sent down. She had also made use of the comb, her hair brushed and slightly damp. It fell forwards as she made herself comfortable, and she tucked it behind her ears before looking at him. 'Has the wound gone bad?'

He blinked. 'No, just hurts a bit.'

She did not look convinced, but she returned her attention to the first letter. 'All right. Where do we start?'

He strained to see what she was looking at. Sighing, as though it were the most inconvenient thing she had done since becoming a prisoner of war, she dragged the stool closer to him and pushed her hair to one side as she studied the words. Nerva's gaze fell to her exposed neck before settling on the letter in her hand. He pointed to the first line. 'My Dearest Nerva,' he said slowly, running his finger along the letters.

Brei examined the marks carefully. 'That's your name?' She pointed.

'Yes.' He watched her as she committed it to memory.

Brei was a stark contrast to the women his mother was always parading in front of him. There was something dishonest about rich women—all that paint on their faces, the overstyled hair, and expensive fabric. There was no illusion with Brei. She was raw and refreshingly honest, from her rich chestnut hair to the handful of freckles dusting her face.

'What are you looking at?' she asked.

He had been staring at her like a fool. 'I was just thinking through the best way to teach you.'

'We always start with letters.'

He frowned. 'Perhaps you could show me something written in your language first.'

'You want me to prove I can do it?'

'I believe you. I am just curious to see if there are any similarities.'

Another sigh, but then she hopped off the stool and walked over to the table. She dragged a blank piece of parchment to her, snatched up the quill, and studied it for a moment.

'You dip the end in the ink,' Nerva said.

She looked around for the ink, then dipped it in. Tentatively, she scrawled a few marks on the page. When she was done, she brought the paper closer to her lips, blowing on it a few times.

'Let's see,' Nerva said.

She returned to his bedside and handed it to him as she sat down.

'What does it say?' he asked, looking over it.

She pointed to the marks, dragging her finger along the letters as he had done. 'Your wound has gone bad.'

Nerva bit back a grin. 'Very funny. I thought I was hiding the pain quite well.'

'The pain, yes, but there is no hiding the colour of your skin peeking out from the bandage. It wasn't like that yesterday.'

His eyes moved over her face. 'You must have been looking very closely.'

'Hard not to notice something so unsightly. Plus your cheeks look fevered.' She brought a cool hand to his face, then quickly withdrew it, eyes returning to the letter. 'Is this from your future wife?'

It took him a moment to understand the question. 'No. One of my sisters—Mila.' He did not know why he told Brei her name.

She looked up at him again. 'Oh.'

A knock at the door made them both jump.

Clearing his throat, Nerva called out, 'Enter.'

The door opened, and one of the crew stepped inside. 'Pardon the interruption, General, but the trierarchus needs to see you urgently.'

Nerva nodded. 'All right. Send the guards in to collect the prisoner.' He turned to her as the door closed. 'We will have to try again tomorrow.'

She looked disappointed as the two guards re-entered, irons in hand.

'Those will not be necessary,' Nerva said. 'She will give you no trouble on the walk back.'

The guards exchanged a look. 'She almost broke his nose on the walk here.'

Nerva breathed out and glanced in her direction. She did not look the slightest bit apologetic.

'He called me a whore,' she said, 'and then my elbow slipped.'

Nerva shook his head. 'Shackle her.'

Brei scowled. '*What?*'

'Rome needs its soldiers in good health.'

She shot up from the stool. 'So I'm supposed to stand still while they *touch* me?'

Nerva closed his eyes as he stood, his leg burning and head pulsing. 'Shackles,' he said again. But when the men stepped forwards to secure her, he caught one by the arm. 'But if I find out your hands have wandered beyond those cuffs, I will break both your noses myself. Are we clear?'

The men nodded, and Nerva walked out.

## CHAPTER 13

'Is everything all right?' she asked, noting the dark circles around Nerva's eyes when he looked at her. He looked even worse than the day before, his cheeks pinched with fever and his forehead shiny. Brei did not dare touch his face again. The familiar gesture had made them both uncomfortable.

'Yes. Why do you ask?'

'Because the trierarchus sent for you yesterday, said it was urgent.'

Nerva nodded and wiped his forehead with the back of his hand. 'There have been sightings of pirates in the area. We will be stopping for supplies in a day or so. That makes us a target.'

'What sort of supplies?'

Nerva rubbed at his forehead tiredly. 'Food. Grain, mostly.'

She was going to ask where they were stopping but knew such a question would sound like she was planning an elaborate escape. Her gaze went to his injured leg. 'The physician changed the bandage.'

'Just this morning.'

'And?'

He exhaled before replying. 'And the wound has gone bad. But you already knew that.'

It was tempting to gloat, but she was also aware of how dangerous an injury like that could be. 'You should lie down.'

'Why?'

Her eyes searched his. 'So I can smother you with a pillow.'

His mouth twitched. 'Do you know what they would do to you if you killed me?'

'Can't be any worse than what they've already done.'

He lay back down and draped an arm over his face. 'Next line. What letters do you see?'

She looked at the parchment in her hand. 'You can barely stay awake, let alone teach.'

'Just keep going.' His voice sounded scratchy when he spoke.

Brei glanced at the jug of water next to his bed and told herself not to touch it. She was there to learn, not tend him. The only reason she needed to learn Latin to begin with was because he had taken her prisoner and was forcing her into a life she did not want. What sort of prisoner would she be if she aided her captor's recovery?

Letting out a resigned breath, she stood and poured some water, then crouched next to the bed and brought the cup to his lips. 'Drink.'

He lifted his arm so he could see her, the small movement looking as though it took great effort. 'Did you poison it?'

She pressed her lips together to stop from smiling. She hated to admit it, but they shared a similar sense of humour. 'Don't be ridiculous. I put an ancient curse on it.'

'That is fine. I am not superstitious.' He pushed himself up onto his elbows and watched her as he drank.

She looked only at the cup.

'Thank you,' he said quietly.

She returned to her stool and stared intently at the next line of text. 'Is that a *b*?' Holding the letter out to him, she pointed at the word. When he did not respond, she lowered the letter and looked across at him. He twitched a few times as he drifted off to sleep. It was hardly surprising given the state of him.

Dropping the letter onto her lap, she held the edge of the stool and looked around the room. A sword lay next to his boots in the corner. Earlier, she had noticed a dagger poking out from the map on the table. Not that she needed a weapon if she wanted to end his life. She could smash the jug over his head, then slice his throat with one of the shards.

But she did none of those things.

It was not only because there were guards waiting on the other side of the door, but because she did not want to harm him. So, she did the next thing that came to her mind. Finding a cloth, she dipped it in the jug of water and began wiping his face and neck.

'What are you doing?' he murmured.

She froze as if she had been caught doing something wrong, but in that moment, it did not seem to matter that he was Roman or that she was Maeatae. He was someone in need of care, and she was able to help him. 'Your fever is getting worse.'

'It certainly feels that way.' His arm slid back, dropping to the pillow above his head. Grey eyes stared up at her. 'You have lovely ears.'

Her eyebrows rose, slowly. 'Ears?'

'Yes. They are neat and perfectly round at the top.' He blinked as he focused on them.

Brei dipped the cloth in fresh water, smiling to herself. There was nothing quite as entertaining as the ramblings of a fevered man. Of all the things for him to compliment her on. 'They are my mother's ears.' Her smile faded. 'My nephew has them also.'

Nerva drew a breath and continued to watch her. 'That is why you fight so well.'

'Because of my ears?' she wiped his face.

'Because of your mother. Nothing motivates a person more than revenge. Though it will eat you up if you are not careful.'

Brei withdrew her hand.

'Tell me what happened.'

She was silent a moment, wondering if she could talk about her mother with her enemy. 'She never returned to the village, so we went back to search for her among the dead. There were bodies everywhere, most of them unrecognisable. Then the Romans came back and began burning them…' She closed her eyes at the image. 'The Maeatae were left on the forest floor for wild animals to pick apart.' Holding on to the edge of the bed, she waited for the wave of emotion to pass. A large, clammy hand covered hers. She waited for that feeling to arrive, the one that would tell her to pull away. Instead, she felt only calm as she stared down at Nerva's hand.

When she found the courage to look up at him, she found his eyes closed. She reprimanded herself for reading into the fever-fuelled conversation. The man hardly knew what he was saying or doing. She pulled her hand free of his and stood, preparing to go to the door and have the guards return her to her cell. But before she had even taken a step, there was a loud crashing noise, and she was thrown backwards. She landed on her side, sliding across the floor and slamming into the wall. Dazed, she pushed herself up and looked around, trying to figure out what had just happened. That was when she noticed Nerva on the floor a few feet away. He had been thrown from his bed.

'Are you all right?' he asked, looking far more alert than he had a few moments earlier.

She nodded. 'I think we hit something.'

Nerva got to his feet and limped over, pulling her up with surprising strength given the state of him. 'Or something hit *us*.'

She was about to ask what he meant when the door burst open and Marcus rushed in. He looked from the empty bed to them. 'We're under attack. They're already aboard.'

Brei looked to Nerva. 'Who's attacking you?'

Nerva limped over to where his sword and boots lay. 'Pirates.' He began dressing. 'How many?'

'Around two hundred men.'

'You easily outnumber them,' Brei said.

Marcus and Nerva exchanged a look that suggested otherwise.

'What?' she asked, looking between them.

'Influenza,' Marcus said.

'It has spread through the ship,' Nerva added. 'Most of the men are about as useful as me right now.'

'Influenza…' Brei looked back at Marcus. 'If they're as useless as him, you have already lost.'

'I am right here,' Nerva said.

Marcus looked conflicted.

'You shouldn't fight,' Brei said, doing her best to remain calm. She knew pirates made their own rules and laws and that she was in just as much danger as the men. 'Your best chance of survival is to hide.'

Nerva wiped a hand down his sweaty face. 'You think I am going to hide? Is that what you think a legate in the Roman army would do when under attack?'

She scowled across at him. 'If he wished to live, yes.'

'You don't look great,' Marcus agreed.

'Gods, not you too.' Nerva finished belting his weapon and looked up. 'I want every able-bodied man on deck. If they can hold a sword, they can fight.' He looked at Brei. 'And take her below.'

Brei crossed her arms and raised her chin. 'You said every able-bodied man is to fight.'

'Yes, *man* being the key word there.'

Her mouth flattened into a line. 'You can't be serious. I'm more able-bodied than the two of you combined.'

Nerva limped for the door. 'You are also a prisoner and a threat to my men.'

'What? I could've killed you seven times over during this visit alone.'

Nerva continued walking as if she had not spoken. 'Get her below deck.'

## CHAPTER 14

Brei paced, wearing tracks in the wooden floor. Never had her cabin felt so much like a cage. Nerva had locked her up and left her defenceless, without even so much as a dagger to protect herself. What was she supposed to do if the intruders made it below deck? She hoped the prisoners coughing their lungs up at the end of the passageway would deter them.

Above her she could hear shouting and banging, things breaking, people breaking. Weapons screeched, some falling to the ground alongside the people who once held them. There was no way Nerva was well enough for the battle she could hear overhead. A frustrated groan escaped her, but then shouting outside her cabin made her freeze. She held her breath as the clash of blades drew close. Then silence—but not the good kind.

Footsteps approached, and the lock rattled. A string of curses followed.

'Get it open' came a voice.

The man spoke Latin, though not the dialect she was familiar with.

She glanced about the cabin for something to defend

herself, her eyes landing on the pail in the corner. Snatching it up, she went to stand by the door. The small window went dark as a face covered it. Someone peered inside. She knew they could not see her, because there was no light, and she was at an angle that made it difficult.

*Bang. Bang, bang, bang.*

She jumped as something pounded the timber door—a foot, perhaps. Her hand tightened around the rope handle of the pail, and she swung it gently, getting used to the weight of it.

*Bang.*

This time the door swung open, smashing against the wall. Brei raised the pail and brought it down on the stranger's head. It broke apart on impact. Dazed, the man staggered backwards, clutching his head. Another man entered behind him, holding a dagger. He looked around, blinking, no doubt waiting for his eyes to adjust to the dark. She lunged forwards and stole the sword hanging from the dizzy intruder's hip. She felt much better with a weapon in her hand.

'Oh, love,' said the other man. 'What do you think you're going to do with that? Why don't you hand it over before you hurt yourself?'

She spun the sword a few times, eyes never leaving him. 'I'll take my chances.'

The two men exchanged a surprised look, then advanced towards her. 'I think we have ourselves a little highlander,' said the first man.

'What you doin' in here, love?' the other asked. 'Looks like them soldiers aren't treating you right.' His smile revealed broken teeth.

'Best you come with us,' the other said. 'We'll take much better care of you.'

At least now she knew the type of men she was dealing with. 'I can take care of myself.'

The pirates chuckled and edged towards her. 'There's a good girl. Hand over the sword before you accidentally cut a finger off.'

'No.' She swung her sword, disarming the man with the dagger. It fell to the ground, and she kicked it behind her. His mouth fell open. 'Now let me past, or I'll kill you both.'

The man closest shook his head. 'Oh, we have a wild one here. How about we—'

She did not let him finish his sentence. Spinning, she slashed at his ribs, and he cried out, hands flying over the gaping wound. Before the other man had a chance to act, she pushed between them and took off at a run. When she reached the other prisoners, she found them huddled against one wall while two men fought in the middle. She did not stick around to be spotted but continued past them to the ladder, climbing the steps two at a time.

On deck, she was met with the familiar sound of battle and a breathtaking backdrop. The sunset painted the entire sky, and it was reflected in the water below. It was a startling contrast of beauty and violence. She searched for Nerva, gaze sweeping the length of the deck. There was a rise of panic when she did not find him. He was probably already dead. The weak and the sick were always the first to die—and he had been very sick. Why on earth had he thought he could fight?

A uniformed man tumbled past her, leaving a trail of blood in his path. She stepped over it, sword ready. But before she had a chance to use it, another man crashed into her, knocking her to the ground before running off without so much as a backwards glance. Rolling onto her stomach, she pushed herself up and looked cautiously around. She was going to need to be more careful. Then she caught sight of Nerva at the bow end of the ship.

He was alive. Now what?

Given that he could barely keep his eyes open before

the pirates arrived, he seemed to be managing quite well. She watched as he stepped back to avoid a blade coming at him, then drove his sword through his opponent's stomach, thrusting it up before withdrawing it. He wavered on his feet, panting and looking around for whoever was brave enough to attack him next. His eyes met hers across the floating battlefield, and his face hardened.

Caught in a flurry of fighting men, another body slammed into Brei, knocking her sideways. At least this time she was able to remain upright. She was not usually so distracted when people were dying around her, but she had also never been so irrelevant during a battle before. The soldiers did not care enough to protect her, and the pirates did not care enough to kill her. She searched for Nerva once more and could not find him. Fingers wrapped her arm, and she immediately threw her elbow up, connecting with a chin. She turned, sword raised, only to find Nerva standing there, cupping his jaw with his hand. 'Sorry.'

'How the hell did you get out?'

Yes, he was angry. 'Some men broke the door down. Was I supposed to wait there for more to arrive?'

One of the intruders ran at Nerva and would have stabbed him in the back, but Brei intercepted and pierced his raised arm with her sword. Nerva spun around and cut his throat before he had a chance to scream; then, taking her by the wrist, he pulled her away from the brawling men.

They made it all the way back to the ladder before he faced her again.

'Find somewhere to hide,' he said.

Her brow creased. 'Hide? It's you who needs to hide.' He looked ready to fall down.

A soldier ran past, and Nerva pulled her out of the way. They were so close she could feel the heat of his body through his clothes. The smell of smoke made Brei look up, and she found the sail on fire. 'That can't be good.' Nerva appeared not to hear her, growing paler by the second. 'Are you all right?'

He opened his mouth to answer, but nothing came out. A moment later his eyes rolled back and his knees buckled. She tried to catch him but only managed to slow his descent to the deck. Crouching beside him, she gave his clammy face a light slap. 'Nerva.' His skin was so hot, despite the frosty air. He did not respond.

Brei looked around for help, but everyone was too busy fighting to take notice of the legate passed out at her feet. Standing, she tucked her sword into her belt and dragged him by one arm into the shadows, where she positioned herself in front of him like a bodyguard.

As she stood there trying to think through her next move, a large, burly man marched past. He carried a sword in each hand, his arms so muscled that every vein was visible. He stopped walking when he caught sight of her and turned. Her mouth went dry. He had a shaved head with jagged white lines striping one side of his skull. He was missing his right ear, and a white film covered his left eyeball. When he blinked, that eye did not close. Her fingers tightened around her sword as she waited to see what he would do next.

The man looked past her to where Nerva lay on the ground. 'What you hiding there?' He took a few steps in her direction, eyes narrowing. 'A soldier.' He grinned at her like a madman. 'What does that make you, then? His whore?'

She was barely listening, too busy measuring herself against him. While she was not short by any means, she barely reached his chest. His shoulders were easily three times the width of her own. She felt like a joke standing there with her sword. 'Keep walking, and I'll spare you the embarrassment of dying at the hands of a woman.'

He laughed from his belly, the sudden noise making her muscles tense.

'You're a bold lass.' His gaze drifted down. 'Look at those sweet little hips. Bet you're a tight little thing too.'

She did not catch everything he was saying, but she understood enough. When he took a step towards her, she swung her sword. He was surprisingly agile, the blade passing in front of his chest as he curved his back.

'I'll take you with both arms missing if I have to,' he said. 'I'm not that fussy.'

She swung again, and he blocked it with his own sword, using so much force that he knocked the weapon from her hand. She blinked and looked around, searching for another weapon or someone who might help her, but there was no one. The only man who cared if she lived or died was lying unconscious behind her. She backed away from her attacker until her heel bumped Nerva's shoulder.

*Wake up.*

The man stepped forwards and grabbed her by the arm. She kicked his leg as hard as she could and was surprised when he did not react in the slightest. Wrenching her forwards, she went down on her knees. Rather than pull her to her feet, he began dragging her along the deck towards the stern of the ship. She clawed wildly at his arm, even tried to bite him, but each time he just pushed her away without so much as breaking stride.

'Nerva!' she called, panic rising. Her time was running out, but the legate did not move.

When her leg hit a hard object, she managed to catch it with her foot and drag it close enough to grab it with her free hand. It was heavy, but she hoisted it up and saw it was an iron hook. She brought it down hard on his arm.

He turned, his mouth pressed into an angry line as he caught her hand before she could strike him again.

Brei was not just going to hand it over to him. Bringing her legs around, she kicked him as hard as she could in the groin. He cried out but still did not let go of her. With his teeth gritted, he tore the metal pole from her hand and tossed it away as though it were a stick. It flew through the air and disappeared over the side of the ship. He yanked her to her feet and slammed her against the taffrail. His hands were large enough to hold both her wrists in one while the other tugged her tunic up.

'No.' She spat at him, knowing it would not stop his advances. He leaned against her, the weight of him holding her in place and preventing her from kicking. 'No.' The word lacked power, but she kept saying it anyway. 'No.'

He gripped her bare thigh and she sucked in a breath, drawing her legs together as tightly as she could. *No.* 'Nerva!'

'I don't mind if you scream,' he whispered, his breath hot on her ear.

She felt the burn of tears as he parted her legs with just the spread of his fingers. Instinctively, she threw her head forwards into his face. Blood exploded from his nose. He let go of her leg to cover it but still managed to keep hold of her hands as he cursed and spat. Brei closed her eyes while he bled all over her. Then she realised her own nose was bleeding too, pouring freely down her face and neck. She was dizzy from the knock and had very little fight left in her.

'You like it rough, is that it?'

His words sounded far away even though they were being spoken directly into her ear. She tried to focus her vision, blinking wildly. 'You'll have to kill me first.'

She braced for just that, expecting him to break both her arms with one squeeze of his hand and throw her to the ground. Instead, she felt his body jolt and watched his eyes widen. His muscles went slack, and he let go of her hands. She pressed herself closer to the taffrail as he slid to the ground. Only then did she see the sword protruding from his back.

She held on to the smooth wood for balance as she looked around. Nerva stood ten feet away in the shadows, sweat dripping from his ghostly face. His gaze dropped a few inches to her bleeding nose.

'He hurt you,' he said, barely coherent.

She brought a trembling hand to her face, wiping at the blood and finding tears also. 'It will stop in a moment.' *The bleeding and the tears.*

He took a step in her direction, dragging his bad leg behind him. The pain must have been unbearable; how he was upright was beyond her. Stepping over the corpse, she went to him. He surprised her by opening his arms, and she surprised herself by running into them. She fought back the sob that threatened to escape. She would not let one more tear betray her.

'It is all right,' he said, his voice like a cool drink of water.

Even in his current state, he offered comfort. Pulling away from him, she looked around for somewhere to seat him. 'Come.' She dragged one of his arms over her shoulders and guided him behind a tall pile of crates that might shield them. She was not naive enough to believe they were safe, so after lowering Nerva to the floor, she went back for the weapons. She returned a few moments later, sinking down beside the legate. They sat shoulder to shoulder, watching the sail burn and listening as the fighting slowly came to an end, the Romans regaining control of their ship. Brei's nose had stopped bleeding, and she made no attempt to clean herself up. She turned the swords, one in each hand.

'Thank you,' she said, not looking at him.

He leaned his head back against the rough wood. 'Do not thank me yet. We may very well drown or burn to death.'

But they did not burn or drown. Eventually, the fighting stopped altogether. Men shouted to one another. The sails were lowered, pails of water thrown over the flames until all that remained was soggy fabric, blackened wood, and foul smoke.

'What happens now?' Brei asked, turning to look at Nerva. He did not reply. She had lost him again. Guiding his head down to her shoulder, she closed her eyes and waited.

CHAPTER 15

The Romans called it influenza. Brei had never seen anything like it. It spread like the plague, had guards and prisoners burning up, wheezing, and taking to their beds because they could not remain on their feet. The realisation that Nerva was likely infected also made her nervous. If healthy men were not immune, what chance did an injured soldier stand fighting it?

The guard who brought her food and water was fine one morning, then by the afternoon had the same wheezy cough that was rattling the ship. He did not return the next day, and no one came in his place. Three days she went without food and water, waking each morning to the splash of bodies hitting the ocean. A cold fear grew in her chest as she realised that Nerva was probably dead. She knew that if he was well enough, he would have come to her. If he had been conscious, he would have sent someone else in his place. But no one came.

Brei replayed those final moments with Nerva: the burning sail, the weight of his head on her shoulder, the soldiers arriving and trying to rouse him. She had called his name as the guards dragged her away, not because she needed his help but because she wanted to see his eyes open.

By the time the ship arrived at the Roman port of Ostia Antica, much of the coughing had ceased. The silence was unsettling. After a long wait, the door to her cabin finally opened. She knew the man standing before her had not sailed with them. He looked much too healthy. Holding a piece of fabric over his nose and mouth, he peered cautiously around the edge of the door, visibly surprised to find her alive.

On deck she was inspected by a physician. Anyone showing symptoms was taken to another part of the ship. She had no idea what became of them, only that they did not disembark. All she wanted was to get off the ship, so when they told her to strip, she did.

'Open your mouth,' the man instructed. He was dressed in civilian clothes and had a way of looking through her rather than at her. It was better that way as she stood naked before him. He checked her teeth, made her stick out her tongue, told her to lift her arms, stand on one leg, cough.

'Clothes on,' he finally said before moving to the next person.

The sun was high in the sky when they finally walked down the gangplank. They were marched along the dock and herded into carts in groups of ten. Brei wiped her face, wondering how she would combat the harsh Roman heat after days without water.

'Is there anything to drink?' she asked one of the guards.

The man did not reply but handed her a waterskin as they departed. She shared it with the other prisoners.

'What about food?' she asked.

'Don't push it' came his reply.

She could survive a little longer without food.

They travelled overnight, sleeping upright with their heads swaying from side to side. When the sun rose the next morning, Brei caught sight of a tall wall in the distance.

*Romans and their walls.*

When they reached it, the cart stopped and more men arrived, shouting instructions at them. Everyone seemed to understand what was being said. That was the moment Brei realised she was the only Caledonian among them. The others must have come from farther south or some other port.

'Out with you,' one of the guards said, losing patience and pulling her down with more force than was necessary.

Brei gritted her teeth and joined the line.

The prisoners were led through the open gate into another world—Nerva's world, the one he had told her she could not fathom. He had been right.

The buildings and structures were like nothing she had ever seen. The houses came closer and closer together until there was no space between them at all. Soon they were weaving through narrow streets swarming with men, women, and children of all ages. Women hung from balconies, chatting with their neighbours who were so close they could touch if they reached out an arm.

The noise, the smells—it was all so overwhelming. As Brei looked around, she half expected people to stop and ask questions of the prisoners being marched through their city, but all she got was a few disinterested glances before they went about their day.

They were taken to a place called *Graecostadium*, which appeared to be a marketplace for slaves, just like the one Nerva had described. Her feet stopped at the frightening sight: people in cages. *Children* in cages.

'Keep moving,' one of the guards shouted, shoving her forwards.

She walked on, her gaze fixed on the children.

'Form a line,' the same guard shouted, pushing them in various directions.

The women were separated from the men, and then a tired looking bald man wandered out to inspect them.

'All right. What have we got?' he asked the guard. 'These the ones from the ship?'

'What's left of them.'

'They've been checked?'

'Yes.'

The bald man did not look convinced. 'That doesn't mean they're not sick, it just means they're not displaying symptoms *yet*.' He strolled along the line of women, pausing to check various things like fingernails and teeth. At Brei he stopped walking, studying her closely for a moment. 'Do you speak Latin?'

She glanced at the other guard before replying. 'Yes.'

'You look strong. Good for labour.' He poked at her toned arm. 'Shame to waste that pretty face though.'

'She's Maeatae. Feisty thing,' one of the guards said.

The bald man frowned. 'Open your mouth.' Brei did as she was told. 'Seems healthy enough, but I want them locked up separately just in case. The last thing I need is influenza ravaging this place.' He pointed at her foot. 'Chalk her up.'

Another man came forwards, carrying a pail of white powder. He crouched in front of her, dusting one foot before stepping back again. Brei stared down at the white limb while the bald man placed a small placard around her neck. He scribbled a few words before moving on to the next person. Brei wished she had progressed further with her lessons. Lifting the board, she turned it in order to see the words. They appeared to be a list of selling points. When the inspector caught sight of her, he straightened.

'Can you read that?'

She remembered what Nerva had told her. Reading added to her value, and the higher her value, the better the household. 'Yes,' she lied. In truth, the only word she recognised was Maeatae.

The inspector returned to her and wrote something else on her placard before stepping back. 'All right. Lock them up and feed them.'

Brei was ushered into a cage—an actual cage. One that would normally be used to hold a large man-eating animal. They were given water that tasted like metal and some sort of coarse dry bread that was at least a few days old. Brei tore off large chunks, swallowing them whole as her hunger awakened. After eating, she tried to talk to some of the other women, but no one was interested in talking to the girl with the chalked foot. They may have shared a cage, but they were not the same.

Many types of people made their way through the market that day. Men in tunics, men in uniform, some in togas who arrived in curtained-off boxes carried by other men. She kept expecting them to emerge with injuries, perhaps a leg missing, but the only ailment she could pinpoint was some extra weight around their middle.

Brei stood at the front of the cage, leaning on the bars, watching them come and go. Those who did wander in her direction took one look at her foot and generally kept walking. It was that way until late in the afternoon, when one man stepped out of a litter, smoothing down his toga as his gaze swept the length of the marketplace. She watched as he wandered along for a moment, then his eyes met hers before looking her up and down. The corners of his mouth lifted slightly, his expression making Brei step back from the bars.

The bald man approached the new arrival with his arm extended. 'Claudius Liberia. A pleasure, as always.'

Claudius tore his gaze away from Brei to greet the man.

'Iunius.' He briefly took hold of the man's arm, then discreetly wiped his hand on his toga.

Iunius clapped once. 'Right, what can I help you with today?'

'A female for house duties,' Claudius replied, his gaze returning to Brei.

Iunius looked around, thinking. 'How was the one I sold you a few months back?'

Claudius crossed his arms in front of him. 'My wife can be rather particular, as you know.'

The merchant wore a knowing expression. 'Well, we must keep the wife happy.'

'Quite.'

'Let me think. We had a solid little worker yesterday, but she went the same afternoon she arrived.'

Even at that distance, Brei got a bad feeling from Claudius Liberia, so she wandered to the back of her confines and sank down between the other prisoners. One of them had started coughing, her cheeks growing pinker by the hour. The others were seated as far away from her as possible.

The sound of footsteps approaching made Brei look up. Seeing Claudius Liberia up close confirmed her suspicion. The man was a predator.

'I'm afraid these women will be no good in a household like yours,' Iunius said.

Claudius was only looking at Brei. 'And why is that?'

'They arrived on a ship yesterday. Most of the passengers were infected with influenza. These are the only female prisoners who survived the journey.'

As if on cue, the sick woman coughed, and Iunius immediately pulled Claudius back from the cage. 'As I cannot guarantee their health, they're priced accordingly.'

Claudius continued to eye Brei, and she felt the need to draw her knees up.

'That one seems healthy. Let me take a look at her.'

Iunius appeared unsure but then gestured for Brei to stand. She did not move.

'On your feet,' Iunius shouted, knowing she understood.

Brei rose while the merchant unlocked the gate and gestured for her to come forwards. Lifting her chin, she tried to make herself as tall as possible as she went to them.

'Let us take a proper look at her, then,' Claudius said.

Iunius tugged down her tunic, but Brei caught hold of it, her fingers tightening on the fabric. Annoyed, Iunius pulled harder, but the tunic did not move. 'Let go,' he said, a warning in his tone.

'I've already been inspected.'

'It is all right,' Claudius said, a smile on his lips. 'Modesty is an admirable quality.' His gaze fell to her chalked foot. 'From Britannia?'

'North of the wall, they say.'

Claudius's eyes shone a little brighter all of a sudden. 'How exotic.' He reached for the placard around her neck, lifting it so he could read. His fingers swept over her breastbone in the process. Yes, he was a predator.

'And she speaks Latin.' His eyes travelled up to meet hers once more. 'Impressive.'

Iunius cleared his throat. 'Historically, you have preferred... quieter girls for your household.'

Apparently he was a regular at the market. Brei could imagine what happened to all the other girls who entered his household.

'It is nice to mix things up occasionally.' Claudius looked at Brei when he said that.

Before he could say anything else, someone called his name. 'Claudius Liberia,' a voice boomed through the crowded space.

Claudius all but rolled his eyes before turning in the man's direction. 'Gallus.'

The brawny man came towards them, his toga as bright as the sun and rings covering every finger. His round cheeks reddened with the effort of the short walk. When he finally reached them, he extended one plump hand, which Claudius reluctantly took hold of. 'We must stop running into each other this way. How is your family?'

It was clear that Claudius had no interest in conversing with the man. 'Well, thank you.'

Gallus turned to look at Brei, taking a moment to read her placard. 'What do we have here?'

'A highlander,' Iunius said.

Gallus looked past her to the rest of the female prisoners. 'Just the one?'

'Influenza,' Iunius said, as if that explained everything.

'Ah,' Gallus said, his face turning solemn. 'General Nerva Papias was on that ship. Terrible business.'

Brei's heart stopped at the mention of Nerva's name.

'Rufus will soon be forced to bury his only son.'

Brei swallowed. 'He's... dead?'

Everyone turned to look at her.

'As good as,' Gallus said, eyes narrowing on her. 'His condition is not improving.'

Brei looked down, reminding herself that he was the reason she was in a cage.

'Let us pray that it does not spread through the city,' Claudius said.

Gallus nodded profusely. 'I hear it can take up to a week for symptoms to appear.'

While the others continued chatting, Iunius signalled to someone to remove the sick prisoner.

'What is the price for this one?' Claudius asked, gesturing to Brei.

Gallus chuckled. 'What do you want with her? If your

wife finds out you brought a contagious foreigner into her household, you are going to be in trouble.'

Claudius glanced tiredly in his direction. 'She looks healthy to me.' He studied Gallus for a moment. 'Perhaps you are interested in the girl for your own purposes. Need I remind you that our beloved emperor banned females from the arena some years back?'

Brei had no idea what that meant. The only thing she knew was that one of them would leave with her. Unless, of course, they thought her contagious. Bending slightly, she coughed, not bothering to cover her mouth with her hand. All three men took an enormous step back, and Claudius's previously cocky expression vanished.

'Oh, dear,' Gallus said, pulling a square of fabric from his pocket and covering his mouth. 'It seems we must continue our search elsewhere.'

Iunius gestured for the cage to be opened and pushed her inside. She felt rather pleased with herself as she turned away from them all and strolled away. The gate locked behind her, and Iunius ushered Claudius away. Gallus remained where he was, waiting for the other men to leave before stepping closer to the cage, eyes fixed on her. Brei stared back at him.

'Clever,' he said. 'We both know it would not have ended well for you if you had left with Claudius Liberia.'

She did not reply but listened. Gallus leaned closer to the bars.

'I see the fighter in you. You will be miserable cooped up in some noble household, fanning your mistress and avoiding the advances of your master.' He glanced after the men. 'How would you like to be a warrior again?'

Brei tried to read him. 'Who would I be fighting?'

Gallus smiled at her response. 'You speak the language quite well. Who taught you?'

She wandered back to the bars. 'War taught me.' She crossed her arms. 'You didn't answer my question.'

There was a hint of a smile on his face. 'Whomever I match you with.'

Her eyebrows drew together. 'What would I be fighting for?'

'Why, for the entertainment, of course. This is Rome.'

She regarded him for a moment, trying to figure out if he was misleading her in some way. 'For fun, you mean?'

He nodded.

'I've no idea why I'm surprised. I've never met such bloodthirsty men.'

Gallus laughed at that. 'You are a long way from home. These are your people now. Play nice, and you might find yourself free one day.'

That made Brei straighten. 'What do you mean?'

A smug expression settled on Gallus's face. He had gotten her attention. 'It means that slaves who please their masters can sometimes be handed their freedom.'

Nerva had not said anything about that. 'Is that what you're offering me? Freedom?'

Another laugh. 'I do not even know if you can fight yet.'

'I can fight.'

His eyes shone at her. 'I sponsor a number of small fights, as well as private events. I am always on the lookout for people like yourself.'

'You mean foreigners who don't know any better?'

'Why do you say that?'

She shrugged. 'I didn't. Your friend said it, that women were banned from the—' She struggled to recall the word. '—*arena*.'

'Which is why people are prepared to pay handsomely for the spectacle. A bit of fun in the privacy of their own home. There are no laws against that.' He rubbed his nose.

'And maybe some of the smaller arenas. No one *really* cares about those.'

Not for one moment did she trust the man standing in front of her, but that did not matter. The question was whether she could outsmart him. 'Do people die?'

'The weapons are blunt, and female gladiators are too valuable to kill off. That does not mean you will not get hurt. The fighting is real.'

She frowned at the unfamiliar word. 'What are *gladiators?*'

Gallus gestured for her to come closer, and she obeyed. 'Gladiators are the greatest show on earth.' He straightened again. 'Now tell me. How are you feeling?'

He was a sharp thinker—just like her. 'Much better suddenly.'

'Wrong answer. With influenza, I shall get you at a much cheaper price.'

Brei's eyes returned to Claudius, who was finalising his purchase of a girl. She looked far too young to be handed over to that man. 'Why should I care what you pay?'

Another hearty laugh from Gallus as he waved a finger at her. 'If this is how you are with words, I cannot wait to see you with a sword.'

## CHAPTER 16

Nerva had always imagined a swift death on a bloodied battlefield. He would stare up at the sky as he bled out while the fight continued around him. It might have been an uncomfortable thought for some, but survival was also uncomfortable. Death was part of war, and he had been told his entire life that there was honour in such an end.

What he did not imagine was a slow, miserable death. That was the death he feared. Fear of being immobile and helpless, being in constant pain, a burden to others. Fear of a fragmented mind that could not grasp what was real and what was not, of suffocating or drowning in his own bodily fluids. He was stuck in a dream, one he would wake up from, then fall back into. Moments of awareness were fleeting, confusing, and made him wish he could hurry death along.

Nerva was aware of some things, like being on a ship. But then he was no longer on the ship. Perhaps somebody told him that—or maybe not. Occasionally he became aware of smells and sounds. At least once, he was convinced that he was back in Caledonia, lying beneath tall pines with snow falling on him. The fever held his mind hostage, and he tired of it.

Despite welcoming death, it did not come. Instead, one afternoon, he opened his eyes and discovered his vision was clear, his body still, no longer ravaged by heat. The pain in his leg had dulled, or perhaps the limb was no longer there. That would make more sense. He turned his head and looked around the room, spotting a young girl seated by the door, humming as she sewed. It took him a moment to recognise her.

'Nona,' he croaked.

Her head snapped up, and a smile spread across her face. 'You're awake.' Dropping her sewing on the floor, she went to him. 'How do you feel?'

On the wall behind her hung a painting of four black horses pulling a chariot. They had once belonged to him. The inside horse was Amator, the greatest stallion Nerva had ever owned. 'Am I home?'

The young servant gave his arm a squeeze. 'Yes. You're finally home.'

*Rome*. Pushing himself up onto his elbows, he looked down at his legs, once again surprised to find both of them still there. He had assumed they would amputate it.

'There was talk of removing it,' Nona said, reading his mind, 'but your mother would not hear of it.' Nona's hand flew to her mouth. 'Your mother. I need to tell her you're awake.' She rushed towards the door. 'Don't move,' she called over her shoulder before disappearing.

He was not going anywhere. Keeping his eyelids open was all he could manage. Soon, the distinctive shuffle of his mother's feet drew near.

'Nerva?'

He would recognise her voice anywhere. Sitting up properly, he leaned against the bedhead. Aquila paused in the doorway, making her entry even more dramatic, then hurried forwards, taking his face in both hands and kissing his cheeks. 'You had us worried out of our minds. The leg, the influenza. You really should be dead.' She sat on the edge of the bed and clicked her fingers in Nona's direction before pointing at the water on the table. The young girl went to pour it, then took it over to Nerva. 'I was planning your funeral,' Aquila continued.

Nerva drank the water and then coughed, taking a minute to settle again. 'How many days was I out?'

Aquila folded her hands neatly on her lap. '*Nine* days on board that death ship, and another six days since arriving home.' Her eyes moved over his face. 'They are saying it killed off all but the strong.'

'It?'

'The barbarian influenza.'

Nerva coughed again. 'I think it is just called influenza.' He had not even realised he had it. Everyone had been focused on his leg. 'How many dead?'

'Rumours are eighty percent of the crew are either infected or dead.'

Nerva frowned. *Eighty percent.* 'Have you heard anything of Marcus?'

Aquila looked heavenward. 'Recovering, thank the gods. I know how fond you are of him.'

He had not had any symptoms when Nerva had seen him last. When had that been? The day they were attacked. An image of Brei trapped beneath a man twice his size flashed in his mind. 'What of the prisoners onboard?'

His mother looked surprised. 'It is not like you to concern yourself with the spoils of war. Hopefully they were all put to death in order to prevent the spread of the disease through the city.'

Some might have been shocked by such a statement, but Nerva was immune to his mother's world views. 'Do you know if they are holding any prisoners for me?'

She feigned exhaustion. 'For goodness' sake. I am not one of your men reporting for duty. Given everyone thought you dead, I imagine they were sold on your behalf.'

He had only been awake a few minutes and Brei was already on his mind. Something had changed between them that day on deck. They had crossed an invisible boundary. Whatever sense of responsibility he felt towards her before, it was tenfold now. 'I would like to go and see Marcus.'

'You have not even seen your own father yet.' Her mouth pinched in disapproval. 'He has been awfully concerned about you.'

Nerva really was not thinking clearly. 'I will see him first, of course. Is he well?'

'Quite well.' Aquila reached out and brushed Nerva's long hair away from his eye. 'I do not think I have ever seen you so unkempt and underweight. Did they not feed you over there? I thought a legate would have had the very best that terrible place could offer.' She sighed. 'But knowing you as I do, you are not one to eat while your men look on hungry.'

He was struggling to follow the conversation, mostly because he was trying to remember if Brei had shown any symptoms the last time he had seen her. Her cool hands came to mind. He had probably infected her. 'There was a woman,' he said, cutting his mother off.

Aquila's eyebrows rose. 'A woman where?'

'On the ship. A prisoner.' He shook his head, knowing his mother would be the last person prepared to help him with something like this. 'She saved my life.'

'A *prisoner* saved your life?'

'A few times, actually.'

Aquila looked as if she had just inhaled a bad odour. 'You were liaising with the prisoners? It is no wonder you got ill.'

'A bit hard not to liaise with Maeatae when fighting them.'

'The barbarians would have most definitely brought it on board. Their type often carries the diseases without showing any signs of them.' She waved a hand. 'I fear we shall have to treat you for fleas also.'

It was always tempting to argue with her, to try and tell her that she was wrong, a victim of propaganda, but he knew better than to try and sway her mind on such matters. He was not well enough to take her on yet.

He was saved by a knock at the door and looked over to see Tertia standing with a tray of food and a warm smile.

'We have sent word to your father that you are awake. Thought you might like something to eat. Broth and some cooked pears—nothing too heavy.'

Aquila let out a loud sigh. 'Just leave it on the table.'

Tertia entered and placed the tray beside the bed.

'Now off you go,' Aquila said, waving her away like a fly. 'You have a lot of mending to get on with.'

Tertia bowed her head, gracious as always, and glanced once at Nerva. 'It is good to see you awake.'

Twenty-nine years they had all been doing the same dance. 'Thank you, Tertia. That was very thoughtful.'

'And her *job*,' Aquila added. She waited until they were alone before adding, 'One would think she would know her place by now.'

Tertia was his father's mistress, and for that reason, his mother despised her. He could not blame her, but he happened to like Tertia. Plus, she was his sisters' mother, which made her family.

'I see your relationship has not improved. Would it kill you to be nice? She is all alone here.'

'Hardly.' She straightened. 'She might be pining after the daughters who abandoned her first chance they got, but she still manages to find her way into my husband's bed.'

Nerva's half-sisters chose to live elsewhere for a number of reasons. 'You know very well they did not abandon her.'

'Good riddance, I say.'

There was another knock, and this time his father's broad shoulders filled the doorway. Nerva had only been gone two years, but Rufus looked like he had aged about ten. His eyes creased at the corners when they met Nerva's.

'You look terrible,' he said, stepping into the room.

'I said the same thing,' Aquila said, standing and fixing her stola. 'Make sure he drinks the broth.' She patted Nerva's cheek before walking to the door.

'Mother,' Nerva called, stopping her. 'Can you make enquiries after Marcus on my behalf?'

'Yes, of course.' She glanced at her husband, then left them.

Rufus Papias came and stood at Nerva's bedside. He was not one for big displays of affection, but Nerva knew he cared deeply for his family, even the illegitimate daughters he never dared mention. 'How are you feeling? You gave us a real fright.'

'It might not look like it, but much better.'

'It does look like it, actually. You were all but dead when they carried you in here.'

Nerva pushed himself up straighter. 'I was not expecting to have both legs when I woke.'

'You know your mother. Having a one-legged son would have ruined all her plans.'

'I suppose I should not be surprised that she would rather me dead than crippled.'

Rufus chuckled. 'The first thing she said when she heard that you were attacked by pirates was that she hoped they took the influenza with them also.'

Nerva's mouth turned up into a smile. 'One can hope. I believe they came for weapons. I barely remember fighting them, if I am being honest.' An image of Brei stabbing a man through the arm flashed in his mind. For a woman who was supposed to despise him, she had certainly had his back.

'You were delirious with fever when you arrived here. You are a soldier in every sense of the word. Even in death you continue to fight.' He placed a hand on Nerva's shoulder. 'Do try to eat something. Your leg was drained more times than I can count and had every ointment thrown at it. Every medicine and potion in existence has been forced down your throat. Your leg is much improved, but the physician has asked you to stay off it for a while. And probably best not to socialise until all your influenza symptoms have gone.'

Nerva nodded; even though he hated the thought of being idle and useless, he did not want to make anyone else ill. 'Is there any news from Britannia?'

'Severus has taken to his bed. They are not expecting him to get up this time.'

'That man has been dying for years. It is torture for Caracalla, who cannot wait to be rid of him.'

'He will still have Geta to worry about.'

'Yes, but for how long?'

Rufus nodded. 'Our friends in the senate will be pleased to hear of your recovery. They are keen to welcome you back.'

They were not Nerva's friends. The senate had been the reason he joined the army. 'I suppose that is a logical next step.'

'Let us speak of this when you are feeling better. For now, enjoy being home. Take some time to recover, and indulge your mother once you are well. She is probably planning a dinner party as we speak.'

'Is it really such a tragedy that I remain unwed?'

Rufus smiled. 'You are nearing thirty. It is not unreasonable that she wishes to see you settled.' He was about to leave, then stopped. 'I asked Tertia to send word to her daughters of your condition. We were unsure if you would make it, and I thought they should know.'

Nerva sighed. His sisters would likely be panicked by the news, as he would be if the situation were reversed. 'I understand. I shall write them and update them on my condition.'

A nod from his father before he left the room.

Nerva thought about asking Nona to bring some supplies so he could write to his sisters but found himself suddenly too tired for the task. He closed his eyes for a moment, and sleep reclaimed him.

## CHAPTER 17

Where were the trees? Brei missed the smell of them. She had not appreciated the crisp, pine-scented air of home until arriving in Rome. The city's air was thick and stagnant. The absence of a breeze meant it never moved.

When she was alone, she liked to close her eyes and go someplace else. If she concentrated hard enough, she could almost taste the sharp, clean air of home. In rare moments of silence, she could hear her nephew laughing, the endless chatter of her sister, and the booming voice of her father. But the moment the noise resumed, the illusion shattered, and she was faced with her reality: a dark room with no windows shared with strangers. It was small, just big enough for three beds, but conveniently located two blocks from the small arena in Caelimontium where she trained. She only went there to sleep; otherwise, she preferred to be fighting.

Gallus Minidius was a practical man, and that suited Brei just fine. He provided her with everything she needed to exist in Rome: food, clean water, clothing, a safe place to sleep, and all the weapons a girl could dream of. While she was never permitted to take them with her, on the sand she could be whoever she wanted to be—and she chose to be a warrior.

It did not take her long to earn Gallus's trust. They had an understanding. Outside the arena, he was in charge. Inside the fighting pit, she was in charge. Everyone got what they needed. At first, the sponsor made a big display of his abilities to protect her from what he described as the 'realities of slave life', but she had figured out very quickly that the only person who could protect her from the hands of men was her. Many tried, and every one of them was shut down. Soon enough, they started giving her a wide berth. What she did appreciate was that Gallus was never one of those men. The only thing he wanted from her was a good fight—every time.

'How long does it take for a slave to earn their freedom?' she asked Gallus one morning. He rarely watched her train anymore, and she took it as a sign of good faith, but that morning he had snuck in and taken a seat on one of the benches.

Laughing at her question, he replied, 'You have only been here six weeks.'

'How long?' she pushed. She had considered trying to escape, but Gallus had advised her in the beginning what happened when slaves ran away. She did not want to be responsible for anything happening to others in his household as a result.

'Years.' He stood, casting her a sympathetic look as though the entire thing was out of his control.

'If you want me to keep winning, I'm going to need a firm answer.'

Another laugh. 'You are an absolute scoundrel. Has anyone ever told you that?'

'Scoundrel?'

'A troublemaker.'

'Oh,' she nodded. 'Yes. People tell me that all the time. So how long?'

Sighing, he made his way along the narrow walkway between the bench seats, looking as though he might topple at any moment. Brei followed him on the sand.

'You give me two years of solid fighting, and then we shall reassess.'

She brushed sand off her arms. 'So I'm just supposed to trust you?'

'My dear, you have no choice.' He glanced sideways at her. 'And if you continue to pester me to an early grave, I will add another year.' Stopping suddenly, he turned and looked at her. 'I have been meaning to ask you. Otho informed me that you have been asking after General Nerva Papias.'

The name made her stop also. She glanced in the direction of the weapons room, where her sparring partner was packing up. 'And why would Otho tell you such a thing?'

Gallus rubbed tiredly at his forehead. 'Perhaps he thinks you are plotting the general's death.'

She scowled. 'Is that what you think?'

'I do not know what to think.'

'I only asked if he knew him.'

'*Everyone* knows the Papiases.'

She chewed her lip for a moment. Despite trying to forget all about Nerva, her curiosity had eventually gotten the better of her. She had asked Otho instead of Gallus to avoid this exact conversation, but Gallus made it his business to know her business.

'He is a good man,' the sponsor added, eyeing her suspiciously.

She crossed her arms. 'Which is why I'm not plotting his death.' She had meant to casually drop the question into conversation, but Otho had given her the same look Gallus was giving her at that moment. Perhaps she would have been better off digging for information elsewhere. She had felt certain if she learned what became of Nerva, she would be able to rid her mind of him. Unfortunately, she had been wrong. 'I was only curious as to whether he survived—and he did.'

He was alive, and hearing that had brought her unexpected relief.

'What is your connection to the man?' Gallus asked.

'He is the reason I'm here and also the reason many of my people are dead.' She looked away. 'Though he spared my life once or twice.'

'Did he?' Gallus looked amused. 'So he took pity on you. You see for yourself that he is a good man.'

'Or perhaps his guilt just got the better of him.'

Gallus tutted. 'Either way, I will feel much better knowing you are nowhere in the vicinity of any of the Papiases. Understand?'

She nodded and looked away.

'The proper response for a slave is *"Yes, Erus"*.'

She bowed before him, as low as she could go. 'Yes, Erus.' Turning, she strolled off across the sand.

'You are lucky I came by the market that day,' he called to her back. 'No one else would put up with you.'

## CHAPTER 18

It was seven weeks before Nerva saw Marcus again. The tribune had been collected from the port the day the ship docked and taken to his family home south of Tusculum while he recovered from the influenza. Once well enough, he had reported to the barracks outside of the city, where he was put to work training new recruits. On his first day off, he went to visit Nerva. Now the pair sat in the Papiases' garden. Nerva always preferred to speak out of earshot of his mother.

'You're looking better than the last time I saw you,' Marcus said, picking up a peach slice and popping it into his mouth.

'Everyone keeps saying that.' He cradled a cup in one hand. 'I am walking without a limp now, and the cough is finally gone.'

'I'm sorry I didn't get here sooner.'

'Do not apologise. You were ill also.'

Marcus studied him for a moment. 'What have you been doing with your free time?'

He had been feeling displaced. Every time he returned

to the city, it was the same. Being a soldier had offered respite. He was making decisions on behalf on his men instead of worrying about his own agenda. Looking back at his life, he saw a pattern: the first twenty years adhering to his parents' wishes, and the next nine in the army. Now he was evaluating his place in the world without those things and was forced to admit he was a misfit.

What had Marcus's question been again? 'A lot of reading,' he lied. If he admitted to staring at blank walls for long periods, more questions would follow—ones he did not want to answer.

'Will you return to Caledonia?'

Nerva shook his head. 'Cordius was promoted to legatus legionis of the third Britannia legion—a permanent arrangement, it seems.' He should have felt betrayed by Caracalla's apparent dismissal, but he had expected it. It did not matter anyway, because he did not have it in him to return to those mountains and take any more innocent lives.

'So that's it, then?' Marcus asked. 'You're officially done?'

'It was always going to be my final campaign.'

'Must feel strange though. It's all you've known for the previous nine years.'

'A little.' He had been Marcus's superior for so long that he had no idea how to present himself as anything but a man in control of things. He took a drink of his wine. 'What about you?'

'They gave me the option of remaining here for the three months I have left, and I accepted.'

Nerva smiled. 'What happened to "third legion for life"?'

Marcus shrugged and reached for the tray again. 'That was before Cordius replaced you.' He was quiet as he ate.

'I'm thinking of returning home to work with my father.' The family bred horses and shipped them all over the world.

'Do you need a stablehand?'

The tribune laughed. 'I don't think I could afford you.'

'Then join the senate with me instead.'

A wry smile settled on Marcus's face. 'You've spent the last nine years telling me how much you despise most of them.'

Nerva placed his empty cup down on the table. 'And I stand by that.'

'Then why return? Do something else.'

'Like what?'

'Stick with your race horses. You've always enjoyed that.'

Nerva leaned back. 'That is a hobby, not a job.'

'It's a job for some.'

'Not a patrician of Rome.'

They were silent a moment.

'You are one of the luckiest men I know,' Marcus began. 'Definitely one of the wealthiest, and yet I find myself feeling sorry for you.'

Nerva laughed. 'That might change when you see some of the marriage prospects my mother is pursuing.'

'Bet they're all goddesses who piss gold.'

Nerva leaned forwards to refill his friend's cup. 'I have attended four dinner parties in the last six days.'

The tribune took a large drink before replying. 'Nothing grounds you like family. Might be just what you need.'

'Says the unmarried soldier.'

'I look to my parents, who are very happy.'

Nerva had watched the facade of his own mother and father the night prior. Once their guests had left, they had gone to their separate rooms without even so much as wishing one another a good evening, and then Rufus had sent for Tertia. Was that what he was supposed to do? Marry well, have children, and then fill the cracks in his life behind closed doors?

The answer was yes.

Marcus straightened. 'I'm afraid to ask, because I hesitate to renew your interest in the subject, but did you find out what became of the prisoner?'

*The prisoner.* It was an accurate enough description of her, but it sounded strangely impersonal given what had taken place on that ship. 'I never found her.'

Marcus appeared sympathetic. 'I wish I could have been more helpful, but as I told you in my letter, it was chaos the day we disembarked. I was in rough shape.'

Nerva had written to him a few weeks earlier, asking for any information on her possible whereabouts. When that had failed, he had made a few enquiries himself. 'I learned a few things.'

'Like?'

Nerva leaned forwards, elbows resting on his knees. 'I believe she is alive.'

Marcus looked surprised. 'Why do you say that?'

'I spoke with the man who brought her up on deck. He remembered her, said she seemed healthy enough.'

Marcus sat with that information for a moment. 'Did he see her disembark?'

'No. He dealt with those displaying symptoms.'

'And do I want to know what happened to them?'

Nerva shook his head.

'The healthy ones would have been sold at market,' Marcus said.

'Yes.'

'Then there should be a record of her.'

Nerva glanced at the portico before replying, paranoid his mother's spies might be lurking. 'The only records contain numbers, not names, and they are far from reliable.' He had visited the Graecostadium in person and asked around. One man had recalled female prisoners arriving from the ship. Some of them had fallen ill soon after. Nerva had checked every holding cell in the place just in case, but she had not been there. 'Trying to track down a slave in Rome is like trying to find a particular fish in the sea.'

Marcus watched him for a moment. 'What happened that day on deck?'

He had woken to the sound of her screaming his name, gotten to her just in time, killed a man three times her size. He had never seen the man's face, but he would never forget Brei's in the moments that followed his death, her broken expression and bloodied skin. The thought of her dying of influenza after surviving all that made him... what? Angry, perhaps. Though the thought of her being sold at market was not easy to digest either. He had imagined numerous times the type of man who would buy her. Pressing the tips of his fingers together, all he said was 'A lot happened that day.'

Marcus leaned back, an amused expression on his face. 'Nine years, and I've *never* seen you in this state over a woman.'

'What state?' Occasionally he woke from dreams where Brei screamed his name over and over, but no one else knew of them.

He gestured with his hand. 'All piney.'

Nerva could not help but smile at that. 'Piney?'

'You know what I mean. It's been almost two months, and she's still at the front of your mind.'

Nerva looked at him. 'I am man enough to admit that she got under my skin, but those feelings would have been put to bed the moment I placed her in a suitable household.'

Marcus was grinning now. '*Put to bed*. An interesting choice of words.'

'You have the mind of a child. Shall we blame the influenza?'

'Blame whatever you like. Doesn't mean I'm going to tease you any less.' Marcus let out a breath and looked around the garden. 'Those poor women your mother has lined up don't stand a chance if your current tastes are anything to go on.'

Nerva put his face in his hands then sat up. 'How does one choose between women so similar?'

Marcus pretended to think hard on the matter. 'If they're all beautiful, well bred, and virtuous, then perhaps it comes down to hair colour or some other preference.'

'I cannot select a wife based on hair colour.'

'Why not?'

'Many ladies dye their hair nowadays or resort to wigs.' He recalled the day Brei had arrived at his cabin smelling of soap with her chestnut hair falling over her shoulders. It was exactly the type of hair that was used for such a wig.

'Don't fret.' Marcus laughed. 'Your mother will be a big help. Though she might need some guidance as to your type.'

'What exactly is my type?'

Marcus waved a hand. 'You know—athletic, good with a bow, horse thief…'

Nerva almost choked on his drink. 'That should be easy enough to find among Rome's nobility.' He reached for Marcus's cup and ladled more wine into it.

'If I drink that, I'll never leave.'

Nerva filled it to the brim. 'Good.' Handing the cup to Marcus, he picked up his own and raised it.

'All right. What are we drinking to?'

Nerva thought for a moment. 'To General Paulus Cordius.'

Lifting his cup, Marcus added, 'And the wig-wearing ladies of Rome.'

## CHAPTER 19

Despite Nerva's reluctance to recommit himself to a political career, it was not long before he was pulled back in. He did not know whether his father actually needed his help campaigning or if he was just trying to awaken his son's political interests. Either way, Nerva was grateful for the distraction. He attended all the meetings his father did not have the time or stomach for, dinners with business owners, senators, patricians, investors, and anyone prepared to support his agenda.

There was one benefit of being busy: it meant his personal life suffered. He could no longer be dragged around the city by his mother, wasting hours eating and drinking with daughters of various acquaintances. Not one to be beaten, Aquila asked Rufus to keep her informed of Nerva's schedule and found ways around it. One woman in particular kept popping up all over the place. Camilla Bavius was the niece of Senator Florus Bavius. She was entirely appropriate, but the only thing Nerva felt in her presence was painfully bored. He spent much of their conversations asking her to repeat herself, because despite his best efforts, his mind always wandered when she spoke. She was attractive, he could not take that away from her, and yet whenever she found a way to accidentally touch him, he felt only indifference.

Nerva was on his way home from a meeting when he spotted a woman standing out front of his house. As he drew closer, he noticed something familiar about her. The moment she turned and looked in his direction, a grin spread across his face. It was Mila. She immediately broke into a run towards him, and he could not hold in the laughter as she flung herself at him. Lifting her off the ground, he hugged her so tight that he felt her ribs bend. 'What on earth are you doing here?' He placed her back on the ground and held her at arm's length to look at her properly.

'I had originally planned on visiting your grave, but now I find you alive.'

'I wrote to tell you I was fine.'

'And I came to see it for myself.'

He let go of her, still in shock that she was standing before him. He had not seen her in almost three years. 'Please tell me you did not travel all the way from Giza to prove me wrong.'

Mila made a face at him. 'The letter my mother wrote made your death sound imminent.'

'A clever tactic to ensure a visit from her daughter.'

'I suspect you might be right.' Mila glanced back at the house. 'Aquila claims my mother is far too busy for social calls, so I have yet to see her.'

Nerva winced. 'She is picking up right where you two left off.'

'I think my sudden return has her reeling.' Mila looked quite pleased by that. 'So, if not dead, how have you been?'

'Bored.'

'Then go back to Britannia.'

He shook his head. 'I will take boredom over the highlands any day. It was always going to be my last campaign.' Nerva let out a breath. 'You know I hate to admit it, but it really is good to see you.'

'I was always good for boredom.'

'You were.' Reaching up, he gave her braid a tug. 'Did Remus travel with you?'

'The whole family.'

'Everyone?'

'Except Dulcia. She remains in Giza with Nero and the children.'

Nerva folded his arms. 'I still cannot believe she convinced you all to move there.'

'She is rather persuasive for one so quiet. Did you receive her letter?'

Nerva nodded. 'What was Nero's reaction to another daughter?'

Mila let out a noisy breath. 'The man is completely besotted.' She watched him for a moment. 'They both wanted to come and see you, but with a new baby…'

'A sensible decision given my recent experience of travelling on a ship.'

Mila's expression turned serious. 'So many dead.'

Nerva nodded as Brei popped into his head. She always did whenever he spoke of that journey. 'I look forward to seeing the children, but it might have to wait until tomorrow. I am attending a dinner tonight with some wealthy businessmen visiting from the south.'

Mila waved him off. 'The boys barely remember you, and Asha has waited years to see you—what is one more night?' She studied him for a moment. 'You despise such dinner parties. Why attend at all?'

'Obligation.'

'Ah.'

'The guest of honour is a little… unrefined. Father is

under the impression that I am better suited to this particular gathering.'

Mila pulled a distasteful face. 'Is that his way of saying you are a bit of a pleb?'

'Have you not heard? The common folk love me. Anyway, there are worse things that could be said about me.'

'Much worse,' Mila agreed.

'You have not changed one bit.' His face turned serious. 'Why not come with me tonight?'

Mila's eyes widened slightly. 'To your tedious dinner party? Do you not have a wife to drag along to those things yet?'

Again, Brei popped into his mind. At some point he needed her out of his head. 'Believe me when I say Mother is working on it.'

Mila's expression softened. 'Oh, dear. Your wife will be absolute perfection.'

'Exactly.'

'You are bored already and you are not even wed yet.'

He had forgotten how well his sister knew him. 'How would you like to meet the frontrunner?'

'Did your mother choose this frontrunner?'

He gave her a look that said she should know the answer to that.

'I see,' Mila said. 'I will not pretend I am not intrigued.'

'Then come tonight.'

She took a step back. 'Nice try.'

'What if I told you there was going to be a gladiator demonstration?' He knew by her expression that it was the right hook.

'Actually, I saw one just this morning.' Seeing his confusion, she added, 'The twins were arguing.'

He stepped closer. 'How would you like to see *actual*

gladiators fighting this evening while you are stuffing your face with fantastic food?'

'What sort of gladiators?'

He almost had her. Two more words would seal the deal. '*Female* gladiators.'

She sucked in a breath, feigning shock. 'How very scandalous. I am coming.' She smiled. 'Will you be travelling by litter, or shall we use our legs like regular people?'

'When have I ever travelled by litter?'

She lifted her shoulders in a shrug. 'I do not know what sort of impression you are trying to make on your new lady friend. Perhaps you can come and collect me on your way there? That way you can see Remus and the children.'

'By children, I assume you are referring to Asha, the twins, and Felix and Albaus.'

Another smile from her. 'I gave the address to Nona in hope that it reaches my mother.'

'I shall see that it does.' He gave Mila's shoulder a squeeze. 'I do not think I said it before, but thank you.'

'It is just dinner.' Her tone was playful.

'For dragging your family back to Rome for my funeral.'

She shook her head, dismissing his gratitude. 'They will be so disappointed. All this way for nothing.'

He gave her a gentle push. 'Go on. Back to the slums where you belong.'

'Actually, we rented a *house*.'

Nerva raised his eyebrows. 'The spice trade is good, then?'

'Very good.'

'How long are you planning on staying?'

She threw her hands up. 'No idea. Maybe a few months, if we can keep out of trouble for that long.'

'If your past record is anything to go on—'

'Shush,' she said, backing away from him. 'I will see you later.'

He turned and climbed the steps to the front door, looking up to gauge the time. He had a few hours at best to organise a gladiator demonstration before Mila realised he was an enormous liar.

~

Brei stood over Otho, panting. A single drop of blood fell from her lip, and she wiped at it before stepping back. She offered him her hand, but his pride prevented him from taking it.

'Suit yourself,' she said as he slowly got to his feet and brushed sand off his backside.

'You're actually mad. Has anyone ever told you that?' His expression was deadly serious.

Brei rolled her eyes. 'You tell me all the time.' She looked over to where Gallus stood talking with a man she did not recognise. They had been speaking the entire time she had been training, their gazes drifting in her direction every so often. Seeing he had her attention, Gallus gestured for her to join them. She exchanged a look with Otho.

'Do you think I'm in trouble for going too soft on you?' she asked.

Otho shook his head and bent to collect his weapon. 'Better give me your sword. Gallus won't take kindly to you approaching him armed.'

Handing over her weapon, she wiped her hands on her loincloth before wandering over to Gallus. Her eyes moved over the other man who was well presented. A businessman, perhaps.

'That looks nasty,' Gallus said when she came to a stop in front of them. He gestured to the large bruise on her thigh.

She shrugged. 'Nothing broken.'

Gallus looked like a proud father whenever she said things like that. 'I told you she was a force to be reckoned with, did I not?' he said to the man.

The stranger nodded, his gaze sweeping the length of her. 'She is most impressive. I look forward to this evening.' He offered his arm to Gallus, who took hold of it, then left them.

Brei watched him walk away before speaking. 'Who was that?'

'A new client,' Gallus replied, turning back to her. 'Take the rest of the afternoon off. Go do something fun.' He thought for a moment. 'Though nothing too fun. We do not want you worn out before this evening's performance.'

'Rather short notice.'

'For whom?' He tutted. 'I can be very accommodating for the right sum.'

That was very true of Gallus. 'And who will I be fighting?'

The sponsor clapped his hands like an excited boy. 'A *legend*. This woman will make every match prior to today seem like child's play.'

Brei took in his rather gleeful expression. 'To be fair, many of the previous matches *have* been child's play.' She could afford to be cocky because she was undefeated.

Gallus chuckled and gestured to the bag containing her clothes and shoes, and they strolled towards it. 'This one has come out of retirement just for the occasion.'

'She's out of shape, then?'

'Even if she were, she might still win. She was Rome's best female gladiator in the years leading up to the ban.'

The ban. In 200 AD, the emperor had issued a decree banning single combat by women in the arena. It had only forced them underground.

Brei snatched up the bag and pulled out her tunic. 'So she's Roman?'

'In every sense of the word.' Gallus was grinning. 'Remember everything Otho has taught you and you will be fine.'

Brei looked in the direction of the weapons room as she slipped on the tunic. 'The only things he has taught me are the rules.'

'Well, you can forget those.' Another chuckle, his eyes shining. 'Fausta seldom plays by the rules.'

∽

When Nerva arrived to collect Mila from their house near the river, he was met at the door by a very excited Asha and two curious little brothers.

'Goodness. You are not *still* growing, are you?' he asked as he bent to kiss her cheek. 'You will catch up to me soon.'

The girl blushed and pushed her brothers forwards. 'Say hello to your uncle.'

Nerva bent and offered his arm to the five-year-olds. 'You must forgive me for stealing your mother away for the evening.'

Caius wore a sheepish grin as he greeted his uncle. Atilius was sizing him up.

'Father says Mother is not allowed near a weapon tonight,' he said.

Nerva's mouth twitched. 'Your father is a very wise man.'

As if on cue, Remus appeared behind the boys, reaching over them to take Nerva's arm and clapping him on the shoulder as he did so. 'Good to see you looking so well. You had us worried.' He glanced back. 'Mila will never admit it to your face, but she was a mess when she got the news.'

'The fact that you are here in Rome is testament to the fact.' He looked past Remus. 'Where are Felix and Albaus?'

'Probably waiting outside,' Mila said, appearing from another room and grabbing her palla from a hook on the wall. She pushed herself up onto her toes and kissed Remus as she wrapped it around herself, then bent down to the children. 'Be good for your father.'

'Ah, what do you mean, *waiting outside?*' Nerva asked, already disapproving of her answer.

Remus cleared his throat. 'It seems they are going with you.'

That was exactly what Nerva had been afraid of. 'Why?' He directed the question at his sister.

'Albaus is my bodyguard,' Mila replied, rising.

Nerva tilted his head. 'What is it you think you need protecting from?'

Mila tried to come up with an answer. 'Snobbery?'

'It is not that kind of gathering.'

She moved closer and spoke in a quieter voice. 'Albaus knows a man who knows a man—'

'Of course he does.'

'And he discovered that Fausta is fighting at a gathering tonight.'

Nerva crossed his arms. 'She is the best female fighter in Rome, so I suggested her.'

Mila appeared offended by that statement. 'The best is probably a stretch. You might remember, I beat her once.'

'During training,' Remus said with an amused expression.

'It does not matter when, only that I won.'

At that moment, Felix and Albaus walked up behind Nerva.

'All right,' Felix said, hands raised in an exasperated gesture, 'who got her started this time?'

Remus and the children pointed at Nerva.

'I know, I know,' Nerva said. 'You think I would know better.' He extended an arm to the tall mute, then to the dwarf. 'If Albaus is playing bodyguard to Mila, what is your excuse for being there?' he asked Felix.

'For Albaus's protection, of course.'

The children laughed, and Nerva shook his head.

'Of course. Everyone ready to go, then?'

Remus rested his hands on his daughter's shoulders. 'Please keep my wife out of trouble.' When Mila turned to glare at him, he winked at her.

As the four of them stepped down onto the street, Nerva felt a hum of contentment. Realising how much he had missed them all, he threw an arm around his sister.

'All right,' Mila said. 'You have until we get there to catch me up on the last three years. I want to hear everything.'

His arm fell away. 'No you do not.'

She cast a stern look at him. 'Yes I do. Something is different about you, and I want to know what has you so… defeated.' She glanced over her shoulder to ensure Felix and Albaus were not listening in before continuing. 'What happened in Britannia?'

Nerva watched the road in front of them. 'A lot. I would not even know where to begin.'

'I see.' She drew a long breath and released it. 'Just start at the beginning.'

CHAPTER 20

The two women prepared in the laundry of the grand house, neither speaking but occasionally catching the other glancing in their direction. Brei's opponent appeared to be around thirty. She was blonde, bleached judging by her roots, and had more muscle on her than the average man walking the streets of Rome.

The small party of fifteen or so were dining in the garden. An area had been cleared for the performance, but the hosts wanted everyone nice and full first. The scent of baked fish and lemon wafted through the house, making Brei's stomach growl. She would eat after the fight.

Otho appeared in the doorway. He had been assigned the role of supervising her. 'I think they're finally ready for you.' He waited for Fausta to stand before continuing. 'You wait for the drums to speed up. Understand?'

Fausta's response came in the form of an eye roll before she pushed past him, her shoulder clipping his. She had arrived alone and was not interested in being managed by a man five years her junior with half her skill. Brei smiled to herself. In another life, they might have been friends.

'Follow me,' Otho said, leading Brei outside.

The women waited in the shadows of the garden, six feet between them. Brei took a few calming breaths, smelling rosemary and a flower she could not place. She could hear the seated guests talking, tinkers of laughter drifting through the potted plants and trees.

'I'm not going to go easy on you just because you're smaller than me,' Fausta said, her voice a whisper. It was the first time she had spoken since they had been thrown into a room together.

Brei looked at her in the dark while adjusting her grip on her shield, the one Gallus had made just for her. It was an exact replica of something she would have used back home. 'And I'm not going to go easy on you just because you're Roman.'

Fausta shifted her weight from one foot to the other, eyes on the light peeking through the trees. A drum began beating slowly behind them, and they both fell silent. The beat was steady, building tension that was palpable. Neither of them moved. Then the drums stopped. The only sound was their breathing and the distant murmurs of their audience.

*Boom, boom, boom.*

The drum was faster this time, and the women turned to face one another. Fausta jumped up and down on the spot a few times, warming her muscles and stretching her neck from side to side. The sword twisted in Brei's hand, and she slowed her breathing. She was ready.

The moment the drum picked up tempo, she lunged at her opponent. The guests would hear them before they saw them, further building the suspense. When the two women finally burst through the trees, the spectators gasped. There was applause as they filled the space, and Fausta smiled. That was the moment Brei realised that her opponent was probably crazier than she was—which was not a good thing. Every time Fausta's sword struck her shield, she could feel the gladiator's hunger. Fausta wanted to win, but so did Brei. She was not fighting for the love of the sport but the chance to return home one day. She was fighting for a life at the end of it all.

Fausta raised a foot, and Brei's shield instinctively moved to cover her knees. It was a dirty way to take down an opponent.

The guests cheered.

Brei lunged forwards again, bringing more strength to every strike of her sword. She could feel the sweat running down her back and chest as she worked harder and harder to disarm Fausta. It would come down to endurance. Brei could see the spectators leaning forwards in their chairs as Fausta's sword came relentlessly at her, every blow delivered with such force and precision that Brei felt it through her entire body. She fought back hard, her concentration faultless. Brei finally knocked the shield from Fausta's hand, but the gladiator dived after it, collecting it with such grace, Brei was in awe of the manoeuvre.

Fausta took advantage of her distracted state, swinging out a leg and hooking the warrior's ankle. Brei fell with far less grace than her opponent, her back slamming into stone and the air knocked from her lungs. Fausta was back on her feet a heartbeat later, then standing over her. Brei got her shield up just in time, the downwards blow sending shock waves along her arm and through her spine. She rolled to avoid the next strike and hit something that felt a lot like a leg.

Rule number one: do not injure your hosts.

While caught up in the chaos, she had brought the fight to their feet. She was about to roll back in the opposite direction when a firm hand grabbed her arm and hoisted her up onto her feet. That was a first. Spectators did not usually intervene.

As she lifted her shield, she allowed herself a quick

glance at the man who had helped her. She froze when she saw his face.

∽

Before he had even seen her face, he knew it was her. It was not only that her skin was painted that ridiculous shade of blue, making a mockery of her heritage, but the way she moved, the shape of her legs, the set of her shoulders, and the colour of her hair. During the short amount of time they had spent together, Nerva had come to recognise her from afar—and there she was. She was fighting Fausta, who had trained at Ludus Magnus, the best gladiator school in the city. He had seen her fight enough times to know the damage she could do. Brei was in over her head. Thank the gods it was not a fight to the death. But that did not stop him flinching every time Fausta's sword smashed against Brei's shield.

'I think Fausta has met her match,' Mila had whispered when they came into sight.

Camilla had leaned in from the other side, her leg brushing against his. 'Is that a true depiction of what the barbarians are like? I thought they would be bigger.'

He might have rolled his eyes if he had been able to move. Why on earth did she have to sit so close? The overpowering smell of her perfume was making the air unbreathable.

Then Brei had fallen at his feet, as though the gods had once again placed her under his protection.

'Jupiter,' Camilla gasped, grabbing hold of Nerva's arm.

He was tempted to end the fight, but instead he pulled Brei upright. When she glanced in his direction, her eyes widened. His heart thudded in his ears. 'Shield,' he mouthed. One word that broke the spell between them.

Brei's eyes snapped forwards, and she raised her weapon just in time.

*Crash.*

Camilla jumped beside him, then laughed. She was still hanging off his arm.

Mila leaned in again. 'Ah, what was that?'

He tore his gaze away from the fight to look at her. 'Brei.' It was the only word he could manage.

Mila's expression collapsed. 'That is *her*?'

He nodded and faced forwards again, his mind still playing catch-up. She was alive, living in his city—and she was fighting for Gallus Minidius. He should have known a man like Gallus would not let an opportunity like Brei pass him by. He would be exploiting her to no end.

'Are you all right?' Camilla whispered. 'You are as pale as a ghost.'

*Ghost.* Nerva knew something of ghosts. He did not dare look away from the fight to reply for fear that Brei would stumble the moment he did. Mila had stilled beside him. He had told her everything, because she was one of the few people he could bare his soul to. She knew his mind, heart, and now his dilemma.

Sweat broke out across Brei's skin, every muscle in her body working. She was a warrior, robbed of her bow, reduced to re-enacting the horrors she had endured at the hands of the very people she was sent to entertain. She was a trophy on display, and shame welled inside Nerva at the realisation. He could tell he had distracted her, that she had not been prepared to see him, and wondered if he could remain seated while she was pummelled with a blunt weapon. But then Brei emitted a roar that shifted the wine in their cups. Her sword and shield worked together, thrusting and blocking, swiping and bashing. For a moment Fausta looked ready to fall down, backed into a corner of the garden with nowhere else for her to go. But the gladiator was not equipped to lose, and she turned the fight around. Nerva sat with his heart in his throat, and Camilla still clinging to his arm, while Brei was shoved backwards and smashed across the head with a shield. It was enough to stun her, and three swift moves later, Brei lay disarmed with Fausta's foot over her neck and a blade pressed to her throat.

Applause broke out, and Fausta stepped back, panting and bleeding from one ear. Brei slapped the ground before sitting up, coughing violently. She was not a good loser either, but at least she could breathe again. Fausta offered a hand, and Brei stared at it for a moment before taking hold of it and being hoisted up. This started off another round of cheers as the audience acknowledged the good sportsmanship being displayed. Brei kept hold of Fausta's hand and surprised Nerva by lifting it into the air, declaring her the victor.

Nerva joined in the applause, Camilla's claws tightening on his arm as he did so. Brei chose that moment to glance in his direction, her gaze flicking to Camilla before falling away. Then, letting go of Fausta's hand, she disappeared into the shadows.

CHAPTER 21

'Oh, please,' Camilla said, a pout in her tone. 'I only want to meet the gladiators, not fight them. There is no need for you to be all protective.'

Nerva was not being protective—not of Camilla. 'I do not think it is a good idea.'

Mila looked between them. 'Perhaps I could take her to meet them. I am sure you have business to finish up here.'

Nerva wanted to speak with Brei, but he wanted to do it alone. The thought of her disappearing again made up his mind. 'I will take you.'

'We will all go,' Mila said, standing. She gave him a sympathetic look as she rose.

Albaus and Felix joined them also, and the small party made their way through the house, their hosts none the wiser. They arrived at the laundry much sooner than Nerva would have liked. He still had no idea what he was going to say, and at some point during their walk, Camilla had reattached herself to him. A man stood in the doorway, blocking their entry. He appeared to recognise Nerva.

'Can I help you, sir?'

Nerva looked past him to where Fausta was having a

wash. Brei was leaning against the opposite wall, foot tapping. She looked over in his direction, and her foot stilled. The man was waiting for an answer.

'We are friends of Fausta,' Mila said, speaking up on his behalf.

The gladiator turned at the mention of her name, grinning when she caught sight of them. Naked from the waist up, she slipped a tunic on before heading over to them.

'Let them in,' she said.

The man stepped aside and went to stand with Brei, who had not taken her eyes off Nerva. His feet seemed to be anchored in the doorway.

'Are we going in?' Camilla asked, her tone too high for the situation.

Mila looked over her shoulder and stopped walking. 'Lady Camilla, come meet the victor.'

Camilla looked up at Nerva, waiting for his reaction.

'Good idea,' Nerva said, pulling his arm free.

Camilla reluctantly went to join Mila. Brei was as far away from the others as possible, and now she had her back to him. The man remained close to her, which annoyed Nerva more than it should have. Of course Gallus would send someone with her, but did he have to hover? Finally, she turned and looked in his direction. Pieces of hair clung to her face and neck, her bottom lip was swollen, and there was a bruise already appearing above her eye. She wore a loincloth, her middle covered by a leather breastplate that was more of a harness. It was similar to what he had seen Maeatae women wear in battle.

'You are alive,' he said, stepping inside.

The man looked between them, remaining at her side. Brei reached for the cloth floating in a basin of water, wrung it out, and began washing herself. 'As are you, General.'

Nerva looked at the man. 'Can you give us a moment?'

Clearing his throat, the man nodded and left. Nerva had no idea where to begin. She had turned her back to him again. 'You are fighting for Gallus?' Out of the corner of his eye, he saw Camilla glance back in their direction. Mila was doing her best to keep her busy.

'He bought me from the market.' She ran the cloth over her face and arms, then dropped it back in the water and turned to him. 'And now I fight.'

'I see that.' He swallowed. 'I am sorry I was not around to… help you.'

'I do just fine without help.'

He nodded. 'Your Latin is much improved.'

Now it was her turn to nod. 'So is your leg.' A pause. 'I thought you might lose it.'

'Me too.' He was standing about four feet from her and took another step forwards to close some of the distance. 'Are you all right?' Such an inadequate question.

Brei searched his face. 'This is the first time I've lost a fight, you know.'

'My fault. I surprised you.'

'You did. Though judging by your face, I surprised you also.'

He glanced over at the others. 'I had no idea what happened to you.'

'Exactly what you said would happen. I was taken to the Graecostadium, and then I was sold.' She continued to watch him. 'Not many of us made it off that ship.'

'I know.' She turned away, and he noticed silver lines on her back, scars from the day Paulus Cordius had lashed her. They were only a few, and they were faint, but the reminder made his stomach turn. She reached behind her, fingers working expertly over the buckles. The breastplate had left deep indents in her skin where the straps had sat.

'There was no food or water in the end. Or at least no one healthy enough to bring it.'

Nerva had an urge to get the cloth and wash her back but did not move. She slipped a tunic on before facing him again. 'I am very sorry about that,' he said.

'It doesn't matter now.' Reaching for the belt that lay next to her sandals, she wrapped it around her middle and fastened it. 'Anyway, you would be surprised how long a Maeatae warrior can survive without water.' She spoke with bravado, and yet she was barely able to look at him.

There were patches of paint on her face that she had missed. Stepping forwards, Nerva reached past her for the cloth and brought it to her face. 'May I?'

Brei looked at him a moment before nodding. She wore her usual defiant expression as he wiped gently. He realised that some of the marks were in fact old bruises. She never flinched when he touched them. 'I am sorry,' he whispered so only she could hear.

She shook her head. 'I told you, it doesn't matter.'

His hand stilled, and he stared at her. 'I am sorry,' he repeated, his throat closing. He had been holding the apology inside for so long. 'For everything.'

She swallowed, nodded. The war was still there between them, all of the pain, the violence, the heartbreak, the small moments of reprieve and acts of kindness. It flowed like water between them.

Before he could say any more, Camilla broke free from the other group and glided over to join them. 'Are you going to introduce me?' she sang, looking between them with a smile that was too large for the space.

Brei took a step back, bumping into the bench. Nerva reached out to steady her, then immediately let go. The three of them stood in awkward silence.

'This is Lady Camilla,' Nerva finally said. 'She was rather keen to meet the fighters.'

Brei's eyes followed Camilla's movements as she threaded her arm through Nerva's.

'So exotic with all that paint and fancy dress,' Camilla said. 'Yet now, seeing you in plain clothes, I might mistake you for a slave in my own household.'

Brei did not respond, and Nerva looked down at his feet.

'You probably do not understand most of what I am saying.' Camilla laughed, then, speaking louder, said, 'You fight good.'

Brei's eyebrows rose. 'Thank you,' she replied before turning away and picking up her sandals.

Nerva closed his eyes. 'Do you mind giving me a minute?' he asked Camilla. 'I will be along soon.'

Her smile faltered, and she looked between them. 'Of course.' She stepped away and left the room.

Nerva drew a breath. 'Sorry about that.'

Brei shook her head. 'Why? She seems nice.'

'She is very… pleasant.' He really did not want to spend the few moments he had left with Brei talking about Camilla. 'Before I go, tell me what you need.'

She straightened and looked at him. 'I don't need anything.'

'Just name it.'

'I told you, I don't need anything from you.'

He drew a breath. 'I have known Gallus a long time. He means to exploit you.'

A hint of a smile surfaced. 'I know that.'

'I want to help you.'

She studied his face for a moment. 'Do you know they put slaves in cages at the market? I could hardly believe it.'

Nerva looked confused. 'Yes.'

She was thoughtful for a moment. 'You knew all the suffering that lay ahead, and yet you marched us north anyway. Instead of watching my people die at your hand,

I was forced to watch them be killed by their own people.'

'I think the conversation has gone off track.' Or rather, it was not the conversation he wanted to have. 'What point are you trying to make?'

She crossed her arms. 'You should have let me die that day in my village.'

'I was saving your life.'

'To what end?' She reached for the bag containing her belongings. 'You can't fix this. Nothing you do now will erase any of it.'

'I am not trying to erase anything, I want to help you.'

She sniffed. 'I'm not sure I can stomach any more of your help.' Stepping past him, she exited the laundry.

Nerva turned and stared at the doorway where she had disappeared, drowning in the heaviness in his chest. Perhaps she was right. Guilt was a powerful motivator for him—always had been.

'Are you all right?' Mila asked, coming up beside to him. The pity in her eyes suggested she had overheard at least part of the conversation.

'Not really.'

Mila nodded. 'Do you want to get out of here?'

He exhaled and straightened. 'Yes.'

CHAPTER 22

Brei was still thinking about Nerva two days after her fight with Fausta. If she was being honest, she had thought of nothing else since. While relieved to see him up and about, with colour back in his face, she also had an odd realisation that he was not the same rugged man she had met on the battlefield. That white toga, the smooth face, and neatly combed hair, the beautiful lady hanging from his arm—it was laughable. What a contrast Brei was. The prisoner of war, the slave, the prop at one of his fancy dinner parties. Running into him had left her embarrassed and feeling oddly betrayed by his other life. It was not logical, as he was only living the life he was born into. He could not be expected to put that life on hold because of a few fleeting moments they had shared on a ship when he was delirious with fever.

But he had been healthy the last time they met, when he had stood too close and told her he was sorry. She had felt the power of those words as they passed his lips and felt a flutter in the pit of her belly as he dragged the cool cloth over her face. She must have looked an absolute mess.

What she concluded with some clarity was that Nerva

was at the top of Rome's class system, and she was at the very bottom. Any liaising between them was not only laughable but inappropriate. The best thing they could do for one another was stay far away.

'Brei,' Gallus called to her. 'A word.'

She was collecting the weapons when she turned to see him marching across the sand. A bad feeling came over her.

'Yes?'

He was puffing by the time he reached her, as if he had run two miles instead of walking ten feet. She waited for him to catch his breath.

'Why did you not tell me you spoke with Nerva Papias the other night?' He was looking at her as though it was a big deal. 'Otho tells me the two of you had a *private* conversation.'

She was going to have words with Otho. 'So?' She adjusted her grip on the weapons. 'Are slaves not allowed to have conversations?'

Gallus huffed and crossed his arms over his belly. 'When those conversations involve a Papias, I expect to be informed of every word exchanged.'

'Is that an actual rule, or are you just being nosey?'

His face hardened. 'Nerva came to see me last night.'

'All right.' She knew there was no point asking what had been said. Gallus would either tell her or not.

'He offered me an amount of my choosing in return for your freedom.'

One of the swords slipped from Brei's hand, landing next to her foot. 'Oh.' That was some gesture. 'And what did you say?'

'I told him I would think on the matter.' He looked ready to fall over with excitement. 'What on earth would make him offer such a thing?' He ran a hand down his face.

'Gods, tell me you did not threaten the life of his family or something.'

'Of course not.'

'Am I supposed to believe this is simply an act of generosity?'

'You're the one who keeps telling me what a good man he is.'

'Even good men do not make open-ended offers like that.'

What explanation was she supposed to give when she did not fully understand Nerva's motives herself?

Gallus's eyes narrowed. 'Did you lie with him, perhaps?'

She tilted her head. 'Must sex be the driving force behind everything?'

'There are kind gestures and there are grand gestures.'

'I wouldn't get too excited. He will change his mind when the guilt passes.'

Gallus looked taken aback by her words. 'Guilt? For what, may I ask?'

She wished she had not said it aloud. 'I don't know.'

'Explain yourself.'

She looked around, trying to form an answer. 'Invading my home? Killing people I love, perhaps?' She walked off towards the weapons room. As expected, Gallus hurried after her.

'Roman soldiers do not invade, they conquer. The only thing Nerva Papias is feeling is pride at his accomplishments.'

'Is that what he said?'

'It is what I know. What I do not know is why he feels this sense of obligation towards you.'

She drew a breath, knowing Gallus would not stop hounding her until he had a proper answer. 'I told you that he spared my life a few times.'

'Yes.'

'Well, it was sort of mutual.'

He was struggling to keep up with her pace. 'What do you mean, *mutual?*'

'I helped him also.'

Gallus grabbed hold of her arm, and she stopped walking.

'What does that mean?'

She glanced down at his hand. 'I helped him stay alive also.' She had fought against the idea that, for a period, they had been allies of sorts. It was strange admitting it aloud.

Gallus nodded slowly and released her arm. 'I see. Nerva is an honourable man, and if he feels indebted to you in any way, he will want to settle that debt.'

It was funny hearing Gallus praise Nerva. He seldom had anything positive to say about anyone. A warm feeling resembling pride bubbled inside her, as if his high opinion of Nerva reflected her own good judgement. 'Are you going to accept his offer?'

They had stopped outside the weapons room.

'I will suggest an obscene amount, one much higher than your worth, and go from there.' He drummed his fingers on his side as he thought. 'Say you did end up a freed woman. What would you do?'

Her plan had always been the same. The moment she was free, she would return to the highlands. 'Go home.'

Gallus laughed, holding his belly. 'Just like that, you would sail back to Caledonia?'

She scowled at him. 'Is that really so obscene? That I would want to return to my family?'

'Not that you would want to, but that you think you could just hop on a boat and stroll through a war zone.' He took a moment to collect himself. 'Even if you walked to the port, you would still need to secure passage on a ship. For that you would need coin.'

'I can earn coin.'

'And what sane man is going to let a Maeatae warrior board his ship at a time like this?'

Brei swallowed. 'The war cannot last forever.'

'No it cannot. But you will need to work in the meantime.'

So that was his angle. 'I know that.'

'Perhaps I could employ you.'

She watched him a moment. 'Perhaps I'll find employment elsewhere.'

Gallus laughed. 'Let us not get ahead of ourselves. First we must see just how indebted Nerva Papias feels.'

Before Brei could respond, Otho ran past them.

'Slow down,' Gallus shouted after him. 'You are going to knock someone down at that speed.'

Otho stopped and took a few breaths before speaking. 'There are rumours.'

'What rumours?'

'They are saying Severus is dead.'

Gallus's face fell. 'Gods, let it be only rumours. It is unthinkable that he should die in that place.'

That place was Brei's home.

Otho was backing away. 'I am heading to the forum to see what I can find out.'

'I'm coming with you,' Brei said, taking off at a jog.

'You have a fight tonight,' Gallus called. 'You need to rest.'

She turned and walked backwards a few paces. 'Have I ever let you down?'

He waved her away. 'Go, and report back what you learn.'

∼

There was a crowd gathering when they arrived. Men, women, and children stood in chilly February temperatures, all waiting to hear if the rumours were true. It was the most people Brei had ever seen packed into the large space. She often went to the forum just to admire the monuments, occasionally wandering inside the temples to watch people pray. It was fascinating to her that they could enter looking completely calm, and then a few moments later be down on their knees weeping before various gods.

Sometimes she would follow behind families who knew something of Rome's history, fathers who would stand before each monument and tell the story of how it came to be built and why it was of such importance. The stories sounded like legends, and she could not help but wonder which parts were true and which were carefully crafted lies designed to inspire young Romans to do things like travel to faraway lands—and massacre all the people.

'Any announcements yet?' Otho asked a woman clutching a palla to her chest. She shook her head. Turning to Brei, he said, 'Wait here in case there's an announcement. I'm going to check the notice board.'

Brei nodded. 'All right.'

The woman next to them glanced disapprovingly at Brei. While her Latin was much-improved, her accent still managed to turn heads.

Brei watched a merchant push his cart through the crowd, the smell of his honeycomb mixing with the smell of possible rain. When she faced forwards again, she spotted Nerva standing just ten feet away with his back to her. He was with Marcus, the tribune who had spent the entire campaign following him around like a little pup. She looked around for Otho, but before she had a chance to flee, Nerva turned and looked straight at her. His gaze was so intense when it landed on her that Marcus spun around to see what had caught his attention. Unable to take both their gazes, she turned and fled in the other direction. Too bad people were packed in so tightly she could barely move.

'Brei.'

She recognised his voice behind her. 'Excuse me,' she said, pushing between people, but everyone was moving towards the podium.

'Brei.'

Nerva grabbed her arm, and she had no choice but to face him. She was still getting used to the sight of him out of uniform.

'What are you doing here?' he asked.

Again, she looked around for Otho and could not see him. 'Waiting for the announcement, like everyone else.'

He did not look pleased. 'Gallus just lets you wander around the city by yourself?'

She frowned. 'I'm with Otho, my... trainer.' Friend seemed a stretch, as all they did was beat and bait one another.

'Well, where is he? It is not a safe time to be on your own.'

She pulled free of his grip and was about to make a snarky reply when someone stepped up onto the podium. He smoothed down his tunic and cleared his throat, staring down at the board in his hand. Nerva turned to listen.

'On February 11, the year 211, our beloved emperor, Lucius Septimius Severus Augustus did draw his final breath while on a brutal campaign in the north of Britannia.'

Brei stepped closer to Nerva. 'He makes it sound like he died in battle instead of tucked up in bed.'

Nerva brought a finger to his lips to silence her, and she looked around at the outpouring of grief. More people were arriving, no doubt wondering what had brought the city to its knees. Nerva looked pensive, while she felt only relief and hope that her people might finally get some reprieve from the fighting.

'Killed,' wailed a nearby woman. 'At the hands of barbarians.'

Brei and Nerva looked at one another.

'Let us get you out of here,' Nerva said, ushering her in the other direction.

'Why?' Brei glanced over her shoulder at him, confused. She kept walking though.

Nerva signalled to Marcus over the tops of people's heads that he was leaving with her. The tribune nodded, then turned back to listen. 'Because grief makes people do strange things,' he said, turning back to her. 'Best not to speak. Your accent might be a trigger for some.'

She knew something of triggers. The death of her mother fuelled the violence inside her every day.

More people filled the forum, making it almost impossible to get out. Brei resisted the urge to elbow her way through the crowd as she was swept away by them.

Nerva reached back for her. 'Take my hand.'

She took it and pulled herself behind him. He managed to clear a path, looking back every time her shoulder clipped against someone. When they were finally through the crowd, Nerva stopped and looked both ways down the street.

'Where do you live? I will take you home.'

He still had hold of her hand, and she did not pull away. 'Vicus Patricius.'

He looked at her with an expression she could not read. 'Which end?'

'Subura.' She felt her cheeks heat as he continued to look at her. The region was well known for its prostitutes.

He stared at her for the longest time. 'Let us go.'

'You really don't have to walk me.' He let go of her hand, and it immediately turned cold.

'No more talking. It is not safe.'

They walked in complete silence the rest of the way. There was too much going on around them to have a conversation. The mood of the city was eerie. News of Severus's death had spread, and people stood in groups in the middle of the street, talking in hushed voices, crying, or consoling those in tears. Brei watched the road in front of her, walking a few paces behind Nerva, like any other slave.

When they arrived at the building, there was a woman standing outside Brei's room wearing a red toga. She smiled at Nerva.

'Hello, handsome. Fancy a drink to honour our emperor?'

Brei gave her a look that wiped the smile from her face and had her strolling away, hips swinging.

'Friend of yours?' Nerva asked as Brei twisted the door handle and bumped her shoulder against it. It groaned open.

'Friend of *yours,* it seems.' She turned to look at him. 'Gallus told me of your generous offer. You should know he intends to bleed you dry.'

There was a hint of a smile on his face. 'I have been dealing with men like Gallus my entire life. I would expect nothing less.'

She looked around. 'You don't owe me anything, you know. Why not use the coin for another good deed? There seem to be a lot of hungry people in your city.'

He regarded her for a moment, not looking offended as she thought he might, but rather amused. 'Why not just say thank you? It does not fix everything, but it does enable you to find employment of your *choosing*. Why risk your life for a greedy man like Gallus?'

His words seemed sincere. 'What else do you think I'm going to do in a city like this? I'll still be an unskilled foreigner. I can't sew or weld, or cook the foods you eat. Even your bread is different to ours.'

'I can find you employment if you need help—'

'That's what I'm trying to say. I don't want your help anymore. And I don't need you to buy my freedom.'

He crossed his arms. 'Do you have a better plan?'

'Yes. I plan on earning it in just a few short years.'

'Is that what Gallus told you?'

She felt her cheeks heat. She did not like to look the fool, especially in front of him. 'That's what we agreed.'

He exhaled. 'Why wait?'

'Because.'

'Because why?'

'Because I can't repay you, and I don't want to owe you.'

Nerva stared at her. 'You will not owe me anything. Consider it a gift.'

She felt an odd sort of panic rise inside her. 'You don't have to keep saving me from these situations. It's confusing.'

'What are you talking about?' He reached out and took hold of her arms. 'What is confusing?'

She pulled free of his grip. 'Every kind gesture, every *gift*, is another tie to you I have to sever. We are not friends.'

He swallowed and straightened. 'I understand.'

She was surprised by his response, but of course he understood. At some point he must have felt that pull between them, the one that should never have been there to begin with.

'Make sure you lie low for a little while,' he said. 'At least until things calm down.'

'I have a fight tonight.'

His eyes returned to her. 'Where?'

'It's a small arena you won't have heard of.'

'You should not be fighting in arenas. It is risky. Gallus knows that.'

'No one cares about a few slaves fighting at an arena that size. Only fits a hundred men.'

'Gallus tell you that also?'

Brei did not reply.

'You should pull out,' Nerva said. 'Now is not the time to play barbarian.'

Brei took in his serious expression. 'I appreciate your concern, but the decision is not mine.'

'It would be if you accepted my offer.'

She sighed. 'You needn't worry. Gallus protects his assets.'

'Gallus will always care more about money than people.' He took another step back. 'I understand why you do not want to accept my help, so I will leave you alone. But if you refuse help, then you are going to need to be smart, because right now you are underestimating the city you live in.' He paused. 'If you need me, for any reason at all, my house is located in region thirteen, halfway up the hill. You can ask anyone where the Papias domus is located. Everyone knows.'

She was torn between telling him to leave and asking him to stay. The conflict of emotions whenever he was around was exhausting. She had no reason to delay him any longer. 'Thank you for walking me home.'

Nerva only nodded, then turned and headed back down the street.

CHAPTER 23

Brei remained in the doorway, watching Nerva until he was out of sight. A small part of her wanted to see if he would look back.

He did not.

The moment he was gone from sight, she felt a pang of something resembling loneliness. When she went inside, she found she could not sit still. After pacing the length of the small room for some time, she gave up on the idea of rest and went to find Gallus to tell him she would not be fighting. He was already at the arena, looking the happiest she had seen him in months. Apparently, he was not as affected by the death of the emperor as the rest of the city. She almost felt bad ruining his good mood, but Nerva was right, it was not the time to put on war paint and fight in front of a crowd.

'You are early,' he said, walking over to meet her.

'And you're happy.' The sight of his beaming face was a little unnerving at a time when everyone else was grieving.

He rocked on his feet, the way he always did when he had good news. 'Two hundred denarii is what I paid for you. Iunius wanted four hundred, but I paid two.'

Brei's eyebrows pulled together. 'Yes, I was there, remember?'

'Nerva Papias, so adored by the people of Rome that I would not be surprised if he became emperor himself one day, just paid me six thousand denarii in exchange for your freedom.'

Brei blinked, staring at him in shock. But as the shock wore off, it was replaced with irritation. She had specifically told him not to go ahead, and he had looked her straight in the eye and told her he would back off. Then he had done it anyway.

'Did you already accept the money?'

Gallus looked at her as if she were crazy. 'Did I... six thousand was my starting point, and he agreed without even attempting to negotiate. Of course I accepted. What sane man would say no to that amount of money?' He rocked on his feet again. 'That sum is far more than I would have made from you in a few years, and I am no longer responsible for your upkeep.'

'My upkeep?'

He waved a hand. 'Your housing and such.'

Brei's face hardened. 'You mean the small room I share with two other women in the slums?'

'Better than sleeping on the street. I must say, you are sounding rather ungrateful.'

'I'm just pointing out that my living arrangements cannot be that expensive.'

'Well, you are now free to leave if you find it so beneath you.' He reached into a pocket and pulled out a coin pouch. 'Here,' he said, tossing it to her. 'While I am in no way obligated to share any of my profits with you, take that as a gesture of my goodwill.'

She had been getting a lot of those lately. Brei stared at the pouch in her hand. 'Coin?'

'One hundred sestertii.' He said it slowly, as though she would have trouble comprehending such an amount.

It was not a lot of money, but given she was starting her freedom from a base of zero, she accepted it. 'Thank you.'

'Oh,' Gallus said, remembering something. 'What is this I hear about you not fighting this evening? Nerva seems to be under the impression that you are withdrawing.'

She had never said no to a fight in her life, so she understood his confusion. The plan had been to withdraw, but now Nerva had once again taken it upon himself to make the decision for her. He had been the one who said that if she were free, she could make the decision for herself. 'Of course I'll fight. I have to pay my way somehow.' She regarded him for a moment. 'But first we need to agree on my cut of the profits moving forwards.'

Gallus chuckled. 'Smart girl.' He pretended to think it over. 'Ten percent.'

She gave him a look that suggested she was not that naive. 'Sixty.'

'Twenty-five.'

'Fifty.'

'Thirty. Final offer.'

'If I refuse, will you go elsewhere for your Maeatae warriors?'

He clicked his tongue, staring her down. 'Will you find someone else prepared to employ a barbarian at a time like this?'

He had her there. 'Forty-five.'

'*Thirty.*'

She sighed. 'Thirty-five percent, or I shall turn to prostitution just to spite you.'

Another belly laugh from Gallus. 'I am not sure I could do that to my fellow Romans. Thirty-five percent it is.'

∼

The fighting pit was tucked away in the heart of Subura. It was a word-of-mouth type of event, and those in attendance knew the risks.

Occasionally, Gallus liked to match Brei with a man, though he was always careful about doing so. He made sure she could outfight her opponent before agreeing to the arrangement. While they did not fight to the death, fighters could still die.

Brei's opponent was a short, muscled man with part of his right ear missing. He was a *dimachaeri* who fought with two swords, and because that type of gladiator was usually matched with another dimachaeri, Brei was expected to fight with two swords also. Gallus had quickly discovered that she could fight with any weapon given to her. She could fight with only her fingernails and a sandal if that was all she had on hand.

'Skip the paint,' he had told her when she was getting ready. 'The crowd is a little antsy tonight.'

'What does that mean?'

'It means we should not throw fuel on the fire.'

That was the first time she felt truly nervous as she waited to enter the pit. Not about her opponent, but the state of the vocal crowd. Her suspicions were confirmed when she was introduced as Venus instead of 'the barbarian all the way from the highlands of Caledonia'.

She quirked an eyebrow at Gallus when she heard the announcement.

'Venus is the goddess of love, desire, sex, and prosperity,' Gallus explained.

'Of course she is,' Brei said, rolling her eyes and picking up her weapons as the gate opened. From the moment she stepped onto the sand, she knew the crowd was not fooled by her change in appearance.

'Show that savage what Roman men do to beasts like her,' one man shouted from the edge of the pit.

Any other time, Brei would have dismissed him as a drunken fool, but the hate in his voice made her feel cold. She looked back at the gate where Gallus gestured encouragingly to her.

*All right.* If she was going to fight, then she was going to win.

~

THE FIGHT CAME to an end with her foot stamped on her opponent's chest and the tips of her swords pointed at either side of his neck. The *summa rudis* declared her the victor, and she immediately stepped back, dropping her weapons. When she offered her hand to her opponent, he surprised her by taking it. Instead of pulling himself up, he pulled her down onto the sand. She fell, landing on her stomach. The crowd *cheered* his bad sportsmanship. She was tempted to pick up her weapons and teach her opponent one more lesson but thought it best to walk away and save the fight for another day.

'I gather by the lukewarm reaction that everyone bet on my opponent to win,' Brei said when she returned to Gallus. She did not slow to talk to him.

'All but a smart few,' he called to her back, trying to keep his voice chipper. 'They are just drunken fools. Pay them no mind.'

The streets were dark as she wandered home that night, the air cold in a comforting way that reminded her of Caledonia. She wore only a tunic despite the frigid air. It could sometimes take hours for her body temperature to drop after a fight, depending on the length of the fight and the skill of her opponent.

Brei was not far from her *insulae* when a man stepped in front of her. She managed to pull herself up just in time. Looking up at him, an uneasy feeling ran through her. He crossed his arms in front of him, eyes narrowed on her. The small hairs on the back of her neck stood on end when she heard the shuffle of feet behind her. She turned. Two more men had entered the alleyway, caging her in.

'You either want coin or sex, and you will get neither from me.' Her tone was calm despite the fear coursing through her. Three men and no weapon was not an even match.

One of the men behind her laughed. 'Sex? With a barbarian? Do you think we all want the pox?'

She recognised him from the fight earlier. He was the one who had heckled her at the beginning. Her unease grew at the realisation. Nerva had been right. She should not have flaunted herself on the evening of the emperor's death. 'Let me pass, and I won't break your face.'

They all laughed at that, inching closer to her. She saw the flash of a blade in one of their hands and was forced to be practical. This was one fight she could not win. She was going to have to run. She looked forwards again, where only one man blocked her exit. He did not have a weapon, so she threw herself into him. It was like hitting a stone wall, but at least this stone wall staggered on impact. As she went to move around him, someone caught her by the wrist and dragged her back into the middle of the circle.

'*Scortillum,*' the man spat at her.

She might not have known every Latin profanity, but she knew by his tone that he was not paying her a compliment. Swinging around, she punched him in the face as hard as she could. He immediately let go of her arm, his hands going over his face. When she went to run, she was blocked again by the same brick wall of a chest.

Brei was not above fighting dirty at a moment like this and threw her knee into his groin. He shifted his leg at the last second, blocking her. A hand came down on the side of her head, knocking her sideways into the wall. Her ears rang, but she had been hit in the head too many times to sit there feeling sorry for herself. When the third man grabbed her by the hair, she threw her elbow back into the centre of his chest, winding him. He did not let go of her, but he was startled enough for her to try again.

Raising her foot, she kicked him in the stomach, causing him to double over. That left one man, and she leapt back out of his reach before he had a chance to grab hold of her. Ducking around him, she took off at a sprint down the alleyway. A string of swear words followed her, but no one gave chase. They may have outmuscled her, but they could never outrun her.

Brei ran until she found herself in region thirteen at the base of the hill Nerva had spoken of. She paused to catch her breath, trying to think through her next move. It was not safe to return in the direction she had come, and she was exhausted. While she was not normally one for tears, she felt the sting of them threatening to spill.

*Absolutely not.*

There was no way she was going to fall down and cry in the middle of the street. No one would care anyway.

She spotted two women walking towards her and straightened, smoothing down her tunic with her hands. 'Excuse me,' she called. The women stopped talking, their feet stilling as they looked at her with an odd expression. 'I was wondering if you could tell me where the Papias household is.'

The women looked at each other, then back at her. 'You are bleeding,' one of them said.

Brei reached up and touched the tender part of her head, then stared at the blood on her fingers. She must have cut her head when she hit the wall. That was when she noticed it had dripped all over her clothes. 'So I am.' She looked up, attempting a smile in hope of appearing less threatening. 'The Papias household?'

The women seemed hesitant to help her, but then one finally said, 'Fourth house on the right, halfway up the hill. It has a blue door.'

'Blue door.' She could remember that. 'Thank you.'

The women hurried off before she had even finished saying the words. Brei felt blood drip on her arm and pressed her hand to the wound on her head. Did she really think she could just show up at Nerva's doorstep, looking the way she did, and he would just invite her in? She blinked slowly and glanced back in the other direction. All the shops were closed. There was nothing but a dark maze of streets and alleyways, and who knew what type of men lurking in them. One thing she knew for sure was that she did not have any fight left in her.

Making her way up the hill, she counted the houses on her right. Four was not many, yet each one seemed to go on for miles. Finally, she stood at the bottom of a set of steps, staring up at a blue door. There was every chance he was not even home, probably off at some dinner party with the pretty brunette who he wore like an accessory. Drawing a breath for courage, she ascended the steps and took hold of the large knocker on the door. She banged it three times before stepping back. Moments later, the door opened and a slave girl poked her head through the gap. She looked Brei up and down before focusing on her bloodied face.

'Yes?' she asked, not opening the door any farther.

'Is Nerva Papias at home?' She tried very hard not to sound foreign but could tell by the servant's expression that it made no difference.

'Who is asking?'

At least the door was still open, even if she did not answer the question. 'My name is Brei.'

'Are you an acquaintance?'

'Yes.' Seeing that the girl was waiting for more of an

explanation, she added, 'The general told me that if I should need anything, I should come here.' She felt quite pathetic in that moment. He had only made the offer that afternoon, and there she was, not even a day later, knocking on his door looking like she had just been attacked by dogs.

The girl thought for a moment, then glanced behind her. 'He is entertaining.'

'Oh.' Brei was already backing away from the door. 'Never mind.' When she went to turn, the girl stopped her.

'Wait here.' She looked unsure. 'Don't move.'

The door shut between them, and Brei heard the sound of the lock. She glanced over her shoulder and considered going anyway. Removing her hand from her head, she was pleased to discover the bleeding had stopped. At least if she ran now, she would not leave a trail of blood in her path. But before she had a chance to decide, the door opened again and Nerva filled the doorway. There was concern on his face, his jaw clenched so tightly she feared he might chip a tooth.

She cleared her throat. 'Sorry to just show up at your door—'

He was standing in front of her before she had a chance to complete her sentence, flooding her senses with the smell of scented oil, the blinding toga, the soft fingertips investigating the wound on her head.

'Come inside. Let us get you cleaned up.'

No questions. No lecture. No 'I told you so'. His arm went around her. Before she knew what was happening, she was being pulled through the door and marched through the atrium. It was the most ridiculous domus she had ever laid eyes on, but she did not stop to admire it. She drank in the sights as he hurried her through the large space, past the conversation drifting in from another room. The servant who had answered the door earlier came out to meet them.

'What do you need?' She spoke in a lowered voice.

Nerva glanced behind him, as if expecting someone to appear at any moment. 'Best take her to my rooms. Get some warm water, clean clothes, and something to clean the wound. Say nothing to my mother. I will deal with her shortly.'

Brei looked across at him. 'I don't want to get you into trouble.'

He shook his head and dragged her forwards. 'Never mind that.'

She said nothing more as she was led into a large room with one of the biggest beds she had ever seen in her life. It literally had pillars at each corner, with sheer curtains hanging from the frame that joined them. She stopped dead in her tracks, looking around and then down at herself. 'I'm going to dirty everything.' She had never felt so uncomfortable.

Nerva let go of her. 'Do not fret. Nona can get a bloodstain out of anything.'

Brei glanced across at the girl, who was looking less wary of her now.

'I must go and make my excuses for leaving early. I will be back.' He nodded towards the servant girl. 'Nona will take good care of you until I return.'

Brei could only nod, overwhelmed by her surroundings and Nerva's kindness. There was that sting in her eyes again.

Nona disappeared and returned with a basin of warm water, a few cloths, vinegar, and towels so soft Brei was afraid to use them. She glanced up at Nona, who looked to be around fourteen. She wore her brown hair in a plait and had heart-shaped lips that reminded Brei of her sister.

'You're so... sweaty,' Nona said. 'I'm going to have to

peel your clothes off you.' She came forwards and reached for Brei's belt.

Brei caught the girl's hands. 'I can undress myself.' She did not mean to be rude but was not accustomed to being handled by strangers.

Nona took a step back. 'Suit yourself.' She dipped a clean cloth into the warm water, wrung it, and held it out for her to take. 'Let's get you cleaned up before Nerva returns.'

It did not go unnoticed by Brei that the girl called Nerva by his first name rather than *erus or dominus*. She lifted the tunic over her head and removed her loincloth, feeling oddly self-conscious in the setting. Taking the cloth, she began washing her entire body before tentatively wiping at her head.

'Your hair is full of blood. Let's wash it properly, and then we can check if the wound needs a physician.' She held out one of the towels. Brei took it and wrapped it around her middle before sitting on the stool. 'Lean forwards over the basin.' The girl guided her down and began ladling the warm water onto her head, rinsing gently.

Brei rested her elbows on her knees and watched the water turn red beneath her. The sensation of having her hair washed made her homesick. Her mother had washed her hair right up until she had disappeared. She realised at that moment how long it had been since someone had touched her without trying to cause her bodily harm. She pressed her eyes shut, and this time she could not fight back the sting of tears. They fell silently, mixing with the bloodied water.

'It's all right,' Nona whispered. 'I won't tell anyone.'

Brei's hands went over her face, and her shoulders shook gently.

## CHAPTER 24

Aquila's steel gaze never left Nerva as he wandered among the guests and bade them good night.

'But it is so early,' Camilla said. 'I thought we might take a stroll in the garden.'

Nerva found a smile. 'It is far too cold for you out there. Please, stay and enjoy the wine and warmth inside.'

He could almost see steam pouring from his mother's ears. 'What on earth could be more important than time spent with loved ones?'

'I shall not bore everyone with the details of my personal affairs.'

Rufus went to sit by his wife, patting her hand. 'Let him go. We are not all born social butterflies.'

No one else seemed surprised. It was not the first time Nerva had left a dinner party early. He was quite well known for his sudden departures.

As he headed back towards his rooms, he realised he was rushing. Partly because he had not seen that broken expression on Brei's face since her friends had been shot down by Maeatae arrows, and also because he was expecting her to flee the house first opportunity she got.

Until then, whatever she needed from him, he would give her.

When he arrived at the door, it sat ajar. He pushed it gently so as not to startle her but need not have worried, because she was oblivious to his arrival. She sat on a stool, a towel wrapped around her, elbows resting on knees. Her hair was wet, and the only sound was the water dripping from it into the basin below. There were fresh tears on her cheeks. He stopped, unsure whether to intrude any further. Just being in the room felt like an invasion of her privacy, despite the fact that Nona was pottering around her. He cleared his throat to let her know he was there and was surprised when she jumped at the noise. That girl could cut a man's throat without blinking; she was not one to startle easily. He saw what looked like defeat in her eyes. That was what moved his feet forwards, gaze fixed on her the entire way. When he reached Brei, he crouched down beside her. 'Thank you, Nona.'

The slave nodded and left the room. Brei squeezed out her long hair, water running over her fingers. Nerva passed her the remaining towel.

'Want to tell me what happened?'

Brei straightened and looked at him as she dried her hair with the towel. 'You were right. I should not have fought tonight.'

'Why did you?'

She looked down, then back at him. 'To spite you.'

He nodded. What other reason had he expected? She was an otherwise intelligent girl. 'So you lost?'

She shook her head. 'I won. The crowd didn't like that. Some of the spectators even went to the trouble of following me home.'

Nerva stood. It was best not to be so close to her when there was that amount of adrenaline coursing through him. 'They did that to your head?' He gestured towards the cut.

'A wall did this.'

His fingers curled into fists. 'But I am guessing the scum who attacked you guided you to that wall.' He paced because he could not stand still. 'What else did they do?'

She was not looking at him. 'Nothing. They were far too repulsed by me.' She tugged the towel down her thigh in an attempt to cover herself.

He knew it was wrong, but his gaze lingered on her bare leg. It was absolute perfection, even with the bruises. He swallowed before speaking. 'But you fled.'

'I was outnumbered.'

'Even if you were not, you do not have to fight everyone. You did the right thing coming here.' When she did not reply, he added, 'Let us take a look at that cut.' He returned to her, crouching down beside her again and gently brushing back her damp hair. Wet locks fell about her face. Her eyes followed him as he inspected the cut on her hairline. 'I do not think you need a physician. The bleeding has stopped.'

'It's nothing.'

He picked up a clean cloth and wiped gently around it. 'It is not nothing. You are hurt.'

'It's just a cut.'

'You should keep pressure on it for a while longer.'

Her fingers brushed his hand as she took the cloth from him. The touch made his stomach knot. His gaze met hers before he withdrew his hand. 'I am a little surprised you came here. You made your feelings rather clear earlier.'

'Not clear enough, apparently. *Six thousand denarii*. You played right into Gallus's game.'

'I did.'

She watched him for a moment. 'How am I supposed to pay you back?'

'You are not supposed to.'

Brei glanced at the door. 'I'm sorry for ruining your evening.'

'Please. You saved me from it.' He held her gaze, unmoving. 'Tell me why you came.'

She gave a small shrug. 'Probably just delirious after the knock.'

One corner of his mouth lifted. 'I suppose I should be thankful it was a hard knock, then.'

Brei swallowed thickly before speaking. 'I want to hate you.' The confession came out on a breath. 'I want to hate you, and I want to blame you for everything. Instead, I come to you for refuge.'

'Why is that?' His own voice was barely above a whisper.

She thought for moment. 'Perhaps because I see you. Not the legate or the senator, just you.'

'And what do you see?'

Her eyes moved over his face. 'A misfit. A man with no real power to change anything.'

'Not true. I could return to the senate and vote on decisions if I wanted to.'

She leaned back so she could look at him better. 'Would that fix what's broken in your world?'

Nona returned to the room with another jug of water. Neither of them broke eye contact. After she had placed it on the table, she picked up the comb and turned to Brei. She froze when she saw them. 'I'll come back later,' she said before fleeing the room.

Nerva waited for Nona to leave before replying. 'No, it would not fix everything.'

Brei held the side of the stool with one hand while the other kept hold of the towel around her. 'Am I a fool to trust you?'

He shook his head. 'You can trust me.'

Her tortured eyes stared at him. 'Would you trust someone you couldn't forgive?' Her eyes were glassy again, as though she might cry.

Without thinking, his hand went to her cheek. The backs of his fingers touched her gently, fearing the slightest amount of pressure would send her scurrying back from him. 'You do not have to forgive me to let me help you. I am not entirely sure *I* forgive me.'

Brei slid forwards on the stool, knees pressed together. 'You took everything from me.'

'We were at war.'

'We still are.' Her voice was quiet.

He shook his head. '*Our* fight is over.'

She tipped forwards and kissed him. His entire body tensed at the sensation of her mouth on his. He remained still, afraid of scaring her off by reacting. He need not have worried, because her hands slid into his hair, fingernails scraping. All of his self-control evaporated. He dropped down onto his knees in front of her, one hand cupping her face as she opened her mouth to him. His other hand went to her bare thigh, higher up than he had intended, the tips of his fingers brushing the edge of the towel. Her knees opened, and before he knew what he was doing, he lifted her off the stool and pulled her against him. Legs wrapped him so tightly that he was lost in the heat of her. When she pushed her hips against him, he had to bite back a moan.

He was not a moaner.

He felt like a young man experiencing a woman for the first time; every sensation felt new and overwhelming. Her fingers gripped his hair so tightly that he was having trouble deciphering between pleasure and pain.

*Pleasure*. It was definitely pleasure.

'I just want to forget,' Brei whispered as she tipped her head back and guided him to her throat.

His hungry mouth consumed her. 'What do you want

to forget?' He spoke the words against her skin, unable to pull away.

'All of it.'

The emotion in her voice, the pain, made him stop and look at her. She sucked in a breath when his lips left her skin. 'You will never forget,' he said. 'The moment you wake in the morning and look across at me, it will all still be there between us.'

She looked down at his lips. 'Who says I'm staying until morning?'

'I am going to need the entire night if you truly want to forget.'

A smile played on her lips. 'You must think yourself quite the lover if that's how you see this playing out.'

He gave her a cocky shrug. 'Roman soldiers are built for longevity.'

She guided his mouth back to her throat. 'Let's see if you can hold the line, soldier.'

∽

Sunlight streamed through the large window, and the bed was cold next to her. Nerva had been very much beside her when she had finally drifted off to sleep before sunrise. She immediately missed the warmth of him.

Blinking, she waited for her eyes to adjust to the blaring light. She knew it was late in the morning from how high the sun was sitting in the sky. Pushing herself up, she hugged the sheet to her and looked around the room in search of Nerva. She gasped when she saw a beautifully dressed woman sitting in a chair just a few feet from the bed.

'I had a similar reaction when I discovered *you* sleeping in my son's bed,' the woman said. Her mouth was pressed into a thin line, her stare venomous.

Brei tugged the sheets a little higher, but the woman's gaze seemed to penetrate the fabric, assessing every inch of her. 'Where is Nerva?'

The woman winced when Brei spoke. 'Gods, and a foreigner too.' She drew a calming breath, one finger tapping on the arm of the chair. 'Nerva is not one for lying about in bed during daylight. A man of his status is *always* busy.'

Brei glanced at the clean clothes Nona had brought her. They were still folded neatly on the table some distance away. 'And who are you?' She suspected she might already know the answer.

The woman's expression darkened. 'I am the lady of this house.'

Brei had been afraid of that. Lady Aquila. She cleared her throat. 'Is Nerva expected to return soon?'

Aquila tilted her head. 'I think it best if you are long gone before he returns.'

It should have come as no surprise to Brei that his mother would not approve of her. It did not help that she was a mess of cuts, scars, and bruises. 'Perhaps if you afford me a little privacy, I could dress.'

Aquila's finger continued to pound the chair as she stared at Brei. 'In the twenty-nine years my son has lived in this house, he has never had a woman in his bed. He is far too private about such things. I am trying to figure out why you are here. Perhaps he is trying to send me a message.'

'Or perhaps the others just leave before you wake,' Brei suggested.

Aquila smiled for the first time, but it was not a friendly smile. 'Absolutely nothing happens in this household without me knowing about it. Now tell me, how did you get your claws in my son?'

What was Brei supposed to say in response to that?

That in their attempts to kill one another on the battlefield, an attraction had formed? 'Maybe ask Nerva about that.'

'I am asking you.' Aquila's hand went to her brow suddenly. 'Oh, please tell me you are not the slave girl he was making enquiries about upon his return.' She looked exhausted by the realisation. 'I thought he had forgotten all about you.'

Brei was having difficulty imagining Nerva being raised by the woman in front of her. 'I'm no longer a slave.'

Aquila looked heavenward. 'Nerva has it in his head that he must help everyone less fortunate than himself. Instead, he should help them accept their proper place in the world.' Her hand returned to the chair, and her finger resumed tapping. 'You understand that last night was nothing more than an act of pity?'

Brei said nothing.

Aquila looked her up and down for a moment. 'What is it you want? Coin? A position in a noble household, perhaps?'

Brei frowned. 'I have employment.'

'Then what?' Aquila appeared to be losing patience. 'Do not tell me you were foolish enough to develop feelings for a man so far out of your reach.'

Brei looked again at the clothing and considered dragging the sheet with her to fetch it. She needed to get out of there. 'I really don't want anything from your son. Right now, I just want to leave.'

Aquila did not even blink. 'But how can I ensure that you do not return? The city is full of rodents. You get rid of one and another appears.' Her tone was so calm, so matter-of-fact, as though she was not aware of the poison coming from her mouth.

Brei sat a little straighter. 'You've made it clear that you don't want me here. I won't be rushing back.' She was getting angry now. It was best she left before she started throwing things.

Aquila leaned forwards slightly in her chair. 'Let me be very clear about something. My son is to be married soon. His betrothed comes from a noble family, the small portion of Rome's elite worthy of such a man. *You* are nothing but a scab on society.' She paused to watch the effect of her words. 'And you will soon be forgotten.'

Brei did not know whether to laugh or take the sheet from around herself and shove it down Aquila's throat. If she had not been Nerva's mother, Brei's reaction would have been very different. 'Now let me tell *you* something.' Her expression hardened. 'Where *I* come from, women like you would not last five seconds. A woman whose only contribution is procreation is an embarrassment. The Maeatae don't need slaves to dress and feed them, and because they are competent mothers, they also raise their own children. I can grow my own food, skin an animal to make clothes, break a horse, and shoot an arrow accurately over two hundred yards. I can outrun wild animals, track my enemy, and kill a man with my bare hands. I am the daughter of a chief, which, where I come from, makes me higher up on the social ladder than you.'

Aquila's eyes widened slightly, the tips of her finger pressing into the chair. 'Get dressed, and get out of my house.' She stood, her back as straight as an arrow. 'And stay away from my son. I can make a nobody like you disappear without a trace, and I will not think twice about doing so for the sake of my family.' With her head high, she glided from the room.

The moment Aquila was gone, Brei leapt from the bed and snatched the clothes off the table.

## CHAPTER 25

Nerva had not wanted to leave Brei alone at the house, but he needed to organise a safe place for her to stay. His sister's return to the city had worked in his favour. The house they had rented by the river could accommodate Brei also. He would tell her the arrangement was for Mila's benefit, that she needed help with cooking and cleaning, some company, and someone to wear the twins out. Any sniff of charity and Brei would not even consider it.

The moment he returned to the house to share the news, he could feel the tension in the air. His bed was empty, not one sign that Brei had ever been there. He had been driven completely mad by her all night. Never had he been so intoxicated by a woman, so wholly at her mercy. Brei had completely surrendered to him, then demanded more and more until he collapsed beside her feeling reborn.

He searched the house for his mother, finding her in the *tablinum*. 'What did you do?' he asked from the doorway. She was sifting through fabric samples and did not even look up.

'Whatever are you talking about?'

He sighed and crossed his arms over his chest. 'Where is Brei? I should have known it was not safe to leave her here alone for one moment. Need I remind you that those are my private rooms?'

Aquila finally looked up, stroking a neat curl of hair that hung down one shoulder. 'If you are asking after the foreign slave girl you had in your bed last night, Tertia saw her scurrying from the house not long after you departed.'

Nerva nodded. He did not have the patience to get into it with her. 'Never mind. I will go find her and ask her myself.' He marched back through the house and headed for the front door.

'Nerva,' his mother called from the other side of the atrium.

He turned to look at her. 'Yes?'

'Do not go to her. No good will come of it.' She clasped her hands in front of her. 'If word of this gets back to Camilla's family—'

'I have made no commitment to Camilla. You are the one leading the girl astray, not me.'

'Be sensible.'

He turned away. 'I have to go. I will speak with you later.'

'Nerva.'

He kept walking. Nona must have heard the exchange, because she was waiting at the door for him. She opened it as he approached.

'Good luck,' she whispered as he passed.

He winked at her and continued through the door and down the steps.

When Nerva could not find Brei at her room on Vicus Patricius, he made his way to the small arena where she trained. He recognised Otho and was about to ask if the trainer had seen Brei when he spotted her in the fighting pit shooting arrows at a pell. 'Excuse me,' Nerva said, stepping past him.

He stopped out of sight, watching her for a while. Her lack of clothing made him feel cold, but then he remembered where she had come from.

When Brei was down to her final arrow, she swung and pointed it directly at him, her expression fierce. 'You should never sneak up on a warrior holding a bow.'

He wandered out, joining her on the sand. 'Please tell me Gallus is not letting you fight with arrows now.'

'Of course not. I'm just keeping my skills sharp in case your mother makes good on her threat.'

He exhaled and brushed a finger over his nose. 'Ah, and what was that threat exactly?'

Brei went to collect the arrows. 'To make me disappear.'

Surprisingly, he had heard much worse threats from his mother's mouth. 'I am sorry about that.'

Brei yanked the arrows out two at a time and walked back. 'I hope you didn't come all this way to apologise on her behalf.'

She lifted her bow again, and he waited for her to shoot before speaking. 'Actually, I have a proposition for you.'

She reloaded the bow. 'All right.'

'I was with my sister this morning, and she is struggling at the moment. She could really do with some help.'

Brei turned to look at him. 'I thought your sisters lived in Giza.'

'Mila is here for a few months on business.'

'What sort of business?'

He cleared his throat. 'Her family imports spices. Mila has become more involved of late.'

Brei was staring at him like she did not believe a word he was saying. 'And what does she need help with?

'The house. The children.'

Brei faced the pell. 'Sounds like she needs to visit the Graecostadium.'

Nerva crossed his arms. 'Mila will not keep slaves. She is looking to employ someone.'

Brei turned back at that. 'Why not?'

'Because she grew up a slave in my household.'

Brei's expression softened. She took a moment to piece it all together. 'So you have asked her to employ me as a favour, hoping I'll stop fighting for Gallus.'

Yes, but he was never going to admit to it. 'She has a room for you. You would be safe there.'

Brei leaned on the bow. 'I already have a place to live, and I don't need your sister's charity.' She stared at him for a moment. 'You know, I don't like your mother. She's not a nice person.'

'Slightly off topic, but fair enough. You are not the first to make that observation.'

'But she's right.'

Nerva's eyebrows rose. 'You are possibly the first to say that.'

Brei shrugged. 'She is. I don't belong in your world, or your bed for that matter.'

'She got to you. It is what she does.'

Brei turned and readied her bow again. 'We both know that last night can't happen again.'

'I did not take you for one who scares easily.'

She glanced at him before releasing the arrow. 'I'm not scared, I'm practical. You shouldn't even be here.'

Nerva walked over and snatched the bow from her hand and held it out of reach. 'You do not get to push me away because you are spooked by what happened last night.'

She focused on the bow. 'I was lonely. Don't read too much into it.'

He handed it back to her. 'You are a terrible liar. Do you know that?'

Brei turned away from him again. 'One of us has to be sensible.'

'If you want to take a step back, that is fine. But do not stand there and tell me last night was no big deal. I was there. I felt it, and so did you.'

The bow dropped a few inches. 'That's why it can't happen again.' She released the arrow with extra force.

Nerva was usually the practical one, but all sense left him when it came to her. 'Fine, but there is no rule saying we cannot be friends.'

She turned back to him. 'We're still at war with one another and you're talking of friendship.'

'And I told you, it is not our war anymore.'

'My people are dying at the hands of your men.' She touched the bow to her chest. 'My family.'

He had to look away, because she was right. He was asking too much of her. 'Can you please just agree to the living arrangements? If I do not have to worry about your safety, I will be much more likely to leave you alone.'

She stared at him while she thought it over. 'Is your sister nice?'

'You are two peas in a pod. Trust me on that.'

She chewed her lip as she thought. 'I will help out in exchange for a place to stay, no money exchanged. And I want to continue fighting for Gallus.'

He swore inwardly. 'Fine.' He would get Mila to work on her.

She offered her arm, the way she had no doubt seen Gallus do when striking a deal. Suppressing a smile, he took hold of it. 'When you are finished here, I shall take you to collect your things and we will go to the house.'

'You don't have to do that. If you leave the address, I can find my own way.'

'I know you can.' He tugged the bow from her hand again and plucked an arrow from her quiver. Taking aim, he pierced the heart of the pell. 'But I want to take you myself.' He handed the bow back to her. 'That is what friends do.'

She eyed him coolly. 'We're not friends, remember?'

He brought his lips to her ear. 'Oh, I remember.' Straightening, he tucked a piece of silky chestnut hair behind her ear, remembering his face buried in it the night before. Judging by her expression, she remembered it too. 'Now hurry up. I do not have all day.' He walked away but could not resist a glance over his shoulder at her annoyed face.

'Very brave to turn your back to me when I'm holding a bow, General.'

He faced forwards so she would not see his smile.

## CHAPTER 26

'Are you ready to cry?' Asha said, twisting her training pole as though she had been born with it in her hands.

Brei kept her face serious. 'Those are bold words from a nine-year-old facing certain death.'

'I beat old people all the time.' She twisted the pole in her hand once again.

Brei circled her. 'Who are you calling old?' She struck out with her own weapon, and Asha blocked it, a smile appearing instantly.

'Felix is really old, and I beat him all the time.'

A throat cleared nearby. 'I am not *that* old,' Felix said. 'I can still hear at a distance of eight feet.'

It was late in the afternoon, and the entire household was outside in the small garden watching what Asha had pitched as 'a battle of epic proportions'.

Brei struck again, this time lightly clipping the girl's ankle. 'You just lost a foot.'

Asha's mouth fell open, but she wasted no time feeling sorry for herself. Lunging forwards, she delivered a sequence of blows that were more than impressive for her age. Light applause followed.

'Better,' Mila said, pride in her voice. She was standing between Remus and Felix with her arms crossed.

Brei fought back but slowed her movements like she used to for her nephew. Any contact would sting, not bruise. Roars came from her left, and the twins charged in with wooden swords and shields that were almost as tall as them.

'It's an ambush,' Asha called, spinning to face them. 'We must work together if we're to survive.'

Remus chuckled and draped an arm over his wife's shoulders, and she leaned her head against him.

'Keep those shields straight,' Felix called to the boys. 'We all know your sister is as cunning as your mother.'

Mila punched the dwarf's arm, but there was a smile in her eyes.

A clash of weapons ensued, and Brei could not help but smile at the serious expressions of the children. She had been the same way as a child, desperate to prove herself, even at an age when her only responsibilities were fetching water and feeding the animals. Spinning and twisting, she allowed the boys a few pokes at her, eventually dropping the pole and clutching her side. Asha turned, disapproval on her face.

'You *never* drop your weapon.'

Brei coughed dramatically. 'Even when I'm dying?'

'Especially when you're dying.' Asha raised her pole just as Caius charged at her. 'Mother, come help us.'

Mila swooped down and snatched up two wooden swords, running into the battle to join forces with her daughter.

'Well that's hardly fair,' Remus said. With a heavy sigh, he picked up the remaining sword and shield and went to stand behind his sons.

'The pointy end faces out,' Felix called.

Remus made a crude gesture at him behind the boys' heads. 'Very funny.'

Felix threw his hands up. 'Just trying to be helpful. I know how long it has been since you held one of those things.'

They were a family of gladiators, even Felix. All three of them had at one time trained at Ludus Magnus.

'What in heavens name have I walked into?'

Recognising Nerva's voice, Brei turned to see his smiling face. She could not help the way her heart sped up every time she saw him—and his visits were frequent.

'It *was* a fight,' Felix said. 'But then Remus joined.'

A wooden sword went flying in his direction, and the twins cheered. Brei moved out of the way, walking over to stand with Nerva.

'I thought you had a dinner party tonight?' She had to speak loudly to compete with the children.

'I am tempted to break the engagement. Your evening looks far more appealing than mine.'

'You can't do that. If you don't show up, your mother's going to come looking for you here. Then both our evenings will be ruined.'

His gaze fell to her lips, then away. He did that a lot, and her mouth turned dry whenever his eyes lingered too long on her.

'She is right,' Mila called while still fighting. 'Please do us all a favour and attend the dinner party.'

'I just got here and already you want me gone. Can I not have a moment's reprieve before I am forced to endure some rather bland company?'

Brei kept her face neutral. 'I've seen the women you speak of, and they're far from bland.'

His gaze snapped to her. 'Is that… is that jealousy in your tone?'

She rolled her eyes. 'Jealousy of what? Their weaving skills?'

'Mila could teach you to weave if you are feeling inadequate.'

She bumped her shoulder into him, reminded of all that muscle she had once explored. The memory made her cheeks heat. Thankfully, Remus spoke up before Nerva noticed.

'There are some interesting rumours arriving with the returning troops,' he said, knocking the sword from Mila's hand, then wandering over to join them. 'Some say the palace has been divided in half, the servants instructed not to talk to those on the other side.'

'And I thought our sibling rivalry was bad,' Mila called to Nerva.

Nerva suppressed a smile. 'At least they both agreed to withdraw from the north.' He glanced at Brei when he said that part. She had been close to tears when he told her. Nerva had stayed at the house, long after the others retired. The pair had sat outside wrapped in blankets, lost in memories they would rather forget. Nothing had happened between them. They had not even touched.

'The senate is also divided,' Nerva continued 'Caracalla was conspiring his father's death well before the cold finally took him. Many are aware of the fact, and those loyal to Severus are now loyal to Geta.'

Remus nodded. 'Sound like trouble's coming.'

'What sort of trouble?' Brei asked.

Nerva looked across at her. 'A very different type of war.'

Brei's mind raced. 'And where are you positioned in this war?'

'My father will support Geta if it comes to that.'

'And who do you support?'

'I support my father, so I suppose that means I support Geta.'

She frowned. 'Won't that make you a target?'

When Nerva did not reply, Remus clapped him on the shoulder. 'I suggest you watch your back, or pay someone to watch it for you.'

'I might steal Albaus if the situation worsens.'

He was referring to the mute bodyguard who was a part of the family of misfits.

'I could protect you.' The moment those words passed through Brei's lips, she wished she could have snatched them back. Everyone in the garden seemed to look in her direction for a moment. 'I only meant if I happened to be around, and you were relying on your own inadequate skills.'

Remus cleared his throat, gave Nerva another pat on the shoulder, and then left them. Nerva's eyes never left Brei.

'You want to be my bodyguard?' he mused.

'I've saved your life enough times. What's one more?' She was looking everywhere but at him. 'I'm only thinking of your family.'

'Do you really think I would intentionally put you in harm's way?'

Everyone had resumed what they were doing, and Brei could finally breathe again. 'No.' There was a long pause. 'Just be careful.'

His expression softened. 'Will you be here tomorrow? I thought I might come by and collect you. There is something I want to show you.'

She walked with him to the edge of the garden, away from the noise. 'I'm training in the morning. I have a fight in the evening.' She watched his face change. He had probably expected her to give it up by now, but she did not know how to be anything else.

'Then I will collect you in the afternoon.'

She did not want him to go but would never admit it aloud. 'Have fun with Camilla.' She said things like that instead.

He reached up and brushed his thumb over her cheek. 'I like it when you are jealous.'

Normally she would have deflected with a joke, but she turned into his touch instead before looking away. He held an enormous amount of power over her—and it made her very uncomfortable. 'You should marry the poor girl and put her out of her misery.'

His hand fell away. 'I cannot marry her.'

Her eyes returned to him. 'Why not?'

He hesitated before answering. 'It is complicated.'

'Complicated how?'

'I do not love her, for one.'

'Do men like you get the luxury of marrying for love?'

He shook his head and watched the children for a moment. 'I suppose not.'

She fought a strong urge to take his hand and press it to her lips. He deserved tender gestures like those. But she did not move. 'At least you have the option. There are probably only a handful of men alive back home, and they will all be taken by the time I get there.'

He glanced at her, swallowed. 'We will wait for things to settle down, and then we will find a way to get you home. You have my word.'

'A pledge?'

'Something like that.'

She trusted him with her life and should have been elated at the idea of going home someday. So why did she feel like her heart was breaking open?

He took her hand and squeezed it briefly. 'I will see you tomorrow.' He left her then.

Brei nodded and looked down at her empty hand.

Every time he touched her, it left another mark on her soul. As much as she wanted to return home, she knew leaving Nerva Papias behind would test her strength.

## CHAPTER 27

Brei circled the harnessed horses and chariot, then turned to Nerva, smiling. 'Can I... have a go?'

Nerva was holding the lead stallion's bridle and laughed. 'You have no idea what you are doing.'

'But I'm a fast learner.'

He patted the neck of the horse before wandering over to join her at the back of the chariot. There were men and horses all around the *trigarium*, casting curious glances in their direction. His little escapade would likely set tongues wagging all over the city. 'All right. Up you get.'

Her eyes widened slightly. 'You're actually going to let me?'

'I am coming with you, of course. These horses are very expensive, and I learned a long time ago that you only have one speed.' He watched as she leaped into the chariot and gathered the reins, eyes lit.

Seeing her like that, he realised he could not recall ever seeing her happy. Afraid, exhausted, sceptical, defeated, heartbroken, amused perhaps, and every shade of angry, but never happy. A vague smile here and there was not the same thing when shadowed by other things.

Nerva had imagined plenty of times what she was like before all of this, before the war came to her home, before she lost so much. He had images of her riding bareback beneath tall trees, bow on her back, and her horse's mane braided in that way he had found so amusing the day they met by the river.

He climbed up behind Brei, reaching either side of her to take the reins also. Her soft hair brushed against his chin, her familiar clean, earthy scent taking over the air. 'We are going to take it nice and—'

Before he had a chance to finish his sentence, Brei slapped the reins on the horses' rumps. The chariot lurched forwards. He was forced to let go and grab the side of the chariot to keep from tumbling off the back of it.

'That is not slow.' He was smiling as he scolded her.

Brei laughed into the wind. She actually laughed, a sound he could drown in if he were not careful. 'Better hold on, General,' she said over her shoulder.

His arms went around her again, taking a firm grip of the reins. He eased the horses around the bend at a canter. 'If you wish to live, let me do this part.' Brei's hair whipped his face as they turned. Once they were on the straight, he handed the reins back to her. 'I am going to let go now.'

'Can we go faster?'

'Absolutely not.'

For once, she listened, continuing at the same pace. When the left wheel hit a stone, the chariot bounced at an angle, causing Brei to squeal and then laugh. Nerva pressed a hand to her belly to steady her, and she turned her smiling face to him. *Forget the gossip.* There was no resisting her mouth in that moment. He bent and kissed her, pulling her closer so that her back filled the grooves of his chest and stomach. Her eyes sank shut as she melted against him.

The horses slowed as they approached the next bend, and another chariot overtook them, the driver muttering something as he passed. Nerva smiled against her mouth as he took the reins back from her and pulled the horses up. She faced forwards again but remained leaning against him.

'I don't want to stop.'

He chuckled, keeping her close. 'We should stop before we crash.'

'You would never let us crash.'

He rubbed his cheek against her hair. 'You are putting a lot of faith in me, and I am very distracted right now.'

She was silent a moment as the horses slowed to a trot. 'I trust you, you know.'

'I trust you also—just not with my horses.' He rested his forehead on the crown of her head as the horses slowed to a walk. 'I will not let anything bad happen to you.'

She turned her face into his neck. 'I want you to come to the house tonight, after the fight.'

'Why?' He breathed the question into her hair.

'Because I want to see you.'

'Why do you want to see me?' He was going to make her say it.

She was still against him. 'Because you're all I have right now.' She turned her face up to him. 'I just want to forget again.'

His hand travelled up to her throat. 'What spell have you cast that has me running to your bed at the click of your fingers?'

She searched his eyes for a moment. 'It's not just me, is it? You feel this too.'

He released his hold on her and pulled up the horses. 'I felt it the first time I laid eyes on you, the day you fell from the sky and knocked me from my horse, and I most definitely feel it now.'

When Nerva arrived home, he was surprised to find Paulus Cordius sitting in the *triclinium*, drinking wine with his parents. He had not seen or heard from the newly promoted legate since returning to Rome. As content as Nerva was to step aside, the news of his replacement had still stung. As far as he was concerned, the man was not fit to lead anyone.

Paulus stood when he spotted Nerva in the doorway. 'There he is. Our fierce leader. You have clawed your way back from death.'

As tempting as it was to turn around and leave, Nerva had no choice but to liaise with the man who had clawed *his* way up to replace him. He found a smile and prayed it looked sincere as he stepped inside the room, arm extended. 'I hear congratulations are in order.'

Paulus's chest expanded to twice its usual size. 'Big boots to fill. However, our emperor seems to think I am up to the task.'

Nerva exchanged a look with his father at the singular mention of emperor. If Aquila had noticed the slip-up, she hid it well. 'Nice of you to make time for a social visit.'

Paulus nodded. 'I think my men and I have earned some time off. It was tough going after you departed. The heavy losses under your command complicated things.'

Rufus shifted in his chair, and Aquila took a long drink of wine. Nerva studied Paulus before speaking. 'It was a tough couple of years for everyone.' He gestured for the legate to sit, then chose the lounge on the opposite side of the room for himself.

'I was just filling General Cordius in on everything that has happened in his absence,' Rufus said.

Paulus nodded. 'It is helpful to take the temperature of the senate given recent events.'

Aquila placed her drink down on the small table in front of her. 'Our young emperors must be truly devastated.'

Rufus cleared his throat. 'It can take time for a household to settle after such a significant loss.'

'We are fortunate to have a strong leader,' Paulus said.

Nerva frowned across the table at him. '*Two* strong leaders.'

Paulus looked at him. 'Is that not what I said?'

'No. We are fortunate enough to have two strong leaders during this transition.'

Paulus sniffed. 'Quite right.' He stood. 'I thank you for the refreshments. I am afraid I must be on my way. I am having dinner at the palace and do not wish to spoil my appetite.'

'But you just got here,' Aquila said, her tone unnaturally high. They all knew he was only there to sniff about and report back to Caracalla.

Rufus stood. 'We appreciate you coming by.'

Another stiff smile from Paulus. 'I am pleased to see Nerva looking so well. I can only imagine the outpouring of grief across the city had he not made it.'

'His strong leadership and enduring compassion have made him very popular,' Aquila reminded him.

'Yes,' Paulus agreed. 'Compassion—even in the throes of war.' The way he said it did not sound like a compliment. He focused on Nerva again, quirking one eyebrow. 'I meant to ask you, whatever happened to the prisoners who returned to Rome with you?'

There was no point in lying, as Paulus likely knew everything already. Still, he was not going to spoon-feed the new legate. 'Many of them died from influenza.'

'Not all, surely.'

He was fishing for a confession. 'A handful survived.'

'I did hear that a Maeatae warrior had been given her freedom and now roams our streets.'

Nerva's stare was ice cold. 'The woman saved my life. I paid for her freedom as an expression of gratitude.'

Aquila rose also. 'There is that famous compassion again.' She kept her tone light. 'Never a bad word to say about anyone.'

Paulus smiled politely. 'It is an admirable quality if directed at the right people. I am not sure his supporters would sing his praises in this instance.'

Nerva tried to keep his hands relaxed. 'Romans have long believed in the fair treatment of slaves.'

'Assuming they know their place, of course,' Aquila added.

Rufus clapped his hands together. 'Let us not delay the general any longer.'

Paulus's eyes were still fixed on Nerva. 'I shall see you very soon.'

Nerva gave a slow nod. 'I am certain you will.'

The legate left the room, and the three of them remained where they were, listening to his footsteps recede. A few moments later, the sound of the front door closing echoed through the house.

Aquila let out a breath. 'He does not like you. That is a big problem.'

'Is it? He will be more likely to stay away, which suits me fine.'

His mother's expression hardened. 'You should be very careful. He is a man with growing power.'

'He is Caracalla's puppet.'

Rufus rubbed his forehead. 'Your mother is right. He might be Caracalla's puppet, but he is also a big part of his agenda. Until we understand the game we are playing, we should be very careful.' He looked tiredly at Nerva. 'Now is not the time to be sympathetic to prisoners of the war that took Severus from the people.'

'The war did not take him, poor health did.'

'No one cares. They need somewhere to channel their grief and anger.'

'What your father is trying to say,' Aquila cut in, 'is do not parade your barbarian lover around the city. You cannot afford to lose popularity right now.'

Rufus shook his head. 'Just be careful.' He left the room, his footsteps heavy on the floor.

Nerva considered leaving also before his mother had a chance to speak.

'It was foolish to take her to the trigarium.'

Too late. Her spies were out in force, it seemed. 'It was not a political statement.'

She stared at him for the longest time before speaking. 'Please tell me you are not foolish enough to fall in love with some broken slave at a time like this.'

'She is not broken.' She was unbreakable, though this was probably not the right time to argue the fact. Nerva went to speak, then closed his mouth again. He was in way over his head when it came to her. Love seemed like a shallow word for what he felt. It was something far more consuming, and it was growing in strength. 'She is going home to her family.' He was not sure if he said it for the benefit of his mother or as a reminder to himself.

'When?'

'As soon as it is safe.'

Aquila gathered up the skirt of her garment and glided past him. 'The sooner the better. For both your sakes.'

CHAPTER 28

*After* the fight, Brei was surprised to find Nerva waiting outside the small arena. 'What are you doing here?' She knew he hated watching her fight, and even if he had stayed outside, he would have been able to hear most of it.

'I wanted to walk you home.'

'Why?' His tense body language and distracted expression made her uneasy. He was looking around as though he was expecting someone to join them.

'Because the city is a dangerous place.' He gestured for her to start walking.

'In case you haven't figured it out yet, I'm less vulnerable than most women. Are you going to tell me what you're really doing here, or am I supposed to guess?'

He glanced sideways at her as they turned onto a dark street. 'What is with all the questions? Perhaps I just wanted to surprise you.'

'Oh, well in that case, I'll just ignore your morbid expression.' He did not even appear to hear her. 'Is this about me fighting?'

That brought his attention back to her. 'No.'

He was clearly not feeling very chatty. 'I won, in case you were wondering.'

'Yes, I heard. Did they call you Venus?'

'Goddess of love, desire, sex, and prosperity.'

He pressed his mouth into a thin line. 'Another reason to walk you home. Does Gallus have you fighting topless also?'

She frowned at that, pulling her palla tighter around her. 'Where I come from, the naked body is an effective way to intimidate one's enemy.'

An abrupt laugh escaped him. 'And where I come from, it is an effective way for men to get off.'

She grabbed him by the arm and stopped walking. 'What's the matter with you?'

He stared down at the marks on her arm, lit up by moonlight. 'You are going to be an assortment of colours in the morning, Venus.'

'And so are you if you don't tell me what's on your mind.'

He shook his head, his expression serious. 'I am trying to figure out a way to get you home.'

Whatever she had been expecting him to say, it was not that. 'I thought you said it was best if we waited.'

'I said *when it is safe*.'

'And is it? Safe?'

He drew a long breath and looked at her. 'I do not think it is going to get any safer than right now.'

The prospect of returning home soon should have made her body sing. Instead, she felt like her heart had fallen into her stomach. There was one very big downside to her departure. 'You're awfully desperate to be rid of me all of a sudden. There are easier ways to back out of our plans this evening, if that's what this is about.'

He stepped up to her, cupping her face, and kissed her with such intensity, all she could do was hold on to his wrists. Afterwards, he pulled away but kept hold of her face. 'Do not say things like that, or I will be forced to take you in the doorway of that shopfront to prove you wrong.'

She swallowed. 'Promise?'

He released her face, head shaking as he took a step back. 'I said I would keep you safe, and it is not safe for you here anymore.'

Her eyebrows came together. 'Talk plainly so I don't have to guess at what's happening here.' When he did not answer straight away, she added, 'Please.'

Nerva linked his hands on top of his head and exhaled. 'Cordius is back in Rome. I am going to assume you remember him.'

Oh, she remembered him. 'I never forget the names of men who slaughter children, nor the ones who tie me up and lash me.' She crossed her arms, waiting.

Nerva's shoulders fell a few inches. 'He asked after you.'

She sat with that information for a moment. 'Well, I'm not afraid of men like Cordius.'

'You should be.'

'I know his type.'

'And I know *him*.' He seemed to hesitate before continuing. 'I fear he will come after you.'

'Why?' But even as she asked the question, the answer formed. It was not about her. 'He's not really coming after me. He's going after you.' She took a step back. 'I'm just a means.'

'That is why I want to get you home.' Nerva closed his eyes. 'If anything happens to you…'

A moving shadow caught Brei's attention. It looked like the outline of a man. Every hair on her body stood on end. She had come to recognise every type of danger inside the city, particularly the drunk men who lurked after dark. Though judging by his even gait and steady pace as he walked towards them, this man was sober. 'We need to go.'

Nerva followed her gaze, eyes narrowing. Brei was not going to hang about so he could assess the situation for himself; she was going to follow the feeling in her gut and hope she was wrong. Grabbing Nerva by the arm, she pulled him in the other direction. In that same moment, someone stepped in front of them. Brei pulled Nerva back this time, just as a blade swung past him.

She was not wrong.

It did not take Nerva long to catch up with what was happening then. He pushed Brei to the other side of him while keeping a close eye on the dagger in the man's hand. Brei glanced back at the other man still approaching behind them.

'Tell me you have a weapon hidden beneath that expensive tunic of yours.' She was looking both ways.

Nerva did not have a weapon.

'Did Cordius send you?' he asked, putting himself between Brei and the man.

She resisted the urge to shove him out of the way. When was he going to realise that she was in better shape than he was?

'Or did Caracalla give the order himself?' Nerva continued.

'Does it matter?' the man behind them asked, a laugh in his tone. 'What'll you do with the information when you're dead?'

Nerva's gaze drifted between the men, one arm outstretched in front of Brei like a horizontal shield. 'Let her go. She has nothing to do with any of this.'

The other man stepped forwards. 'No one's going anywhere.' He pulled a small dagger from a sheath and wet his lips. 'Don't be too afraid. Wherever you're headed, your father's waiting there for you.'

Even in the dark, she saw Nerva pale. He seemed to stop breathing as the words reached him. They were surely toying with him, making him suffer in his final moments. Rufus Papias was entertaining in his home. That was what Nerva had told her that afternoon. And yet Nerva's expression seemed to contrast everything she thought she knew.

'No one is dying.' Nerva spoke the words like he was giving an order, his voice deep and firm. 'Unless you try something foolish. Then I make no guarantees.'

Brei's breathing quietened, and her fingers twitched at her sides. If they made a move, she was ready.

'Is Caracalla sending thugs instead of soldiers to do his dirty work now?' Nerva asked.

Brei took in their plain clothes and weapons. They were different to the ones Roman soldiers carried during battle.

'Ask yourself why,' Nerva continued. 'These desperate acts are going to upset a lot of people.'

He was trying to talk them off the ledge, but everything about their body language suggested it was too late.

One of the men went for Nerva, the other for Brei. She hated that Nerva was unarmed and was not particularly pleased about being unarmed herself. When her attacker thrust a knife at her middle, she curved her body so it missed. She responded with a hard kick to the offending limb. The knife flew from his hand, landing in the shadows some distance away. His eyes widened in surprise, and then he turned to her, his bushy brows pinching together to form one fierce scowl. He pulled another knife from a sheath on his leg and swung it at her with such force that she barely had time to get out of the way. She panicked when the blade brushed her neck, and her hand flew to her throat, surprised to find the skin intact. He came at her again, and she dropped into a crouch, kicking out at his knee. He cursed but kept hold of the weapon.

'Run,' Nerva called to her.

*Run?* She could see him fighting in her peripheral

vision. There was no chance of her leaving him there to die. No, she was not going anywhere.

A growl erupted from her throat as she ran at her attacker, grabbing hold of the arm clutching the knife and turning sharply into him until she heard the snap of bone. When the weapon dropped from his hand, she kicked it in Nerva's direction. 'Dagger,' she called as it slid towards him.

Without taking his eyes off his attacker, Nerva swooped down and snatched up the weapon. At least the fight was even now.

Brei shoved the injured man as hard as she could and watched him fall to the ground, clutching his arm and roaring through gritted teeth.

'Run,' Nerva said again.

If she was going to leave, this was her opportunity. Instead, she charged at the other man, knocking him sideways. She heard the smack of skull on stone and watched his body roll once before going limp.

Nerva grabbed her by the arm and pulled her away. 'Let us go—now.'

She resisted. 'But they're all still alive.'

'Now!' He broke into a jog, dragging her with him.

What on earth was he running from? Then a realisation hit her: he was not running away from the danger, he was running to his father. 'All right.' She sped up, and he let go of her.

As they sprinted through the streets and alleyways of the city, Brei could feel the tension coming off Nerva in waves. He surprised her by keeping up the same pace, even as they ascended the hill. Nerva finally slowed when he spotted a group of men on the street outside his house, talking in hushed tones. She watched hope bleed from him. The group turned when they reached them, and their expressions made Brei look down.

'Where is my father?' Nerva asked, looking between the men.

They shifted uncomfortably, smoothing out invisible creases in their togas. Finally, the grey-haired man closest to the steps cleared his throat.

'Please accept our heartfelt condolences.'

That was when Brei saw the bloodstain on the cobbled road behind the men. She knew the moment Nerva saw it by his sharp intake of breath before he stepped back and collapsed to his knees. She had no idea how to help him, knew the burden of grief could not be shared. Nerva tipped forwards, fingers pressing into the stone. His head hung just a few inches off the ground. Brei went to him then, crouching down beside him and placing a hand on his shoulder.

Silence rang out around them.

## CHAPTER 29

Nerva walked a few paces behind the bier that carried his father. His mother was in the litter behind him. Far behind her were the women in Rufus Papias's life who no one would acknowledge—the slave woman he had loved and one of his illegitimate daughters. His other daughter, Dulcia, would have likely received Nerva's letter by then. He wished he could have told her in person, like he did Mila.

'Dead?' she had asked, blinking and swallowing as she waited for him to confirm it. While her relationship with Rufus had been strained, he was still her father.

'Yes. I am sorry.'

She had hugged him then and held on for some time. '*I am sorry. He did not deserve such an end.*'

The high-pitched wailing and chest beating of the paid mourners pulled Nerva's attention back to the procession. He looked either side of him at the people lining the streets to pay their respects. Many cried genuine tears. Rufus Papias had done much for the city, and those who truly knew him felt the loss.

The bier was taken outside of the city, the body placed

in an elaborately decorated coffin without any worldly possessions. He would be buried, as per his wishes.

Nerva let someone else take care of the eulogy. He was barely holding it together as it was. The constant sniffs from his mother were not helping. Theirs might not have been the greatest love story of all time, but trust and respect sat in place of affection.

He glanced over his shoulder at Mila when his father disappeared through the mosaic entrance of the tomb. She offered him a weak smile. The man they had grown up with was really gone.

His gaze drifted to Brei, who had insisted on joining the procession despite his objections. He had wanted her to stay at the house where it was safe, but she could not be told. There was so much sympathy in her eyes, so much understanding and comfort, he was forced to turn away for fear he would embarrass himself with tears. He had gone to her every night since it happened, after his mother retired for the evening. He would bury himself in her until the pain eased enough to let him sleep. Waking up with Brei curled against him was the best form of comfort. She always knew what to say, and when to remain silent.

'You must rejoin the senate,' Aquila whispered to him, brushing an inconvenient tear from her cheek. 'Every man present here today will support you.'

'Must we discuss this now?'

'Yes,' she whispered. 'Now is the time to show the people of Rome that the Papias name continues to be a force in this world.'

He looked around to ensure no one was listening. 'They are coming for me either way.'

His mother swallowed and waited for the eulogy to continue before speaking again. 'Geta has promised you protection.'

'In exchange for my loyalty.'

Her head snapped in his direction. 'Where else would your loyalties lie after what Caracalla has done?'

'My loyalties have always been with Rome.'

She faced forwards again. 'Well, Rome is divided. In this city you choose a side or one is chosen for you.' She looked around before adding, 'And where is your pride? Those men came to our home and murdered your father in the street…' She could barely get the words out.

He pinched the top of his nose. 'Can we save the political conversation for *after* the feast? They have not even finished burying him yet.'

They fell silent as the eulogy came to an end.

She was right though. Everyone would be expecting him to step up and take his father's place—and he did not want to. At some point the city had stopped feeling like home and had become a constant reminder of all the things he stood against. His political views had often been in opposition to his father's.

Caracalla was no fool. He knew the death of Rufus Papias would put Nerva firmly on Geta's side. The time for appearing neutral had passed.

He glanced over his shoulder again, eyes meeting Brei's. It was time to get out of the city—before it was too late.

CHAPTER 30

If there was one time Nerva needed Brei to do as she was told, it was after his father's death. He made three requests of her: stop fighting, do not go anywhere without Albaus, and be prepared to leave the city at a moment's notice.

Four days after his father's funeral, he stood across from her, staring at the welts and bruises covering her body. He could not touch her. In fact, he could barely look at her.

'Nothing is broken,' she said, throwing her hands up. 'Everything you see here will heal.'

It was a good thing there was a bed sitting between them.

'I told you, whatever amount of coin you need, I will give it to you.'

She crossed her arms. 'I can make my own money.'

He could feel the blood pulsing in his ears. 'Did Albaus go with you?'

'He dropped me there and collected me after.'

'But did not stay with you?' He was going to have firm words with the bodyguard.

She exhaled in frustration and shook her head. 'He can't protect me in the arena. Only I can do that. It's sort of the point.'

He looked over at the dressing table against the wall. A comb and a few other items sat on top. 'Have you even packed?'

Now it was her turn to look away. 'I only have about five things. It won't take me long to throw them in a bag if the time comes.'

His gaze snapped back to her. '*If*? You will be leaving any day now.'

She looked wounded by his words. Falling forwards onto the bed, she crawled to him. 'Are you going to spend this time mad at me?' She tugged on his arm. 'Let fear drive you?'

She was right. He was terrified of failing to protect her. If his father could be killed outside his own home, then Brei could be murdered anywhere. He sank down on the bed beside her, closing his eyes as she touched his face and chest. 'I need you safe. I cannot let anything happen to you because of me.'

She kissed him and moved closer. 'Tell me about the last few days. Has it been unbearable?'

Yes, it had been unbearable. The visitors, the outpouring of sympathy, his mother. All of it. He had even been forced to let Paulus Cordius into his home so he could deliver a speech about how sorry he was for their loss. Aquila had stood there nodding, and Nerva had stood there imagining what it would feel like to cut his throat and watch him bleed out on the rug his mother had imported from Egypt. But he had no solid proof Paulus was involved in Rufus's murder. 'The hardest parts are surely behind me,' he said, kneading Brei's hair between his fingers. He did not want to think about the even harder part in front of him. Her departure would leave him utterly depleted.

'Grief is a strange and unpredictable beast.' Brei stared down at her lap when she spoke.

Before Nerva could respond, there was a pounding on the door. They were normally left alone when he visited, as it was the only mutual territory they had. Standing, Nerva walked over to the door and opened it. Mila stood on the other side, looking flushed and out of breath. His stomach fell at the sight. 'What is the matter?'

'Aquila sold her.'

Nerva's shook his head, confused. 'Who?'

Her hands went into her hair. 'I went by the house to check on her, and Aquila would not let me in.' She took a breath. 'Nona says a man came by to collect my mother after you left the house this morning.'

*Tertia.*

Nerva hit the door frame and swore. His father had always planned to free her if anything should happen to him. 'The will is being read tomorrow. Mother must have known of his plans.'

'So she got in first,' Brei said behind him.

Mila did not know where to look. 'Nona does not even know where they have taken her.'

Brei came to stand next to Nerva. 'She can't have gone far. I can help you look. We can split up and comb the city.'

'It is not safe for you to be wandering around the city,' Nerva said.

Brei rolled her eyes. 'Then we will stay together and take Albaus with us.'

Nerva took in his sister's distressed face before nodding. 'Fine. I will pay a visit to my mother.'

∽

Nerva was pacing in the atrium when his mother finally returned to the house. Conveniently, she had managed to stay away the entire day.

'Goodness, what has you in such a state?' Aquila asked, pretending to be puzzled by his hostile manner.

He was not playing her games this time. 'Where is Tertia?'

Aquila pretended to be confused by the question. 'How would I know? By now you have likely heard that she is no longer with us.'

'Yes, I know that part. Mila tells me you would not even let her into the house.'

His mother removed her palla and gave him a puzzled look. 'Why should I? Those women are no longer my problem.' She tossed the palla at Nona, who had wandered in to tend to her. 'Can you actually stand there and blame me for this? Thirty years is quite enough.'

Nerva took a few steps towards her. 'No, I do not blame you. Father did not blame you either, which is why he made provisions for Tertia. It was always the plan that she leave.'

Aquila threw her hands up. 'So, I am supposed to house his mistress in the meantime?'

'The reading of the will is tomorrow. You have deliberately sabotaged her freedom.'

'I owe that woman nothing. She should be grateful I did not poison her.'

Nerva rubbed his brow. 'Please just tell me where she is. She can be housed elsewhere until Father's wishes are known.'

His mother raised her chin, mouth pursed. 'I am afraid you are too late.'

'What do you mean?'

Aquila brushed invisible lint from her stola. 'She is no longer in the city.'

It took a moment to register what she was saying. 'Oh, Mother. What have you done?'

She looked straight at him, unblinking. 'I have cleansed my house of sin.'

Nona, who had been staring at the floor, cleared her throat and left the room. Nerva watched her walk off before continuing.

'Where is she?' The words came out loudly, and Aquila jumped. He had never raised his voice at her before. She took a moment to compose herself.

'On her way to Elba.'

Nerva blinked. 'Elba?' His mind raced. 'Why did you send her there?'

'The mine is always in need of workers.'

Nerva took a step back from her, head shaking. 'How could you? That is low, even for you.'

'What do you mean, *even for me?*'

'I mean that you are a terrible person who does terrible things, but this is an entirely new level of cruel.' He searched her face, hoping to glimpse some remorse. Nothing. 'She is an excellent seamstress. If you really could not bear her presence for one more day, any number of noble households would have welcomed her. But you know that. Your actions were *very* deliberate.' He could not look at her any longer. 'You better pray I find her.'

Aquila drew a breath. 'She is not your problem either.'

'I disagree. She has been a loyal servant in our household my entire life. She did not deserve that. Mila and Dulcia do not deserve that.'

His mother crossed her arms in front of her. 'They are almost a full day ahead of you. If you really must interfere, perhaps you can write a letter.'

He stepped past her and headed to the door. '*Write a letter*? You must be joking. I am going to Elba.'

Aquila's mouth fell open as she spun around. 'You

cannot leave the city so soon after your father's death. It is entirely inappropriate. The reading of the will is tomorrow.'

'You dare lecture me on propriety,' he called over his shoulder.

The front door slammed shut behind him.

CHAPTER 31

The moment Nerva announced he would be leaving the city, Brei knew she would go with him. Everyone in the household was prepared to go, but Nerva did not want to attract attention. He also feared that since he was still very much a target, he would be putting others in danger.

'Nerva, be sensible,' Mila said. 'There are men who want you dead. It is not safe for you to go anywhere without protection. Let me come with you.'

He had appeared amused by her offer. 'I mean no offence when I say that Caracalla's men will not be deterred by the presence of my sister.'

Mila opened her mouth to say something, then closed it again.

Remus came up next to her. 'You're not going to Elba,' he said, giving her hair a playful tug.

She dug her elbow into his ribs. 'She is my mother. And whose side are you on?'

'The side of good sense.' Remus looked at Nerva. 'I'll go with you.'

'Can I go too?' Atilius called, running over to join them.

'No,' Mila and Remus replied in unison.

Brei was leaning against the wall between Felix and Albaus, silent. She was not going to have a conversation about it and give Nerva the chance to shut her down in front of an audience. She was going with him.

Felix let out a dramatic sigh, drawing the attention of the room. 'Albaus and I will travel with you. Remus should stay here in case Caracalla grows desperate and comes after your family.'

Nerva did not object because Albaus was a sensible choice, and it was a well-known fact that wherever he went, Felix went also.

'Part of the journey will be via boat,' Nerva said, frowning at the dwarf.

'Yes, I know. It is *such* a pity I like you.'

Remus walked over and clapped Felix on the shoulder. 'It's only six miles off the coast.'

'You would be surprised how long six miles feels when your head is hanging over the side of the boat.'

Albaus grunted, his lips turning up in his own version of a smile. Brei's leg bounced as she made plans in her head. When Nerva glanced in her direction, she could see the toll the previous few days had taken on him. It was the wrong time for him to be riding off to play hero, and yet every time he did, she fell a little harder.

Mila went to Nerva, eyes glassy. 'I cannot tell you how much I appreciate you doing this at a time when you are supposed to be mourning.'

'I am sorry it happened at all. I will do everything in my power to find her.' He looked over at Felix and Albaus. 'Meet me at the stables at first light. I want to try and make the journey to Populonia in three days.'

Felix nodded, Albaus grunted, and Brei headed for the garden. She needed air. Nerva must have known something was up, because he followed her out and caught her by the arm. She spun to face him.

'You are awfully quiet,' he said. 'Have you nothing to say on the subject? No objections?'

She stared at the potted tree behind him. 'What objections could I possibly have? Tertia is your sisters' mother, and you are doing what any good brother would do for his siblings.'

He watched her for a moment. 'Why are you not looking at me?'

She dragged her eyes to meet his. She considered herself a reasonable liar if the occasion called for it, but there was only truth between them. 'I'm going with you.'

He looked annoyed but not surprised. 'Absolutely not. You will stay here with Mila and Remus.'

She had no trouble looking at him then. 'I'm free to go where I please. I'm not asking your permission.'

Nerva's eyes closed as he drew a breath. 'Can you please just do what I have asked for once in your life?'

She almost felt bad for him. 'Caracalla is waiting for an opportunity to kill you.'

'Which is exactly why you need to stay here.'

'I can protect you.'

Anger flashed in his eyes. 'I have Albaus for that. I need *you* safe.'

She let out an exasperated huff. 'I'm safest with you. We're safest with each other. That's been proven time and time again. Just look at this past year.' Her voice was raised now. 'You don't get to strip me of my weapons and just send me below deck anymore.' She saw him flinch at that.

He took a moment to think through his next words. 'If you want to leave this city, you cannot be seen with me.'

Every time he brought up her leaving, she felt a little sicker. She tucked her long hair behind her ears. 'I'm done talking about it. I'm coming with you.'

'You will stay here, or I will have Geta's men drag you back and guard the house until I return.' His tone was sharp as a blade. The heat of his glare made her eyes burn. He was the only man on the planet who held the power to bring her to tears.

'I wish you would stop treating me like a slave.'

'And I wish you would stop playing the enemy. We are on the same side now.'

She looked down at his feet. 'And what am I supposed to do if you don't come back?' There was that burn in her eyes again.

Nerva took hold of her chin, forcing her to look at him. 'Of course I will come back.'

She searched his face for a moment, then fell forwards against his chest. His arms went around her, and she felt that familiar sensation of invincibility. Mustering her remaining strength, she said, 'I'm coming with you.'

Nerva's chest expanded and then collapsed with a resigned breath. 'You do not leave my sight.'

Brei closed her eyes and pressed her lips to his chest. 'I promise.'

∽

THEY MADE the journey in three days, stopping only to rest their horses and eat, never lingering in one place for too long. Nerva insisted the group camp rather than paying for rooms, as he was worried he would be recognised. Nights were cold, so they slept around a lit campfire, someone keeping watch at all times. To avoid drawing unnecessary attention, the guards Geta had assigned travelled behind and camped separately from them.

Once they arrived in Populonia, Felix secured them passage on a boat that would take them to Elba. Nerva had hoped to catch up with Tertia before they crossed the sea to the island, but without knowing their route, he was forced to simply pray that she would be there when they arrived.

When it was time for them to board the boat, Brei stopped at the bottom of the gangplank, holding everybody up. Nerva placed a hand on her shoulder, and she jumped at his touch.

'What is the matter?' he asked, gesturing to Felix and Albaus to wait.

Brei looked up at him. 'It seems I don't like boats anymore.' She appeared embarrassed by the confession.

'Geta's men are staying here until we return. You are welcome to stay with them.'

She immediately shook her head. 'I'll be fine.'

Nerva felt like he had been punched in the stomach. He had done that to her, locked her up, left her in the dark with no food and water. 'I will be at your side the whole time.'

She nodded and walked on.

The voyage to the island was accompanied by a harsh wind that tugged at their clothes and seemed to fuse their bones. Brei barely appeared to notice. She spent the entire journey staring out at the horizon, frozen hands clasped in her lap. Her hair was out, long strands blowing in all directions. Nerva found himself watching her most of the journey, fascinated by her resilience and lost in her beauty. He did that more than was healthy, often trying to imagine life without her. There was not one woman among Rome's elite who could hold his attention like she did. No one would ever feel as good in his arms, make him lose his mind to lust like her. He knew because he had been with many women before she robbed him of his horse and heart, and none had come close.

Brei looked across at him and frowned when she saw his expression. 'Are you all right?'

She saw right through him. 'Not really.'

They stared at one another for a moment, all the things they could never say aloud between them. Turning back to the horizon, Brei slid an icy hand across the bench seat next to his. He brushed his little finger along hers. It was their common language.

As they neared the island, Nerva took in the houses built along the coastline, mini palaces perched on the edge of paradise.

'How could a place that looks so beautiful harbour so much cruelty?' Brei asked as the boat was secured.

'Leave it to the Romans,' Felix replied. He was ghostly pale but had managed to keep down the food he had eaten that morning. 'Patricians have a talent for blocking out the unsightly things and laying claim to everything else. They will only give thought to the mines if the noise disturbs their peace or the smoke impedes their lovely view of the water.'

Nerva patted the dwarf's shoulder as he stood, taking no offence as he agreed with everything he said.

'Let us move quickly,' Felix said, running a hand down his clammy face. 'I am about two boat rocks from being sick.'

Brei gestured for him to go ahead. 'After you.'

Albaus rose behind the dwarf, shoving him forwards. Felix was too sick to object to the rough treatment.

Once ashore, they found an ox cart, and Nerva paid the driver to take them part of the way. The man's eyes widened when the cart groaned beneath Albaus's weight.

'Ah, we'll need to redistribute some weight so I don't lose a wheel on the way.

'Well, do not look at me,' Felix said, getting comfortable.

Nerva rose and plonked himself down on the other side as the cart lurched forwards.

'You have business at the mine?' the driver asked. 'They usually send a cart to meet the boat.'

'Something like that,' Nerva said. 'We are trying to track down a woman, a new arrival.'

'The only women who go into that mine don't tend to come out again.'

Nerva glanced at Brei, whose expression mirrored his own. 'Have any new slaves arrived in the last day or so?'

The man made a throaty noise, then spat over the side of the cart. 'They still bring in newcomers to replace the ones who don't make it out of the vein mines. Those things are always collapsing.' He rubbed at his nose with the back of his hand. 'Not for too much longer though. Most of the iron is coming in from Spain nowadays.'

Brei leaned forwards on her crate. 'How many slaves do they have working in the mines here?'

'Thousands, maybe.' He said it like it was no big deal.

Albaus shook his head, and Felix looked away. Brei seemed to be waiting for Nerva to dispute the high number, but he knew it was probably accurate.

They continued along the east coast of the island. No one said anything further until the driver pulled up and pointed down the hill.

'Just follow the noise,' he said, grinning.

Nerva paid him as the others jumped down, then watched the cart pull away. As soon as the driver was out of earshot, Nerva turned to look at the others. 'We are all going to remain calm and polite. Let me do the talking.'

'In this place, your coin will do the talking,' Felix said.

Albaus cracked his knuckles. Brei's fingers brushed over the dagger she had strapped to her thigh, looking off down the hill. The sound of stamp mills and trip hammers drifted up from the mine.

'Brei,' Nerva said, pulling her attention. She turned back to him, waiting. 'Did you hear what I said?'

'Yes.'

'Stay beside me and say nothing. They might grow suspicious if they hear your accent. Understand?'

She nodded, then headed off down the hill.

The man in charge of the mine was Ennius. He was a stocky man with leathery skin and a whip coiled at his hip, similar to the one Brei had been beaten with by Paulus Cordius. She shifted uncomfortably beside Nerva. He took a small step closer to her.

'She could have only arrived in the last day,' Nerva explained. 'She was not that far ahead of us.'

Ennius sniffed and looked around the group. 'You expect me to keep track of the slaves who come and go in this place? More than sixty dead yesterday after a collapse, and sixty in to replace them this morning. I don't ask their names or where they come from.'

Nerva kept his expression neutral. 'Of course not. I imagine you are a very busy man. Perhaps you would allow us to search for her.'

His eyebrows shot up at that suggestion. 'I can't have you people wandering about the place, getting under workers' feet. Besides, it's not safe. You don't want to be here when a tunnel gives way.' His gaze settled on Felix. 'Fancy a job? You'd do nicely in this place.'

Albaus took a step in the man's direction, and Brei reached out and grabbed hold of his arm. She was playing by the rules for once.

'Tempting,' Felix said, his tone flat, 'but I am afraid I do not do well in confined spaces.'

Nerva cleared his throat. 'Perhaps someone in your charge might be able to accompany us. I am happy to pay for the inconvenience.' He gestured to Albaus, who slid a bag off his shoulder and pulled out a coin pouch, handing it to Nerva.

Ennius's eyes glowed a little brighter suddenly. 'Say we

do find this woman who was *mistakenly* sold.' He gave Nerva a look that suggested he did not believe that part of the story. 'What's she worth to you?'

'Name your price.' Nerva shook the coin pouch so that it jingled.

Ennius wet his lips as he pondered the question. 'Two thousand denarii.'

Felix snorted. 'Are you returning her to us gold-plated?'

'Done,' Nerva said, casting a warning glance at Felix. 'Assuming, of course, she is in good health and unharmed.'

Ennius extended his arm, and Nerva took hold of it.

'I will help you find her myself,' Ennius said.

Felix looked around. 'I assume, at that price, we will be travelling by litter.'

'You are welcome to stay here,' Ennius said. 'I'm certain your companions won't miss you.'

Nerva stepped forwards. 'He will accompany us, in silence.'

Felix put his hands up in mock surrender. 'So silent you will not know me from Albaus.'

They followed Ennius along a maze of narrow dirt paths, taking in the horrendous working conditions of the slaves. Most of the miners were severely underweight; many seemed barely able to keep hold of the hammers they used to break up the rock. Some walked with a limp, and others had fingers turned at unnatural angles and scars on their faces from lashings. Nerva made Brei walk in front of him. He watched her shoulders grow tenser as she looked around. Each hungry face chipped away at her facade.

'Brei?'

They were almost at the opening of the mine when someone spoke Brei's name. The entire group stopped and turned in the direction of the voice. There stood a thin woman with swollen knuckles and blackened fingernails. A layer of dust covered her hair and skin, making her indistinguishable from others around her. Yet the longer Nerva looked at her, the more familiar she seemed.

Had she really called Brei by name?

The straggly woman took a few steps in their direction, but a nearby guard shouted at her to stop. She did as she was told, but her wide eyes never left Brei. The hammer fell from her hand.

'Mamaidh?' Brei breathed out, ghostly pale.

Nerva's heart slowed as Brei took off towards her.

Felix looked up at him, confused. 'Ah, who is Mamaidh?'

Nerva watched as Brei embraced the woman with such ferocity that he feared her malnourished bones would splinter beneath the pressure. Tears spilled down both their faces, and sobs shook their bodies.

Nerva tore his gaze away to answer Felix. 'Mamaidh is a Maeatae word.' He swallowed. 'It means *mother*.'

CHAPTER 32

It seemed wholly impossible, but there was no mistaking the familiar scent and feel of her mother. Keelia was alive. Everyone had thought her dead for so long, grieved her, even started to heal from the loss. Brei had never considered the possibility that Roman soldiers would take her prisoner, that she would board a ship to Rome, as Brei had once done.

'Mamaidh,' Brei choked out, eyes pressed shut for fear if she opened them, she would find her gone. Her mother's body shook against hers.

'My girl.'

Her supervisor stepped forwards, a whip flicking in his hand. 'All right, all right. Break it up. Back to work.'

Brei's eyes snapped open at the sound of his voice, and she reached for the dagger strapped to her leg.

'Brei,' she heard Nerva say behind her.

A moment later, she was standing between her mother and the man, the dagger pointed in his direction. 'You lay one finger on her and I will cut out your eyes.'

The man's nostrils flared as his hand tightened around the handle of the whip. 'Who the hell are you?'

Before she could reply, Nerva was in front of her, hand outstretched. 'Give me the knife.'

Her gaze flicked to him, confused. 'What?' She shook her head. 'No. I'll put it away when this pig lays down his whip and steps back.'

Nerva moved closer to her. 'Brei, give me the weapon.' His tone was firmer this time.

Her inner voice was screaming, demanding blood be spilt as she imagined what her mother would have endured over the past year and a half.

'Trust me,' Nerva said.

His voice was water, extinguishing the flames dancing before her eyes. Slowly, she lowered the knife, never taking her eyes off the man holding the whip. 'She's coming with us.' She would not leave without her.

By that stage, the others had wandered over to see what was going on. Ennius looked Keelia over.

'Is this her?' he asked, visibly confused.

Nerva shook his head. 'No, but I will be taking her also. How much?'

Ennius crossed his arms, a smug expression settling on his face as he realised the opportunity in front of him. 'Well, she looks like a strong, solid worker.'

Felix peered around Brei, inspecting Keelia. 'Are you joking? She looks as though she has risen from the dead to steal the souls of children.' He turned back to Ennius. 'I can practically see through her.'

Nerva silenced him with a glance. 'How much?'

'Who are these men?' Keelia whispered.

'It's all right,' Brei replied. 'You can trust them.'

Ennius sucked on his teeth for a moment as he thought. 'Another two thousand denarii, or she goes back to work.'

Brei lurched forwards and grabbed him by the neck. 'How about you hand her over, or I tear your throat out.'

Before Ennius had a chance to react, Nerva pulled her

back and pinned her against his chest. 'Calm down,' he said into her ear.

She stilled. Albaus came forwards and took her from him. Brei knew she would have more luck charging through a stone wall than breaking free of his iron grip.

Ennius coughed and gasped, leaning on his knees.

'I will pay you the two thousand denarii,' Nerva said.

The man straightened and glared at Brei over Nerva's shoulder. 'That's four thousand denarii total.'

'Oh,' Felix said, 'and he has thrown in a lesson on adding numbers.'

Ignoring the dwarf, Nerva looked back at Brei. 'Are we good?'

Her hate-filled eyes remained on Ennius. 'Yes.'

'Let her go,' he told Albaus.

The giant released her, and blood rushed to her hands.

At that moment, a line of slaves passed them in single file.

'Nerva!' a woman called.

They all turned to see Tertia at the back of the line. Her dark hair was in a simple plait, lips blue from the cold and lack of clothes.

'Halt,' Nerva boomed, the volume of his voice making everyone stop, including the guards. He walked over to Tertia and checked her for injuries while the guards looked between each other. 'Are you all right?'

She nodded. 'What are you doing here?'

'Getting you out.' He turned to Ennius. 'This is the woman. Unshackle her.'

Ennius glared at Brei as he passed her. 'Take the irons off that one and bring her to me.'

Brei walked over to her mother and took hold of her callused hand. 'We're getting you out.'

∽

Nerva paid Ennius extra to have someone transport them back to the small port. They bought some bread on the way and ate it perched on rocks overlooking the sea while they waited for their boat to depart.

Keelia told the story of how she came to end up on the island. Brei sat still next to her, picking at her bread. She just let her mother talk, speaking up only when Keelia's limited Latin confused the story.

The Romans had wanted to make an example of her, because a woman who could fight as well as them threatened everything they thought they knew about the world. Only once they were satisfied they had broken her spirit did they load her onto one of the naval ships bound for Ostia Antica. She had been sold at the same market as Brei.

The man who bought her struggled to communicate with her. The language barrier resulted in frequent beatings when things were not done as he had instructed. He sold her as a labourer, and she ended up working on construction projects around the city. As she settled into her new life, she began making friends with some of the women she worked alongside. But just as she was beginning to accept her fate, one of the supervisors got drunk and broke her friend's arm because she refused to lie with him. Keelia had tried to protect the woman and was beaten with an iron rod for interfering. Unable to work, she was sent to the mines to die. But death did not come easily to a Maeatae woman raised in the highlands, where mountain life was crueller than any Roman man.

The three-day journey to Elba Island enabled her to rest, and by the time she arrived at the mine, she could hold a hammer as well as any other.

When Keelia finished talking, Nerva cleared his throat. 'I am going to get you and Brei back to Caledonia.'

Keelia watched him cautiously. 'And why would you do that?'

It was a fair question. She had no reason to trust him. 'Because I made a promise to your daughter.'

Keelia looked between the two of them. 'I see.'

When Nerva glanced at Brei, he was met with a tortured expression. 'As soon as I can secure you safe passage, you will leave together.'

'Don't worry,' Brei said, looking out at the water. 'It won't take my mother long to pack.'

Her bitter tone was not lost on him. Did she think he was pleased by her leaving? He would have kept her in Rome forever if there were any hope of a future together, but that was not the world they lived in. He was a patrician of Rome. She was Maeatae, a warrior, a prisoner of war. *His* prisoner. He might have bought her freedom, but that did not mean she belonged in his city.

It was a miracle that Brei had found her mother, and he wondered if the gods had brought her to Rome for that purpose—not for him, but to reunite a family his army had torn to shreds.

Brei pushed off the rock and strolled away. Felix tutted.

'What?' Nerva asked.

The dwarf's expression suggested he should already know. 'While Brei is obviously thrilled at having found her mother, I get the distinct impression she is not happy about leaving you.'

Keelia was looking after Brei with a concerned expression.

'Perhaps,' Tertia said, speaking up, 'you could remind her that her departure will be hard on you also.'

If he admitted that aloud, he might never let her go. 'What purpose does that serve? Ours is not a love story but a tragedy. We are the start of a bad joke.'

Felix turned to Albaus. 'Did you hear the one about the legate and the highlander?'

Nerva shook his head and glanced over at Keelia, who was now watching him intently.

'What power do you hold over my daughter that would make her reluctant to return home?' Keelia said. 'I know she has thick walls around that warrior heart.'

'Romans are experts when it comes to walls,' Felix said, looking pleased at himself.

Tertia tutted, and Albaus grunted.

Nerva rose and went after Brei. She was standing on the rocky beach at the edge of the water, looking out at the sea. He came up beside her, looking out also.

'Want to tell me what is going on in that head of yours?'

Brei let out a long breath. 'I think I'm still in shock.'

'Understandable.'

'I will pay the coin back.'

'I do not care about the money.'

She glanced at him. 'You're a good man, General.'

'Oh, we are back to "General" now.'

A seagull landed behind them, cawing at Brei, who was still holding her bread. 'I'll never see you again.'

He nodded. 'It is unlikely.'

'Not even in battle.'

He smiled. 'Just as well. It turns out we make terrible enemies.'

'And fantastic lovers, which is rather inconvenient.'

He laughed, easing the tension. 'Terribly inconvenient.'

She was silent a moment. 'I don't suppose you would come with us?'

Nerva turned to face her properly. When she did not look at him, he took her by the arm and turned her. 'You know I cannot just disappear.'

She studied him for a moment. 'If you were just an ordinary man, not a Papias, would you at least want to?'

'I have dreamed many times of running away from this life, but a man in my position cannot be that irresponsible.'

'That wasn't the question.'

'The answer makes no difference.' He was trying very hard not to complicate things further. The last thing either of them needed was an outpouring of feelings.

Brei's gaze returned to the water. 'So instead you'll stay here and become your father.'

'Probably.' He was silent a moment, recalling the sight of his dead father laid out on the marble floor inside the house, eyes still open. It was a powerful reminder of why he needed her gone. Not only did he want her out of harm's way, but he also wanted to ensure she never had to witness his own death.

'The thing is,' Brei whispered, 'I don't want to leave you.'

It was the exact conversation he had wanted to avoid, but he could not stand there and pretend to be unaffected by her words. He took her hand and brought it to his lips. 'I truly wish there was a reason for you to stay, but you deserve more than what I can offer you.'

She withdrew her hand. 'You should have left me alone when I asked you to.' Her voice barely carried.

'I was trying to protect you.'

'You just kept showing up.'

He blinked. 'I did.'

'And here we are.'

'Here we are.' He shifted his weight to his other foot. 'At least we found your mother.'

'At least there's that.'

They both turned to watch the boat approach, their arms brushing.

'What are you thinking about?' he asked when he could not take the silence any longer.

She exhaled. 'I'm trying to imagine an ocean between us.'

He looked up. 'Even with land and sea between us, we will still be under the same sky.'

She turned her face up and drew a deep breath. 'That's all we get? After everything? One sky?'

'One *enormous* sky.' He watched the clouds pass overhead for a moment. 'I know I did a lot of things wrong, but I am going to do the right thing this time. You and your mother are going home.'

After a long silence, Brei turned away from the water and headed back towards the rocks.

## CHAPTER 33

If there was one quality Brei both admired and loathed in Nerva, it was the way he stuck to his word.

A few days after they returned to Rome, he showed up at the house looking like his father had died all over again. She knew what he was going to say before he even opened his mouth.

'When?' she asked. They were standing in the garden because it felt like neutral territory.

Upon their return, he had asked her if he should stay away. She had said yes.

Their first lie.

Nerva did not stay away, and when he showed up the following night, she took him by the hand and led him to her room. They could still face each other in the dark, but the sun always exposed them in the morning, bringing them another day closer to their inevitable end. Another memory. Another piece of her lost to him.

'In three days,' he said.

*Three days*. She tried to draw breath, but her throat

seemed to have closed. He stood with his hands on his hips and his eyes on the ground between them.

'Marcus will travel with you.'

She nodded because it was the only response she was capable of.

'I will come by later,' he said, turning away. He did not even wait for her to reply, just fled like he was late for a dinner party. Maybe he was. Camilla was probably loitering at the house, waiting for him to set a wedding date.

Brei could not just sit around for three days staring at her packed bag, so she did what she needed to—she fought.

Gallus had no idea she was leaving. Nerva had insisted she tell him nothing. She continued to show up and train, needing the distraction.

The day after Nerva broke the news of her departure, Gallus came to her while she was training. 'I have a good one for you tonight,' he said, rubbing his greedy little hands together.

She and Otho exchanged a small smile as she laid down her weapons. 'Oh?'

'Festus Betitiius wants you for a private party tomorrow night.'

Brei wandered towards Gallus. 'Did he ask for me by name?' It must have been good money, because the sponsor's cheeks looked like two red saucers, a sign he was excited.

'He did when I pitched "*the barbarian*".'

She winced. 'What happened to Venus?'

'Oh, I pitched her first, and when he showed little interest, I tried again.'

'Ah.'

'He is an enormous fan of the games and most definitely misses the spectacle of women at the Flavian Amphitheatre.'

She just nodded.

'A display like no other. That is what I promised him.'

'In other words, you want me to paint my skin and carry a bow, even though I'm not allowed to use it.'

'Exactly. Otho will accompany you.'

Brei looked over to where her mother sat watching them. Gallus had been excited at the prospect of a mother-daughter warrior act, but Brei had quickly shut the idea down. The only thing Keelia needed at that time was to gain some weight and strength for the long journey ahead of them.

'All right,' Brei said. 'I'll be there.'

That evening, she showed up at the grand house and was ushered out back to wait in the cold. Her opponent was already there and looked up in surprise when she arrived. He had clearly not been told he would be fighting a woman. Brei stripped down and covered herself in paint that in no way resembled the pastes she had used during actual warfare. Those pastes enabled her to blend in with the unique landscape of home. *Home.* She thought about how hard her sister would laugh at this ridiculous version of her people. Perhaps not as hard as she would laugh at learning Brei had fallen into bed with the legate who had torn through their village.

*'What were you thinking getting mixed up with a man like that,'* her mother had said when they had finally had a few moments alone.

*'You mean the one who saved your life?'*

Keelia knew he was a good man. She was just far too logical to fathom a connection between them. Brei barely understood that connection herself. It was as though they were joined at the heart, and they had no choice but to bleed into one another. Somehow, a few stolen moments here and there had sustained a bond so deep that she had resigned herself to drowning in it.

She too had been logical once.

'I don't like fighting girls,' the man said, pulling her from her thoughts. He was watching her with a look of irritation.

She turned to look at him. 'Me neither, so stop whining like one.'

Otho coughed and handed Brei her weapons. 'They're ready for you.'

∽

BREI HAD BARELY FOUND her rhythm when she glanced at the guests and found them all looking in the other direction. What on earth could be more exciting than the fight happening in front of them? She signalled for her opponent to stop. When he continued to fight, she made the gesture of surrender. He wore a confused expression, because it had been clear from the beginning that she was going to beat him. She had just been drawing things out for the sake of their audience.

They both turned to see what held the attention of the guests, and Brei spotted Paulus Cordius standing beneath the portico with eight soldiers behind him. He was arguing with the host, who stood like a confused lamb. When the legate looked over the heads of the guests, his eyes locked with hers. Her breath caught. One side of his mouth lifted in a grin that was more of a snarl. He turned away then, giving instructions to his men that Brei could not hear.

Otho looked equally as confused. She realised at that moment that she had more clarity than anyone else there. Looking behind her at the tall wall at the far end of the garden, she wondered whether there was any point in trying to jump it. Running would only make the entire thing more enjoyable for Paulus. Instead, she dropped her sword on the ground, where it clattered loudly, drawing everyone's attention, and waited for the soldiers to reach her. Out of the corner of her eye, she saw her opponent slink back into the shadows as the men approached.

Two of the men took an arm each. Her instinct was always to fight, and she might have broken free of two men —but not eight.

'What's this about?' Otho said, rushing forwards.

Paulus marched over. She wished she had at least one arm free to wipe that smug expression off his face.

'This woman is under arrest for illegal gladiator fighting.'

'This is not an arena, this is a private gathering,' the host cried, casting apologetic looks in the direction of his guests, who were likely finding this far more entertaining than the fight.

'He is right,' Otho said, his chest expanding. 'You can't dictate what people do in the privacy of their homes.'

Paulus turned to him. 'We have evidence that this woman has also been fighting in arenas across the city.'

'What evidence?' Brei asked.

Paulus's gaze snapped back to meet hers. 'Eyewitnesses.'

She fought the urge to break his nose with her foot. As if he cared where she fought. He needed her for something, as bait to get to Nerva, perhaps.

'Take her to Mamertine Prison,' Paulus instructed the men.

Brei's eyes were practically burning holes through him. She had heard all about Mamertine Prison from Mila, who was one of the lucky few to have lived to speak of it. Looking at Otho, she said, 'Tell Gallus. Only Gallus. Understand?'

He nodded as she was led away.

'You should have died in the highlands with the rest of them,' Paulus called to her back.

She looked over her shoulder at him. 'Oh, I plan to.' The last thing she saw was his jaw tick as she turned away.

~

'I JUST ADORE A SUMMER WEDDING,' Aquila said, a brilliant smile etched on her tired face.

Another dinner party. Another awkward wedding conversation with Camilla attached to his arm. He was running out of excuses, finding himself less and less interested in marrying the woman every time he saw her. There was not a thing wrong with the poor girl, yet he felt constantly distracted and irritated in her presence. Worse than that, his mind tended to wander to Brei whenever he looked at Camilla. How long now until he could slip from the room and go to her? He needed to be crushed between those silky thighs and taste the blood on her lips from the fight. She had become a drug—one he would soon have to survive without.

'The *beginning* of summer is always a popular time,' Camilla said. 'Before everyone leaves the city to go to their villas.' She turned to Nerva, a delicate hand landing on his bicep. 'I would love to visit your villa next time we are in Antium.'

Was there no escape from her? 'Mother would love that.' He could tell it was the wrong reply by the way her face fell. Aquila's smile also wavered.

'The villa belongs to Nerva now,' his mother said. 'As Rufus's only living son, he inherited *everything*.'

Camilla squeezed his arm. 'I was so sorry to learn of your father's passing. I had planned to attend the funeral, but my father thought it best I stay away due to... the circumstances surrounding his death.'

Murder. *His murder*. No one was brave enough to call it what it was, because that would mean acknowledging the risk to Nerva. Thankfully, he was spared from replying when Nona entered the room and whispered into his ear.

'Gallus Minidius is waiting in the atrium for you.'

A cold sensation spread through Nerva's chest. 'I am afraid you will have to excuse me,' he said, standing.

Aquila's hand drifted to her throat. 'Whoever it is, tell them you are entertaining and to come back tomorrow.'

'I am afraid it is urgent.'

Camilla reluctantly retracted her claws. 'Then you must go.' She gave the most brilliant version of an understanding smile.

Nerva nodded and fled the room.

When he entered the atrium, he could tell something was wrong by Gallus's expression. The man was usually so jovial. 'Where is Brei?' The question was out of his mouth before even a greeting.

Gallus waited for him to get closer before speaking. 'I apologise for barging in unannounced—'

'Where is she?' he asked again.

Gallus cleared his throat and folded his hands in front of him. 'Ah, at present, the girl is in Mamertine Prison.'

Nerva felt his stomach fall at his feet.

'I thought you might want to know.'

'Mamertine?' Nerva's hands went into his hair. 'I saw her just this morning.'

'My source tells me soldiers arrived at the house where she was fighting and arrested her.'

Nerva took a few steps back, his mind racing. 'On what grounds?'

Gallus's cheeks brightened. 'Illegal fighting.'

'Of course.' Nerva exhaled and swore under his breath. 'And what of her mother?'

'I do not believe anyone knows of her existence—yet.'

'Good.' He would send word to Mila and ensure it remained that way. 'Who made the arrest?'

Gallus thought for a moment. 'Otho did tell me his name. Cordius, perhaps. Unfortunately, there is little I can do about the matter. While I am rather fond of the girl, I am not prepared to join her in prison.'

So that was why Gallus had come to him, knowing Nerva would act on his behalf. He was probably fretting over the coin he would lose if she did not return.

Nerva crossed his arms and stared at the sponsor. 'Given you are mostly to blame for her ending up in there, I hope I can count on your help getting her out?' When Gallus did not immediately reply, he added, 'I have always thought us friends.' He doubted the man was capable of friendship, but the suggestion had the desired effect.

Gallus appeared flustered for a moment. 'Yes, of course. Always happy to help a friend in need.'

Nerva nodded. 'Good, because we are going to need to be very careful with how we handle this.'

'I agree wholeheartedly.' Gallus rubbed his shiny forehead, then looked around to ensure no one else was listening. 'All right, then. Tell me what you want me to do.'

CHAPTER 34

For the first time since arriving in Rome, Brei felt truly cold. The air in Mamertine Prison was icy and rank with death, and she wore only a breastplate and a loincloth trimmed with fur. It was a costume, and she suddenly felt ridiculous in it. Hungry eyes had been watching her from all corners of the cell, ever since the guards dropped her through the hole above.

A violent cough made Brei look at the person sharing her section of the wall. She watched as the woman gathered phlegm in her mouth and spat it on the ground between them.

'What's that on your skin?' she asked, lifting a tired finger and pointing it at Brei's arm.

Brei took in her pinched face. Green eyes shone from two dark sockets. It was difficult to tell her age due to her filthy state. 'It's warpaint.'

A man on the other side of the room, who Brei had assumed asleep or dead, laughed hysterically, then fell silent.

'Don't mind him,' the woman said. 'Mad as a meat axe,

but harmless enough.' She smiled, revealing yellow teeth with black spots on them. 'You a foreign girl, then?'

'Something like that.'

More coughing ensued. The woman took a moment to catch her breath before speaking. 'What you doing in here, then? Go to war with the wrong man?'

Yes, that was exactly what she had done. 'Illegal fighting.'

The woman's eyebrows rose, assessing Brei for a moment. 'Gladiator? Don't see ladies fighting these days.' She wheezed. 'You look fit enough to take a bear. Though it won't do you much good. They'll just send another one to finish the job.'

'Finish the job?'

'To kill you.'

She said it so matter-of-factly, Brei thought she may have misheard. 'Is that where we go from here? To die in the arena?'

'Those who live long enough. The rest of us will probably end up in the sewer.'

Brei shifted on the icy floor. 'Women fight bears?'

The woman laughed, then broke into a coughing fit. It was some time before she was able to talk again. 'Not really a fight. More of a feed. They'll likely tie you to a post or the tail of a horse. Something will kill you in the end.'

Brei looked up at the faint light coming through the round grate. So that was how it would end for her.

Closing her eyes, she thought of her mother. Nerva would still get her out of Rome if he could. He had probably learned of her whereabouts by now. She hoped he stayed away and did not play into Paulus Cordius's game. She knew that was the reason she was in there—live bait. The legate was counting on Nerva coming to her rescue so he could label him a sympathiser, a traitor, give Caracalla a legal reason to go after him.

Brei kept her eyes closed and ignored the sting of tears.

∼

FOUR DAYS WITHOUT FOOD. The one time the guards had thrown down bread, prisoners had lurched from dark corners with surprising agility to snatch it up before it had hit the urine-soaked floor.

Brei could survive without food. Nerva knew that too.

The water they gave her was bitter but quenched her thirst. Other than that, the only thing that broke up the long days was the arrival and departure of prisoners. Brei wished she could pace to keep warm, to stretch her muscles and stop her bones from setting in place, but there was no energy to be wasted on walks with no destination.

On day five, the woman with the cough did not rise with the sun. Brei had seen a lot of death in her time, but there was something unsettling about being trapped in a small space with a corpse. All of her experiences of death had either been on a battlefield or surrounded by grieving loved ones in the comfort of someone's home. In her village, people would sit beside the deceased and hold their hand as they cried. And there was Brei thinking about taking the clothes off the corpse. No one would blame her. It was the sensible thing to do. Instead, she remained shivering against the wall. In the afternoon, when the body was dragged away by a guard, she decided she would not die in that place.

Somehow *damnatio ad bestias* seemed like a more fitting end than rotting in the sewer.

On day six, Brei scurried for the bread with the rest of them. She ate it alone, staring up at the hole it had come through. She could feel her mind beginning to splinter. Where before she had wanted Nerva to stay away, now she began to question why he had abandoned her. He was not the sort of man who did nothing in these situations. He was the type who would find a way to get food to her, a message, something. Perhaps he was already dead. No, if she was alive, he was alive. Perhaps he knew something she did not. It was the only explanation that eased her growing fear and the one thought she kept hold of.

Rats scurried past her blackened feet, searching for breadcrumbs. But the prisoners were too hungry to leave crumbs. Leaning her head against the stone wall, Brei closed her eyes and slipped into a fitful sleep.

∼

'You are doing the right thing,' Mila assured Nerva for the hundredth time.

He had barely slept in five days, and his mind was beginning to suffer. Doing nothing had been harder than he anticipated. He knew there were ways to see that she was fed, given clothes, maybe even fresh air. But to what end?

'Cordius will have eyes everywhere,' Marcus reminded him. 'You better believe there is a prisoner in that place whose sole purpose is to watch her.'

'Without a doubt,' Gallus agreed. 'And you will not be any good to her locked up or dead.'

Nerva understood the logic, but that did not make it any easier to sit in comfort while she suffered in that cesspool of a prison. He looked around the room at his small team of helpers. Mila, Remus, Felix, Albaus, Gallus, and Marcus. They each had a role to play. 'So, tomorrow, then.'

'We all know our parts,' Remus said.

'The Megalenses Ludi,' Felix said, nostalgia in his voice. 'You know, I fought at that festival once.'

'Did they celebrate it back in those days?' Remus asked.

Felix glanced sideways at him. 'Have you considered writing your jokes down? That way they can be enjoyed for generations to come.'

'Save that mouth of yours for tomorrow,' Mila said. 'We are counting on it.'

Nerva nodded at his sister. 'If everyone plays their part well, this time tomorrow, Brei and her mother will be out of the city.' He swallowed down the thickening feeling in his throat. 'I cannot tell you how much it means to have your help with this. I shall not forget it—even you, Gallus.'

The sponsor straightened. 'As I said right from the beginning, I am always happy to help a friend.'

Nerva and Mila looked at each other but said nothing.

'You saved Mila from certain death once,' Remus said to Nerva as he pulled his wife to him. 'We owe you.'

Albaus grunted, and Felix drew a breath before speaking.

'While I am not one to keep score'—he looked between Mila and Nerva—'you are both now severely indebted to me.'

'I've saved your arse enough times,' Remus said.

'I was not talking to you.'

Nerva clapped the dwarf on the shoulder. 'Like I said, I shall not forget it.'

'We all have your back,' Mila said. 'I am just sorry it ends with Brei gone.'

'Well, that is life,' Nerva said, hardly believing those words actually came from his mouth. He was fooling no one with his detached facade.

Felix looked around. 'This is the part where someone tells him there are plenty of fish in the sea.'

'I am familiar with the saying,' Nerva replied. He knew Brei was no common fish. She had set his life ablaze. Theirs was that rare type of love that tore souls to shreds, even if neither of them had ever admitted it aloud.

Mila stepped forwards and patted his chest. 'I wish we could offer more than bad jokes right now.'

'Not sure I could handle anything more than bad jokes right now.' He tried to smile, then turned away. 'I will see you tomorrow.'

## CHAPTER 35

Light blinded Brei as she was pulled up through the hole into daylight.

'Hands,' the guard said.

She held out her arms as she took in the faces of the other prisoners around her. Judging by their expressions, they were all headed to the same execution. The guard secured her wrists with irons that weighed down her wasting arms.

'Where are we going?' she asked as he jerked the shackles.

He moved to the next prisoner. 'You wanted to fight. Now's your chance.' The guards exchanged a smirk.

'And who am I fighting?'

He shoved her to get her moving. 'Wild beasts with a taste for human blood.'

Her heart thudded in her ears as they were ushered through the *comitium*. The city must have been celebrating a festival, because there was a procession moving through the forum. People lined the streets; the cheering and clapping was deafening. The applause stopped when the prisoners came into view, turning to boos and insults. People spat in their direction as they passed. Some of the prisoners looked down while others wept. A few begged the crowd for mercy, as if that would somehow change their fates. Brei looked straight at them. Perhaps if they knew her story, they would weep alongside her instead.

Brei's eyes moved between each face, looking for something—or someone. Did she really think Nerva would be standing among the plebeians watching the procession? He might have already left the city with her mother. Or maybe her mother had come after her and been caught. Paulus Cordius might have learned of her existence and planned on surprising Brei by dropping her into the pit also.

Her toe caught the edge of a paving stone, and she stumbled.

'Keep moving,' shouted the guard, yanking her upright.

The Flavian Amphitheatre rose in front of them. She had never been inside, despite wanting to see what all the fuss was about. Nerva had told her not to go.

'*You do not need more reasons to hate this city,*' he had said.

And she had stayed away.

The prisoners entered the amphitheatre through a separate corridor and disappeared into a maze of underground tunnels. Brei tried to keep track of the turns but was distracted by the caged animals that hissed and growled as they passed. Claws and teeth snapped between the bars, making the prisoners jump. Some of the animals Brei did not recognise: striped horses and cats with paws as large as a man's head. Others she could not make out at all, glimpsing only glowing eyes and heavily shadowed figures. Finally, they came to a stop.

'Four in each cell,' one of the guards instructed.

Brei was locked up with three other prisoners from Mamertine. One man slid to the floor, his head in his hands. Another prayed. The woman sat expressionless against the wall in a pool of her own urine. Brei remained standing, forcing herself to breathe. Falling apart would not change the outcome, so instead of fear, she chose to let in the anger she had shut out all week.

*Where is Nerva?*

He had spared her life countless times. Now he was letting her die in the most horrendous way the Romans could come up with. Her hands curled into fists at her sides. What better person to be angry at than the man responsible?

*Bang.*

'On your feet, the lot of you,' shouted a guard, pounding on the iron bars behind Brei.

When she turned to look in his direction, she was surprised to see Gallus, Felix, and Albaus standing with him. The slightest shake of Felix's head wiped the surprise off her face.

'We have a *very* funny performance planned,' Gallus was saying to the guard. 'We just require a few extra props.'

Brei's pulse was racing, but she was careful not to let her feelings show on her face.

Gallus nodded towards the door. 'Go on, then. Open up. No one will get far with my friend here.' He nodded in the direction of Albaus, whose head was tilted to prevent it from hitting the low roof.

The guard hesitated before stepping forwards to unlock the door. 'Don't get any clever ideas,' he warned the prisoners as Gallus and Felix stepped inside.

Felix crossed his arms and looked them all over for a moment. 'Which ones are most likely to survive until the climax, do you suppose?' He looked up at Gallus, waiting for an answer.

'Probably none. Perhaps we should look elsewhere.'

'I do not like our chances at short notice. *Why* must prisoners die at the most inopportune times?'

Gallus nodded in agreement. 'Perhaps we should take all four to be safe.'

Albaus grunted and looked off down the corridor. Above them, gladiators were already fighting, their movements sending dust floating down on them.

'I agree,' Felix said. 'And we might need slower beasts for that particular part.'

Gallus turned to the guard. 'We shall take all four. I will need their shackles removed.'

'Removed? It is safer to—'

'How about you leave stage direction to those with some skill, eh?' Gallus waved his hand. 'Come now. The show must go on.'

The guard hesitated before approaching the prisoners and removing their irons. When he got to Brei, he winked and said, 'Enjoy the show.'

She looked down at her feet so he could not read her expression.

'Come along,' Gallus said. 'Form a line and follow me.'

'Keep an eye on that one,' the guard called, gesturing to Brei.

Albaus dragged her to the back of the line using far more force than was necessary, earning another grin from the guard. Brei stared at the man's head in front of her. Albaus shoved her into motion when the line began to move.

They walked through the orange flickering light of torches. More turns, more tunnels. Brei had no idea what direction they were travelling in. Nothing looked familiar. They turned another corner, and a pair of hands reached out from a dark nook, pulling Brei into the shadows. A hand went over her mouth.

It took all of her willpower not to push it away. Albaus continued forwards without breaking stride, confirming that it was part of the plan. It took a moment for her eyes to adjust. Mila's face came into view. She brought a finger to her lips, waited a moment, and then slowly removed her hand from Brei's mouth. For Nerva to put his own sister at risk spoke volumes.

Brei kept quiet as Mila unbelted her tunic and tugged it over her head. Underneath it was an identical tunic, belted in the same way as the one she had just removed. She gestured for Brei to dress, then reached beneath her tunic, pulling out a pair of leather sandals which she placed at Brei's feet. When she was dressed, Mila reached down and picked up two ceramic jugs, handing one to Brei.

'Wash your face,' Mila whispered.

Brei poured a small amount of water into her hand and rubbed it over her grimy face, careful not to dirty the clean tunic.

'Stay behind me,' Mila said into Brei's ear. 'Do not speak. Do not look the guards in the eye.' With that, she stepped out into the tunnel and walked calmly in the opposite direction. She clearly knew her way around the tunnels, because she turned corners that Brei would have otherwise missed. Eventually they entered a passage lit by natural light. At the far end was a closed door with armed guards standing either side of it. Brei was sure the men would notice her heart beating through the fabric of her tunic. She did exactly what she was told, eyes down and completely silent. Her heart reached a frantic thrum as the door opened in front of them. She was certain her appearance would give her away. Her legs and feet were filthy, and one toenail was bleeding. Never had she looked so much like a prisoner. She lowered her head farther so that her matted hair fell over her face. Her vision blurred, and the small amount of water in the bottom of the jug was sloshing in her unsteady hands.

When she reached the guards, one of them grabbed her

arm. She immediately stilled. Mila stopped also, but she did not turn back or say anything.

*Breathe.*

A hand landed on Brei's backside with a sting, and then the guard gave it a squeeze.

'I'll come find you later,' he said.

The moment he let go of her arm, she kept walking, matching Mila's pace. She continued to stare at the ground in front of her until they reached another large tunnel. Mila looked in both directions before stepping inside. Only then did she turn to Brei.

'Go to the very end. I am going to wait here and ensure no one follows.' She pulled Brei to her with her free hand, hugging her close. 'Hurry, but do not run.' With that, Mila gave her a gentle shove to get her moving.

Brei knew it was the last time she would ever see Nerva's sister. There were so many things she had wanted to say, like 'thank you for giving me a family when I had no one'.

'Go,' Mila said.

Brei nodded and turned away. Her legs moved automatically, ears straining as she listened for approaching footsteps. She made it all the way without running into anyone, but new panic surged as she approached the end of the tunnel. Where was she supposed to go from there?

A figure stepped into the light just as she reached the end, causing her to suck in a breath. It took her a moment to register Remus.

'This way.' He gestured for her to keep moving. 'Stay a few paces behind me.' He spoke without looking back at her.

She did as she was told while sneaking glances at her surroundings, taking in the barracks and training area. Men walked around carrying various weapons or stood talking beneath the portico. She realised where she was then. There was a tunnel that joined the Flavian Amphitheatre to Ludus Magnus, the gladiator school where Remus had been raised. They made it all the way to the front gate with just a few disinterested glances in Brei's direction. The guard at the entrance nodded at Remus before opening the gate. He did not ask any questions as she followed him through.

Once outside, Brei looked both ways down the street and spotted a plainly dressed Marcus seated on a horse across the road. Nerva was not with him. She realised then that she might never see him again. He had done all this to see her free, and she would not even get the chance to say thank you.

'Go,' Remus said, touching her shoulder.

When Brei looked up at him, he gave a small nod of encouragement.

'Thank you,' she whispered before stepping out onto the street.

When she reached Marcus, he offered his hand. She took hold of it and swung herself up onto the horse behind him. 'Where's my mother?'

He pushed the horse into a walk, then looked around before replying. 'Waiting for you.'

She nodded and fell silent.

When they were some distance from Ludus Magnus, Marcus passed a bag to her. Inside were a waterskin, food, and a palla. Nerva had thought of everything. Brei thanked Marcus, then took out the waterskin, drinking greedily. She used a small amount of water to wash her hands and face, shuddering as the cold liquid ran down her neck and soaked into her tunic. Pulling out the palla, she wrapped it around her shoulders.

'Eat,' Marcus said. 'Even if you're not hungry.'

She took out the small parcel of bread, hard cheese, and some dried pear, eating slowly. 'Are we going to the river?'

'Yes' was his only reply.

She had more questions, but he was focused on other things at that moment. His rigid body language suggested he was prepared for trouble.

They descended a slope towards the water where a small boat waited for them. Her mother was already inside. Brei saw the relief on her face when she spotted the horse approaching. Brei looked both ways down the river. Nerva was not there. It was not safe for him to be involved. If there was one day Paulus Cordius would be watching him, it would be the day of her execution.

A boy walked up to meet them. He helped Brei down, then went to take the horse.

'We must keep moving,' Marcus said as he joined her on the ground. 'The ship will not wait.'

Brei looked behind her, disappointment bitter in her mouth, then turned and headed for the boat.

CHAPTER 36

The women ate and slept on the boat, taking turns with Marcus to watch the busy river. Brei had been rescued from the jaws of death, found her mother, whom she had long thought dead, and was on her way home to be reunited with the rest of her family. There was so much to be thankful for, but it was impossible to appreciate just yet. They would not be safe until they passed through Hadrian's Wall.

'You've barely said two words since leaving Rome,' Keelia said on day two of their journey. 'You watch those trees like you're expecting someone to run through them.'

Brei dragged her gaze from the riverbank to look at her mother. 'What if Cordius finds out I didn't die in that arena?'

'How?'

'When he didn't see me die, maybe?'

'You heard Marcus. Those types of executions are so chaotic no one can tell who is who.' Keelia sighed. 'But Cordius isn't the reason you cry when you think I'm asleep.'

She had never been a crier before *him*. 'It's been a big couple of weeks.'

They watched the sun slip behind the horizon. The clouds had lifted for the journey.

'You don't always have to be brave for my sake.'

Brei turned away so her mother would not see her fighting back tears. 'I wish I could turn it off,' she whispered.

Keelia reached out and took her hand. 'I see why you care for him.' She hesitated. 'But he did the right thing for both of you. It might not feel that way, but you belong with your family, not in that place.'

She refused to cry in front of her mother. 'I understand the logic.'

'And yet you wait for him.'

She swallowed. 'Sometimes home isn't a place but a feeling.'

Keelia pulled her daughter to her. 'I'm sorry. I really am.' Her arms wrapped her tightly. 'You know, I always wondered what sort of man you would fall in love with. I started to wonder if there was anyone in those mountains who could handle a woman like you.'

'You make me sound like a wild horse.'

Keelia smiled. 'You're a handful. Always have been.'

'I get that from you.'

Her mother laughed. 'You are ten times fiercer than me. Who would have guessed you would fall for a man like Nerva?'

'You mean a Roman?'

'No, someone gentle.' She stopped speaking as a boat passed by headed in the opposite direction. 'While I'm sorry you return home with your heart in pieces, I'm so grateful that we're returning home at all.'

Brei closed her eyes. 'I never told him how I felt. I can't

figure out if that's a good thing or a bad thing. I suppose I was trying to protect us.'

'Nerva is a smart man. He didn't need words to know how you feel. Did he ever tell you how he felt?'

Brei shook her head, and a tear ran down the side of her face and into her hair. 'I'm a smart woman. I didn't need words to know how he felt.' She smiled, but it faded quickly.

∽

The merchant ship was being loaded with grain and other supplies that would be taken to Britannia. Both uniformed and plain-dressed men swarmed the port of Ostia Antica, making the women nervous.

'Should we board?' Keelia asked, growing more anxious by the second.

Marcus shook his head. 'Soon. They need to finish loading supplies before boarding passengers.'

Keelia fell quiet again, hugging her bag to her chest.

Brei was waiting for Paulus Cordius to show up, to glimpse his smug expression amid the crowd. He would drag her back to Rome, execute her himself—she was sure of it. She could not relax. Every face was beginning to look like his. She kept glancing around, her mother's tense state feeding her own.

'I think they've finished,' Keelia said, looking to Marcus with a hopeful expression.

He gave her a tight smile. 'Not too much longer.' His gaze swept the dock again.

Perhaps he was expecting Paulus also. Brei shifted her bag from one hand to the other, checked behind her, right, left. A familiar figure caught her attention, and she narrowed her eyes on the man. She sucked in a breath.

'What's the matter?' her mother asked, panic in her voice.

Marcus took a step forwards, then relaxed. 'I wasn't sure if he would make it.'

Nerva stood at the far end of the dock. He was searching for someone. Searching for *her.* She could tell by the way his expression softened when he found her.

The bag fell from Brei's hand. Without thinking, she took off at a run towards him. Behind her, Keelia made a startled noise, and Marcus told her not to run. It was not the most sensible thing to do while trying to keep a low profile, but there was no stopping her feet. She watched the emotion play out on Nerva's face as she got closer. When she reached him, she grabbed hold of his stubbly face with both hands, pressing her forehead to his. He took hold of her arms, gripping her too hard.

'You came,' she said, slightly breathless. 'Tell me you're coming with us.' When he shook his head, something in her chest tore. It was as though his hands were wrapping her throat suddenly. 'Come with us.'

'You know I cannot go with you. It was a risk coming here at all, but I needed to see you board that ship with my own eyes.' He looked her over for a moment. 'Are you all right? Did they hurt you?'

His questions went unanswered. 'You're really not coming?' She wished she could speak without choking on the words.

'No, Brei. I am not coming with you.'

She shook her head, rejecting his reply while gripping his face harder. 'You don't understand. I can't go without you.'

'Of course you can.'

'I love you.' It was strange how easily those words slipped from her.

His grip on her tightened to the point of pain. 'Stop.'

She let go of him suddenly, as if his skin had burned her. He wore a tortured expression, the same one she had seen on his face the day he had invaded her village and walked past the dead children to mount his horse. 'Stop?'

Not 'I love you too', but '*stop*'. The pressure on her arms eased as he got control of himself.

'I came to make sure you are all right, to make sure you boarded. I have been going out of my mind—'

'I'm fine.' Her lips felt numb.

He searched her eyes for a moment. 'Marcus will see you all the way to the wall. You can trust him as you do me.'

She stepped out of his grip, feeling confused, hurt. His hands remained in the air, holding nothing. 'I'll decide who I trust.' Her words were as cold as the northerly wind coming off the water.

Marcus and Keelia had caught up, but they froze a few feet away, likely repelled by the tension. Marcus cleared his throat. 'It's time to board.'

Another pain in her chest. Her eyes never left Nerva. 'Why did you come?'

He glanced at the ship, his hands going to rest on his hips. 'I told you. I needed to make sure you were all right.'

She hugged herself. It was so cold suddenly. 'Well, now you know.'

His hands went into his hair. 'This is hard for me too.'

She knew that. It was there in his voice, his body language, the grief coming off him in waves. 'Then come with us!' Her voice was raised this time, surprising even her. Marcus and Keelia looked around to see if anyone else had heard the outburst. She was holding them up, jeopardising everything.

'You know I cannot.'

'Then I'll stay.' The declaration spilled out of her,

making her mother flinch. 'If you won't come, then I'll stay here with you.'

'You cannot stay. It is not safe.' Nerva's voice was low but firm. 'It is time for you to board.'

Her hands went over her face as she tried to rein in everything she was feeling. 'I can't.'

He took hold of her arms again, holding her up as her knees shook. 'You can. You are the strongest woman I know.' He brought his lips to her ear. 'Your mother is counting on you. Your family is waiting for you.' He kissed her hair, his breaths uneven. 'I need to stay here in order to protect you. Now do this one last thing for me. Get on that ship, and go home.'

Brei's hands fell away from her face, and she stared into his grey eyes, where her own misery was reflected back at her.

Keelia stepped forwards and took her hand, pulling gently.

'Get them aboard,' Nerva said to Marcus. When he let go of Brei, his fingers were like rigid claws as they returned to his sides.

'I don't need a bodyguard.' The words came out of her harsher than she intended, but it was better to be angry than hopeless.

'You will need one all the way to the wall,' Nerva replied. He looked away, then back at her. 'Brei, I—'

'It's all right.' She shook her head and began backing away. 'Don't say anything else.' She could not take any more. A tear betrayed her, and she turned quickly before he saw it.

Her mother kept a firm hold of her shaking hand. Brei could feel Nerva's eyes burning holes in the back of her head as she stepped onto the gangplank. One trembling foot in front of the other.

'Brei,' Nerva called.

If she stood any chance of boarding the ship, she had to keep walking.

'Everything I have done since the day we met has been for you—especially this.'

The pain in her chest was already so immense that she barely noticed it growing. She just hoped her knees held until she reached the ship.

'It will be all right,' her mother whispered behind her. 'Just keep walking.'

Nerva was done talking, and she did not dare look back to see if he was still standing there. Finally, her feet landed on the deck, and she waited while someone gave Marcus instructions she could not follow. Next thing she knew, they were descending a ladder into a private cabin with plenty of light.

Nerva had done that also.

Marcus said something she did not hear. Keelia replied on her behalf.

Brei stumbled forwards, almost tripping on the door of the cabin as she headed for the safety of bed. She closed her eyes against her mother's voice as she lay down. The door creaked shut, and a hand rested on her back, rubbing circles.

'I just need to sleep. Leave me.'

Her mother did not retract the hand.

'Did you hear what I said?' Her voice broke that time.

'I heard.' The soothing circles continued.

Brei covered her face as a sob tore through her.

## CHAPTER 37

The weeks onboard passed painfully slow. Despite the calm waters of the Atlantic Ocean, Brei was constantly sick. She only left her bed when her mother forced her to take air on deck; otherwise, she tried to pass the time by sleeping.

When they anchored in Spain for supplies, Marcus encouraged her to spend some time on land to see if her condition improved. It did not. She could hardly blame her body for giving up. She had been fighting for such a long time, imprisoned, starved, and then had left her beating heart at Nerva's feet for the birds to pick apart.

'I'll be fine,' she assured her mother when they boarded again. 'It'll pass.'

Keelia said nothing but continued to watch her with a newfound intensity.

A strong westerly wind fought the ship across the North Sea, making the final part of their journey the roughest to date. Brei's nausea was no worse for it. It did not change with the weather but with the time of day. She began to notice a pattern, and then a cold realisation hit her.

On the day they were due to arrive in Arbeia, Brei and Keelia sat on upturned crates on deck, watching the horizon. Brei was thinking about how it would feel to set foot on her homeland after all that time away. She dragged a clammy hand down her face. The fresh sea air was not enough to cool her body, which seemed to be operating at twice the temperature of late.

'Are you all right?' her mother asked.

Brei glanced across at her. 'Yes. Fine.'

Keelia nodded and looked at the horizon again. 'Best not to say anything to your father just yet.'

'About what?'

Keelia was quiet a moment. 'About the pregnancy.'

Brei gripped the edge of the crate she sat on little tighter. 'How long have you known?'

Her mother smiled and shook her head. 'The real question is how long have *you* known?'

Brei drew a breath. 'Just a few days.' She hesitated. 'What will happen to the baby?'

Keelia reached out and took her hand. 'I won't let anything happen to it.'

The faint silhouette of land appeared on the horizon at that moment. *Home.*

'Nerva will never know,' Brei whispered.

Her mother squeezed her hand. 'And that's for the best. What's an honourable man to do with that information?'

Brei blinked, that heavy feeling closing around her heart once more. Before she could reply, Marcus walked up to them, pointing to the horizon.

'Not too much longer now. How's the sickness?'

She attempted a smile. 'I'll be fine once I'm on land.'

'I've no doubt.'

The three of them disembarked at the mouth of the River Tyne just as the sun was setting. Brei walked up the grassy slope, staring up at the fort that dominated the landscape. The port was so busy that no one seemed to take much notice of them. Marcus found a woman selling horses and negotiated the sale with surprising ease. His charming persona made it hard for women to say no to him. Nerva had been the same way.

'Are you sure you want to come the rest of the way with us?' Brei asked as she mounted the chestnut filly.

Marcus kicked his horse into a trot. 'I'll see you through Hadrian's Wall. After that, I'm afraid you're on your own.'

Brei caught up to him. 'There're really no troops north of there?'

He shook his head.

'How far to Portage?' Keelia asked, catching up to them.

'Around thirty miles.'

The three of them rode north until they could no longer see the horse in front of them, then moved off the main road and set up camp, skipping the campfire so as to not attract attention. The war might have been over, but that did not mean there was no danger.

They huddled beneath wool blankets, and Brei could not stop her mind from wandering to Nerva. Whenever he had slept in her bed, she had woken in the middle of the night and kicked off the linens. The warmth of his body made her overheat. He held her tightly, as though she might disappear while he slept. She had felt invincible in those moments, could almost forget how dangerous the world was outside of his arms.

The moment the sun kissed the hills in the east, they packed up their few belongings, saddled the horses, and continued north. They rode all day without stopping, reaching Hadrian's Wall a few hours before sunset. Soldiers moved in all directions like disturbed ants.

'What exactly is your plan?' she asked Marcus, keeping her voice low. She was suddenly aware of her change in heart rate. They were significantly outnumbered.

'Let me do the talking,' Marcus said. He retrieved a rolled piece of parchment from his bag and held on to it as they approached the tall, heavy gate. Two guards assessed the women before turning their attention to Marcus.

'What is your business here?' asked one.

Marcus held up the piece of parchment. 'I have a letter for your commander.'

Brei and Keelia looked at one another as it was handed down to the guard. The man studied the seal, then nodded to the other guard, who marched off to fetch his superior.

They all waited in silence, with the guard watching the women. Brei tallied his weapons and studied the gate, trying to judge how long it would take her to open it and bolt through it if the need arose. She could feel the draw of home now.

The guard returned a few minutes later with his commander, who held the open letter in his hand. The commander looked the women up and down before turning to Marcus.

Marcus saluted him. 'I am Marcus Furnia, sir, previously of the third Britannia legion.'

'At ease,' the commander said. 'I gather from the emperor's letter that this is a personal favour and not an army matter.'

Brei tried not to let her surprise show on her face. *The emperor*? Nerva had gone to Geta on her behalf. It was no wonder he could not leave. If he was not indebted to the man before, he certainly was now.

Marcus nodded. 'That's correct, sir.'

The commander's gaze returned to the parchment in his hand, then to Brei. 'The people on the other side of that wall do not take kindly to trespassers. I cannot guarantee your safety if you go through.'

'We can take care of ourselves, Commander,' Brei said. 'All we need is the gate opened.'

The commander glanced at Marcus a final time before turning back to the guards. 'Let them through.'

Brei heard the air leave her mother's lungs. They were really going home. She turned to Marcus. 'How am I supposed to adequately thank you for everything you've done?'

'Just make it home safe.'

She nodded. 'We will be absolutely fine.' She said that for Nerva's sake, wanted those to be the last words reported back to him. The man deserved to sleep knowing he did not send her to her death.

Marcus gestured to the bag hanging from her saddle. 'I put some extra supplies in there. Make sure you have a look once you're on your way.'

She nodded.

'And try to keep moving as much as you can,' he finished.

The gates sat ajar, just enough so the horses could pass through in single file. Brei looked at Marcus one more time. 'Thank you, Tribune.' She pushed her horse into a walk, listening as her mother said goodbye behind her.

The women nodded at the wary guards as they passed them. Brei looked over her shoulder as the gates closed behind them. 'Take care of him,' she called, unable to say his name aloud. She saw Marcus nod as the crack narrowed.

When the gate was secured from the other side, she looked across at her mother. 'Ready to go home?'

There was light in Keelia's eyes. 'Ready.'

CHAPTER 38

'I hate leaving you like this. It feels a lot like abandonment,' Mila said, watching Nerva with an expression that bordered on pity.

They were standing across the street from the Papias house. *My house*. He was still adjusting to his inheritance.

'It is not abandonment. You are being practical, and remaining here is not practical—or safe, for that matter.' He looked over at the two guards waiting by the bottom step. This was his life now; men followed him about, ensuring no one stabbed him in the back.

Mila sighed. 'You have taken care of Dulcia and me our entire lives.'

He rubbed his forehead. 'Dulcia needs her sister, and I need you safe. Everyone wins with you gone.' Nerva's head pulsed with the same headache he had carried for weeks, ever since he had watched Brei board that ship without so much as a glance back at him. Of course, he did not blame her. She was not one to speak her feelings, and the day she had, he had told her to *stop*.

'*I love you*,' she had said.

Her words had almost knocked him over. Not because he was unaware of her feelings, but because there was an unspoken agreement between them that they would never say them aloud. For a split second, he had considered going with her. The word 'stop' had been aimed at himself. Without it he might have said things he could not take back. *I love you. I need you. I am coming with you.* They were the kind of phrases that sat on the edge of his tongue. And gods, did he love her.

'Are you absolutely sure?' Mila asked.

He nodded. 'I never thought I would be this man.'

'The brooding kind?'

He crossed his arms. 'I suppose that is accurate.'

Her expression softened. 'You have to give yourself some time. You are heartbroken.'

'Must you?'

'You are.' She tapped his chest. 'You have the biggest heart of any man I know. It was only a matter of time before someone crushed it. Not that this is Brei's fault, of course.'

The corners of his mouth tugged. 'But a Maeatae warrior. I mean, the entire thing is laughable. You cannot deny it, because I recall your reaction when I first told you about her.'

'I was a little surprised is all.' Mila leaned against the stone wall, watching the guards who looked up and down the streets. 'And yet fate keeps bringing the two of you back together.' She fell silent for a moment. 'I liked her, you know. Yes, she was wrong for you in lots of ways, but not in the ways that matter.' She glanced at him. 'We both know you will bore of Camilla in no time.'

'I was bored after one conversation.' He could feel his headache growing and rubbed at the spot again. 'Why did Brei have to be so perfect?'

Mila suppressed a smile. 'You really love her.'

He exhaled. 'At what point am I supposed to accept that I am never going to see her again?'

Mila reached out and squeezed his hand. 'You lost the woman you love and your father in a matter of weeks. It is a lot. Even for someone who is as resilient and practical as you. You are going to absolutely hate me for this, but—'

'Please do not say to take one day at a time.'

'You need to take one day at a time.'

He shook his head. 'You just had to say it.'

Her response came in the form of a grin. Before she had a chance to speak, the sound of horses approaching made them both turn. Two mounted soldiers came towards them, and the guards crossed the street to block them.

Nerva sighed. 'It is all right,' he called to them. 'They are Geta's men.'

The guards stepped aside to let the horses pass.

'What is it?' Nerva asked when they were close enough to hear him.

One of the soldier's spoke up. 'The emperor would like to see you at the palace.'

It was the third time Geta had sent for him that week. Nerva was performing the role of advisor despite having never agreed to it. The day he had gone to Geta and asked for that letter had sealed his future. The man was keeping his secret, and now Nerva had a debt to pay. Of course, that was not the only reason he remained in the city he had grown to despise. He wanted to ensure their fleet of ships never touched the shores of Caledonia ever again.

He turned to Mila. 'You will have to forgive me.'

'Go.' She waved him away. 'Just make sure you come and say goodbye when you are done.'

## CHAPTER 39

It was over one hundred miles from Hadrian's Wall to Antonine's Wall. The two women travelled north on Dere Street, always bracing for trouble. Thankfully, the extra supplies Marcus had been referring to were two daggers. They felt much better with weapons on hand.

They reached the wall in three days, finding it abandoned and covered by low-hanging clouds that made the sight more eerie. The tall gate sat ajar. All that fighting. All that bloodshed. For what? The moment Severus had died, his sons had withdrawn their troops and retreated south. It would take decades for the Caledonii and Maeatae to recover from the loss.

A flame ignited in Brei's belly, all the anger she had pushed down for so long bubbling to the surface.

'We should rest before we go through,' Keelia said. 'Who knows what we face on the other side.'

'Our people. That's what's on the other side.'

Keelia gestured towards her horse. 'Does your horse look like a highland horse? Your saddle? Your dagger? Your clothes? What of your Roman braid?'

Brei sighed. 'Shall I strip down and paint myself?'

Keelia's mouth pressed into a thin line. 'You have a baby to consider. We rest first.'

Brei closed her eyes for a moment, then swung her horse and pushed it into a trot, heading for the abandoned fort. That night they slept inside, imagining how much warmer they would be with a fire. But they could not risk the smoke. The last thing they needed was local tribes thinking the fort had been reoccupied.

'What I'd give for some hot food,' Brei said, chewing on leathery salted meat. 'I'd happily eat one of the horses if we could cook it.'

Keelia smiled. 'At least your appetite is returning.'

Dragging her bag closer, Brei lay her head on it and was asleep within moments.

The next morning, they saddled the horses and passed through the wall. On the other side, they stopped, staring out at the familiar landscape. Brei had expected everything to look different, but the only evidence the Romans had ever been there was the wall behind them.

Taking a deep breath, Keelia pushed her horse forwards. Brei glanced over her shoulder before following after her. It would take at least three days to reach their village, and they had no idea what they would find when they got there. The war had continued for months after Brei had been taken prisoner.

'What if they're all dead?' She could not stop the question from tumbling out.

Keelia kept her eyes ahead. 'Then we make a new home. This land belongs to us, and we can live where we choose.'

The first day passed without incident, though there were times when Brei suspected they were being watched. She would have felt safer with a bow, but a dagger was better than nothing.

That night they lit a fire because they were sure the

tribes in the area already knew they were there. They took turns sleeping. In the middle of the night, Brei jumped as an arrow struck the ground a few feet from her leg. If they wanted her dead, she would be. It was a warning, a test to see how she would react. She gently woke her mother so as not to panic her, then got to her feet, turning in circles.

'We are Maeatae,' she shouted, 'returning to our family, our home. Kill us, and you will be killing your own.' Her right hand rested protectively over her belly. 'We fought to defend these mountains, and we are now free to travel through them.'

No more arrows fell that night.

As soon as there was light, the women put out the fire and gathered their few belongings.

'Leave the saddles,' Brei said as she sprang onto the mare's back.

Keelia mounted and looked across at her. 'You let out your hair.'

It was the mountains, cleansing her of Rome. Not of him though. He coursed through every vein in her body. 'Thought I better look the part.' Her gaze drifted to the trees. 'Let's go.'

That afternoon they moved to higher ground, weaving through tall trunks and listening to birds take flight around them. Eventually they went in search of water, and it was there by the stream that she truly felt a presence amid the trees. She was crouched down to fill her waterskin and glanced over at her mother to see if she had sensed it also. Keelia's rigid posture answered her question. Brei stood and walked around the other side of her horse to get a better view. She waited, her eyes trained on the trees, watching for even the smallest of movements. The sound of a bow pulling taut made her turn. She caught sight of someone and, snatching up her dagger, threw it. It pierced the tree they were hiding behind. 'Show yourself!'

She felt reborn in that moment. Something about her stance, strength, the words echoing around them made it clear the warrior had returned.

Men emerged from the trees and rocks around them, weapons still in hand but looking far more curious than threatening. She searched the faces, recognising some of them.

'Brei?'

The sound of her father's voice made her breath hitch. She spotted him, all broad-shouldered and scar-faced. His dark eyes took her in. She broke into a run towards him, and he caught her in his arms like she was five years old, burying his bearded face in her neck. Neither of them moved for a moment. She was crying, and he was making shushing noises he did not mean. Then, remembering her mother, Brei pulled away and turned.

Keelia stood with a tear-streaked face, watching them. It took Seisyll a moment to comprehend who he was looking at. Brei could not blame him; no one expected loved ones to return from the dead. Finally, Seisyll's face collapsed, tears spilling over and disappearing into his beard. Keelia moved forwards then, never taking her eyes off her husband. Brei stepped back, watching as they met in the middle, not touching, only looking at one another.

'You're really here,' Seisyll said, not bothering to wipe his face.

A choking noise escaped Keelia. 'I'm home.'

Seisyll scooped his wife into a bearlike hug, and a small piece of Brei's broken heart was restored. She blinked back happy tears, swallowing furiously to keep her emotions in check as the other men looked on.

'Alane?' Keelia asked.

Brei held her breath as she waited for her father's reply.

'She's well. Drust too.'

'What about Lavena?' Brei barely had the courage to ask the question.

Her father looked at her. 'She was taken in by a tribe, healed, and returned to us a few months ago.'

Brei folded and rested her hands on her knees, then straightened and looked up at the sky. 'Thank you,' she whispered.

CHAPTER 40

Summer came and went. Autumn. Then winter arrived.

Nerva's life had become an endless sequence of meetings and social events. Was there anything more soul-destroying than a dinner party where half of the guests wished you dead? It was a game of sorts, one he was unfortunately good at—and he hated himself all the more for it.

As political conflict continued, so did the threat to his life. As a precaution, Nerva sent his mother south to their villa in Antium. He had good reason not to trust Caracalla when it came to the women in his life.

When he was not running about doing Geta's bidding, he sat alone in the empty house with a handful of servants who had insisted on remaining behind. Interestingly, Nona's company was ten times more enjoyable than many of the people he spent time with.

'When do you suppose your mother will return?' Nona had asked him one evening when he arrived home.

He was a little drunk and did not want to think about it. 'Safer for her to remain in Antium.' Her safety was not the only reason he had sent her away. Their relationship had been more strained than usual since his father's passing.

'What do her letters say?' Nona asked. 'I bet she misses you.'

Nerva should have put his cup down and gone to bed, but instead he filled it again. 'It is the city she misses, and the fast access to gossip.'

Nona took his cup from his hand. 'She's the only family you have left now.'

He hung his head and leaned forwards in his chair. 'Must you remind me?'

'A bitter mother is better than no mother,' she said, looking away.

He rested his elbows on his knees. 'How old are you now?'

Her gaze returned to him. 'Fifteen last week.'

He laughed through his nose. 'Just fifteen and wiser than most people I know.'

She resumed cleaning up. 'You should go to bed. Don't you have a dinner tomorrow, or today?'

He rubbed his forehead. 'I always have a dinner.'

'Will Camilla be there?'

He shook his head. Camilla had given up on him. The last time he had seen her, she had been attached to another arm. He should have felt jealous, but he only felt relief. His mother would have likely heard the news also. She would blame him for dragging his feet. 'No' was his only reply.

Nona straightened and sighed, taking in his expression. 'I didn't like her anyway.'

Nerva laughed. 'I suppose I should be getting over there before the sun sets.'

The dinner party was hosted by Senator Maximilianus Orfius, who had been a big supporter of Caracalla's since his coming of age. It was Nerva's job to change that.

'We all want to trust our leaders,' Nerva said to Maximilianus. They were seated on lounges in the triclinium and had just finished eating. 'You have likely heard about the festival of Saturnalia.'

'I was shocked.'

'We all were. I think it says a lot about Caracalla that he would try to assassinate his brother during a Roman celebration.'

Maximilianus sat with a sombre expression. 'I have supported the man from the beginning, as you know, but this feud is taking time and resources away from more important matters.'

Nerva gestured for their cups to be filled. It would be a long night.

∼

LATER THAT EVENING, as Nerva made his way home with two guards flanking him, he made the mistake of looking up. It was winter, and he should have seen nothing but cloud cover and drizzle. Instead, he was met with endless stars.

*'That's all we get? After everything? One sky?'* Brei had said that day on the beach.

One enormous sky.

His gaze fell to the street in front of him, the reminder too much. How long could he avoid looking up for? The problem was, it was not only the sky that reminded him of her. She was everywhere. Certain smells, particular foods, every gladiator demonstration and piece of amber jewellery that burned as bright as her eyes. The smallest thing could trigger a memory of her.

'Sir,' one of the guards said, grabbing him by the elbow.

Nerva stopped walking and looked around. He had not even realised they had arrived at the house. It was unusually dark. One of the servants always left a flame burning until he returned. Even the guards knew that.

Something was wrong.

When he went to move, the guard kept hold of him. 'I'll go ahead of you.' He then marched past Nerva, heading for the steps. But before he reached them, a figure emerged from the shadows, plunging a dagger through the man's belly. Nerva grabbed for his own weapon as the other guard rushed forwards. He ran after him, but by the time he got there, the second guard lay dead. Without hesitating, Nerva slit the stranger's throat in one mighty sweep before he even had a chance to raise his weapon. The man collapsed to the ground, eyes wide and clutching his neck as he bled out in the same spot Rufus had died. Nerva ran up the steps, then stopped when he heard the scuff of a boot on the street behind him. His fingers tightened around the dagger as he turned. Two armed men stood at the bottom of the steps wearing hard expressions.

The front door opened behind him, and his head whipped around to see two intruders exit.

They had been *inside* the house.

Nerva's thoughts went to the servants, to Nona. 'I pray you were not foolish enough to harm anyone.'

The men looked far from apologetic. 'Just be thankful your mother had the good sense to leave,' one replied.

A flame lit in Nerva's belly as the two men ran at him. He leapt sideways, watching the knives cut through the air. The others ascended the steps to join the fight. It was not the most ideal location, but he was not given a choice in the matter. Blades swung in all directions, and Nerva did his best to avoid them. He managed to grab hold of an arm, twisting it until the weapon fell from the man's hand. Nerva swung him then, sending the intruder crashing into his companions. Taking advantage of the distraction, Nerva pushed past them and ran down to the street. He could have run at that moment, but he was too angry to flee. Instead, he turned and faced them.

The men descended like locusts, and he swung his weapon in a giant sweeping motion to keep them at arm's length. But one made it through. Nerva caught him by the arm, twisting it while spinning the man to face the other way. He tugged the weapon from his hand while keeping him close, like a human shield. A moment later, he held a blade to his attacker's stubbly neck. 'You all walk away right now, or you all die here tonight. Choose now.'

The men glanced between themselves, then went for him. Nerva cut the throat of his hostage before shoving him forwards into one of the others. He felt the sting of a blade at his side. There were too many weapons coming at him at once. Despite the unfair odds, he fought back, all of the pain and frustration of the previous year fuelling him. He used every weapon he had: dagger, fist, foot, knee. But it was no use. One of the men finally disarmed him, and he found himself trapped in the middle of a triangle, panting while blood seeped through his tunic. More bloodstains on the road for his mother to step over. Nerva felt sorry for her. He could picture her eternally stoic face collapsing at the news of his death.

'You chose the wrong side,' one of the men said through bloodied teeth. He took a step towards Nerva, dagger raised, then froze. His eyes burned a little brighter for a moment, and then he coughed, sending a spray of blood through the air. Nerva looked past him and found Marcus standing ten feet away, breathing like he had come at a run. Caracalla's man collapsed with a knife wedged in his spine. Before the others had a chance to play catch-up, Nerva threw his elbow up, hitting one of them in the face. He heard the crack of bone as the nose broke. The distraction bought him enough time for Marcus to join the fight.

The men brawled in the middle of the street like dogs,

until all of Caracalla's men lay dead. Afterwards, Marcus leaned on his knees, panting, then looked up at Nerva.

'I came as soon as I heard.'

'Heard what?' Nerva tried to catch his breath.

Marcus straightened, a look of confusion on his face. 'Geta. He's dead.'

Nerva closed his eyes and brought his bloodied hands to his face. *So, Caracalla finally got to him.* 'What a mess.'

'You're bleeding.'

Nerva glanced down at the superficial wound. 'It is nothing.'

'Good, because you need to get out of Rome—now.'

'I am not running. Caracalla needs to be held accountable.'

'You don't have a choice. His men are combing the city killing anyone who supported his brother. He won't stop until every memory of him is erased.'

Nerva understood then.

The front door creaked, and both their heads snapped in that direction. Nona peeked out of the doorway, looking terrified. 'Oh,' she said, taking in the sight before her.

Nerva jogged up the steps. 'Are you all right?'

She nodded. 'I hid when they arrived.' Her face was ghostly pale. 'The others are… the others are dead. I checked them.'

Nerva blinked, guilt pounding his insides. It was not uncommon for a man's slaves to be killed alongside him, but what Caracalla probably did not realise was that none of them were slaves. Nerva had granted them all their freedom upon his father's death and kept them on as employees.

'Marcus is right. He'll just send more men,' Nona said. 'You should run if you want to live.'

And go where? Going to his mother would only put her

in danger. He would have to run now and think later. 'Do you have somewhere to go?'

Nona looked around before replying. 'I'll be fine.'

She was lying. Nerva knew she was an orphan.

'Nerva,' Marcus called, his tone urgent.

'Give me a minute,' he replied, stepping around Nona and dashing inside.

'We might not have a minute,' Marcus hissed.

Nerva went straight to his rooms, trying not to look at the two dead servants bleeding out in the atrium. Snatching up a bag, he shoved his swords into it before heading to the tablinum to get the denarii he had stashed away. Then he fled the house he had been born in, knowing he might never see it again. Passers-by had stopped on the street, hands over their mouths as they took in the massacre before them. Nerva ran straight past them to Marcus and Nona, who were looking more nervous than when he had left them.

'Did you seriously pack a bag?' Marcus said.

'Well, we need money.'

The three of them powered towards the stables, Nona practically running to keep up.

'Where will you go?' she asked.

Nerva glanced at her. 'You mean where will *we* go? You are coming with us.'

Marcus looked over at him. 'I suppose I can't go home either.'

Nerva shook his head. 'Not if you want your family safe.' He checked behind him before speaking again. 'How do you both feel about Giza?'

Nona's eyes widened. 'The city?'

'Yes, the city. Tertia is there with my sisters. You always liked her.' He knew the women would take care of the girl. It was what they did.

When they reached the stables, they found the caretaker dead outside the stalls. Nerva stepped over the corpse and got to work saddling a horse. When he was done, he mounted and pulled Nona up behind the saddle. 'Hold on.'

As the three of them made their way through the city, they noticed entire families outside in the cold, talking in hushed voices. The news of Emperor Geta's death had spread. By some miracle, they made it out without being stopped or questioned. The moment they were free of the walls, they kicked their horses into a canter and rode west. Two hours later, they stopped at a roadhouse to rest the horses and make a plan.

'We might not have the luxury of a direct voyage to Egypt,' Nerva said. They were seated around a small table with a plate of food between them. No one had an appetite. 'We should board the first ship we can get passage on.'

'Agreed,' Marcus said.

The two men glanced at Nona, who had fallen asleep at the table, her head resting on her hands.

'Had she really nowhere else to go?' Marcus asked.

'If she did, I would have sent her there. My sisters will take her in.'

'They do love a stray.'

Nerva gently woke Nona so they could get moving again, and Marcus asked for the food to be wrapped so they could take it with them. He also managed to buy some waterskins from the owner.

It was an hour past sunrise when they finally tasted the salty air of the Tyrrhenian Sea. Their horses' heads hung low to the ground, legs trembling beneath them. Nerva and Nona dismounted, and he patted the mare's neck. 'You can rest now, girl.' He turned to Marcus. 'See what you can get for the horses.' He looked at Nona. 'Do not leave his side.'

Nerva went straight to the merchant ships to find out what their options were.

'None sailing to Alexandria today,' said the third captain he approached.

'I see. Where are you headed?'

'Barcino.'

Not ideal, but they needed to go somewhere. 'Do you have room for three passengers?'

The captain looked him up and down suspiciously, taking in his expensive clothes. 'For the right price, I can make room.'

Nerva nodded. 'We can pay our way. We have a young girl travelling with us. I trust she will be safe aboard your ship?'

The captain smiled. 'All part of the service.'

After Nerva had paid the man three times what that service was worth, he went to buy some supplies for the voyage.

'What the hell are we going to do in Spain?' Marcus asked him as they prepared to board. He was carrying the wool blankets they had purchased from a merchant.

Nerva glanced back at Nona, who was chewing her lip behind him. 'Hopefully find a way to Egypt.'

The three of them were silent as they made their way up the gangplank, every step putting more distance between them and Rome.

Three days later they arrived in Barcino, where they were told they would need to take a ship to Carthago, then another to Alexandria. It would be a seven-day wait for the next voyage. Nerva raked his fingers through his hair when he heard that part. He did not like the idea of sitting idle for seven days.

The three of them wandered along the port until they spotted a ship preparing to leave with the tide. 'Where is this ship going?' Marcus asked its captain.

'Britannia.'

Nerva turned back at the word, and his heart stopped

beating in his chest for a moment. *Britannia*. That ship they were standing in front of would dock just a few hundred miles south of Hadrian's Wall. Why he let his thoughts go there, he had no idea.

'What is that look?' Marcus asked him.

'What look?'

Marcus shook his head. 'You know exactly what look.'

'You do have a look,' Nona agreed.

Nerva cast a disapproving glance in her direction. 'I am simply trying to figure out the most effective route to Egypt.'

'Well, I can tell you this,' Marcus said. 'It's not via Britannia.'

The captain spoke up. 'Londinium, to be exact.'

'Oh, he's not fussed about the details.' Marcus crossed his arms in front of his chest and continued to watch Nerva with an amused expression.

'What?'

'Nothing.'

Nerva tilted his head. 'I know what you are thinking, and you are wrong.' He looked down at Nona. 'I told you I would take you to Giza, and I will.'

Marcus just continued to watch him.

'Why are you looking at me like that?'

'Because the moment our captain friend here said he was headed to Britannia, your eyes went as wide as spoons.'

Nerva looked away. 'They did not.'

'They did,' Nona said.

Even the captain was nodding in agreement.

Nerva rolled his eyes. 'So?'

'So, after all this time, you still want to go to her,' Marcus replied.

'Who?' asked the captain.

'Brei,' Marcus and Nona replied in unison.

The captain's eyebrows came together. 'Who's Brei?'

'His one great love,' Nona said.

The captain pulled a face. 'Living in Londinium?'

'No, she is north of Hadrian's Wall,' Nerva said. 'Which is why, even if I wanted to, I could not go to her. In case you have forgotten, Rome's troops are now *south* of that wall.'

The captain still looked confused. 'The north is nothing but a graveyard now.'

'Do not worry yourself, as I have no intention of travelling there.'

The captain was still trying to piece the story together. 'You fell in love with a *barbarian?*'

'She is not a barbarian.' Nerva's tone was abrupt.

'He could not make it work,' Marcus continued. 'Too many complications, commitments, and responsibilities in Rome. Isn't that right, friend?' He squeezed Nerva's shoulder.

Nerva stared at him. 'I know what you are doing. I am not going to travel blindly through the highlands and, on the odd chance I find her, disrupt her life all over again.'

'You wouldn't live long enough to find her,' the captain mumbled.

Nerva gave a small nod of agreement. 'We are sailing to Cathargo in seven days.' As he spoke the words, he glanced up to the grey sky above them.

That enormous sky.

He turned away from the others as an icy breeze came off the water, whipping his clothes. 'We go to Giza as planned.'

CHAPTER 41

The snow was relentless, but it did not stop Brei from going outside. She loved nothing more than layering up in furs, her sleeping daughter tucked against her chest as she hunted with Drust and Lavena. Never mind the fact that they usually came back empty-handed thanks to Adhar making noises at the most inopportune moments. It had been fine when all she did was sleep, but now that she was a few months old, she seemed to have decided that sleep was for the weak.

The pregnancy had dragged on forever, made longer due to the fact that her father had not spoken to her after learning the news. But the two months following Adhar's arrival had flown by in a blur of sleeplessness and adorable first smiles. Her father's resolve to shun her and the child had lasted all of five seconds from the moment Keelia put the tiny baby under his nose. Now Seisyll was fine—as long as Brei never mentioned *him*.

It was mid-January when they finally got a day's reprieve from bad weather. A thick layer of snow covered every surface of their village, and every person living there was trying to jam months' worth of chores into one day.

Brei worked alongside her mother, dyeing leather that would be used for clothing. She cleared a work area with a shovel and laid a blanket over the icy ground so Alane and Adhar could watch her. Her sister was always happy to be the caregiver while Brei worked, an arrangement that suited everybody.

'Did Father leave early this morning? He was gone before I woke,' Alane asked.

Brei finished hanging a section of leather, then brushed her hair off her face with the back of her hand. Seisyll had gone to meet with the chief from a neighbouring tribe and would likely be gone a few days. 'He didn't leave early, you just slept late.'

Keelia looked up from her work, eyebrows raised. Brei looked between her and her sister, who was also staring at her. 'What?'

Alane looked down at Adhar.

'You replied to her in Latin,' Keelia said, resuming her work.

'No I didn't.'

'Yes you did,' Alane said, looking up at her. Adhar let out a squeal as though agreeing with her aunt.

Brei wiped her hands as she watched her daughter try to push herself higher off the blanket. 'Do I do that often?'

'Yes,' Keelia and Alane replied together.

'It puts your father in a mood every time,' Keelia added.

Brei picked up another section of leather. 'So strange. It's been months.'

Alane picked the baby up and sat her on her legs. 'And yet you think about *him* every day.'

Brei dunked the leather while glaring at her sister. 'How would you possibly know that?'

'Because you spend most of the day looking off down the hill, like you're waiting for him to appear.'

Brei flicked some water at her sister but stopped when

she realised she was getting her daughter also. 'Do you blame me? It wasn't that long ago that Romans came through those trees and killed half the people who lived here.'

'But you are not waiting for an army, are you? Just one man.'

Brei did not want to discuss Nerva, because every thought of him took up another section of her mind. Soon there would be nothing else in there. It was a good thing no one was brave enough to say his name aloud or she might spiral. 'She will bring up her milk if you keep bouncing her like that.'

Alane's legs stilled, and she looked at Brei with pity. 'I don't blame you, you know. It's hard to forget a man when you're reminded of him each time you look at your daughter.'

Adhar's eyes were the exact shade of grey his were. She also had his light hair and devious smile—and Brei's ears.

'*You have lovely ears,*' he had told her that day on the ship, fevered out of his mind.

Brei squeezed her eyes shut as her chest tightened.

'Are you all right?' Keelia asked, her tone gentle.

Brei opened her eyes and looked up at the sky, and the air returned to her lungs. 'I'm fine.'

∞

NERVA INSISTED that Marcus take Nona to Giza as planned. It was his foolish decision to return to Caledonia, his risk, possibly his biggest mistake. He did not want them to be a part of it.

It took ten days to sail to Londinium. When the ship docked, he went in search of a horse and supplies, then rode north to Eboracum. It was tempting to call upon people he knew there, but he could not risk news of his whereabouts getting back to Caracalla. The man had sole control over the Roman army now, and if he wanted information, he would get it.

After a day's rest, Nerva began the 130-mile journey to Hadrian's Wall. Despite all that thinking time, he struggled to come up with one logical reason why he was proceeding with his insane plan. Simply wanting to see her was not an adequate reason to disrupt her life again. Needing to know she was home and safe came close, but there were other ways to get that information without him travelling halfway around the world. His family was waiting for him in Giza, his mother had no idea where he was at all, and he was about to ride solo into hostile territory with only a few names and a marked-up map. It was not uncommon for tribes to move around, especially during times of conflict, which meant there was every chance he might die from cold or hunger before he ever found her—if he did not receive an arrow through the chest first.

And yet he did not turn back.

When he reached Hadrian's Wall, he gave the guards a fake name and told them he was a horse breeder in search of highland ponies. The men exchanged a doubtful look.

'You are going to round up wild horses by yourself?' one man asked.

'My job is to locate the herds and make a note of their numbers and condition.'

'You understand there are no troops past this point?'

'Yes.'

The guard shook his head and went to open the gate.

It was another one hundred miles to Antonine's wall, and while the days passed without incident, the air grew colder and his mind more fragmented. When the wall finally appeared in front of him, he stopped his horse and stared at it from afar, feeling a strange sadness creep over him. He remembered it alive with soldiers, and now there was nothing but ghosts.

He slept the night in the abandoned fort, and in the morning, he ate in silence while reading the graffiti on the eroding walls. When he finally passed through the gates, he stopped his horse on the other side and gave himself one more chance to turn around. No harm done at that point, only time wasted. Brei would never know he had been that close to her.

His gaze travelled up to the low-hanging clouds. Pressing his heels into his horse's sides, he continued on.

Nerva travelled north-east for two days before he realised he was being followed. He tried not to panic. The fact that he was still alive meant they probably wanted to know who he was before killing him. He kept riding, bracing for an arrow in the back. Only when his horse was too tired to continue did he stop, forced to acknowledge the presence. The feeling of being watched climbed his spine. He could sense them amid the trees, as he had done many times before. This time he did not have an army to intimidate, to fight for him, to tear roots from the ground until there was nothing left to hide behind. He had no armour or real power of any kind. In that moment, he was vulnerable.

Dismounting, Nerva slowly removed his sword and laid it on the ground in front of him. Then he did the same with the dagger strapped to his leg and the one hidden in his bag. Afterwards, he raised his hands and stepped back from them. His gaze swept the trees. 'I do not mean you any harm.' He spoke in their language. 'I am searching for a woman, a friend. Her name is Brei.'

Silence.

Nerva remained patient, not moving as he gave his watchers time to evaluate his story. Just as he was losing hope, a man emerged from behind a tree, holding a spear.

His clothing looked distinctly Maeatae. His thick brows were drawn together as he eyed Nerva with suspicion.

'Tell me again the name of the woman you search for.'

A few more men emerged from behind trees, watching him with interest.

'Her name is Brei. Her father is Seisyll, chief of one of the tribes. I am not even certain he is alive, or if she is, for that matter.'

Of course she was; he would have felt her death as though it were his own.

The man's expression darkened. 'And how do you know this woman?'

Nerva swallowed, wondering what answer to give. *We met on the battlefield, I took her from her home, sent men to destroy her village. I made her my prisoner, put her on a ship, locked her up, abandoned her, found her again, loved her.* Instead, all he said was 'We met during the war. I just want to make sure she is all right.' That was partly true. He also wanted to feast on the sight of her happy, back home where she belonged.

The man's fingers moved on the spear as he processed the new information. 'You are very foolish to set foot on our land, *Roman*.'

Nerva looked down at his weapons, dusted with fresh snow. 'Foolish. Desperate.'

The man continued to study him. 'Tell me your name.'

'Nerva Papias, formerly General Nerva Papias of the third Britannia legion.' It came out like a confession. He watched the man's eyes widen slightly and braced for that spear to pierce him.

'Tie him up,' the man said.

As two men came for Nerva, his gaze went to the weapons, barely visible through the snow now.

What had he done?

CHAPTER 42

Brei was sitting on the stump of an oak with Adhar on her knee, bouncing her daughter extra fast just to see her laugh. Whenever the baby squealed, her eyes shone a little brighter.

'Why do you get to have all the fun?' Alane called. She was crouched beside their goat, taking milk.

'Because I'm her mother,' Brei replied. She brought her nose to Adhar's, causing another fit of hysterical laughter. Brei could not help but laugh also. 'Was I this cute as a baby?' she asked her mother.

'No,' Keelia replied flatly. She was skinning a deer Brei had caught that morning. 'You were the most serious child I'd ever come across.'

Alane laughed. 'Adhar clearly gets her easy nature from her father.' The moment she said it, the smile fell from her face. 'Sorry.'

Brei rolled her eyes. 'It's fine. I won't fall apart at the mention of his name.' Not true. Sometimes just the thought of him knocked the wind from her lungs.

Alane was about to say something when Drust and Lavena burst through the trees, running up the hill towards them. 'They're back!' Drust shouted. Lavena tripped in the knee-deep snow, and Drust pulled her straight back up. He was too young to travel with the warriors, and Seisyll had convinced him the reason he had to remain behind was for the protection of the village. Drust took the responsibility very seriously for a boy of eight. The moment he had risen that morning, he had woken Lavena, and the pair had rushed off to climb the tallest tree they could find. They had kept watch all day.

'Good,' Alane said, straightening. 'Now maybe you can help me for a while.'

The children came to a stop, Lavena desperately trying to catch her breath. 'They have a *prisoner*,' she said. 'A man.'

The three women turned to look at them, and then Brei rose, slowly. Her eyes went to the clearing as she settled Adhar on her hip. 'What man?'

Drust's eyes were wild with excitement. 'A *Roman*.'

A cold sensation gripped Brei. There would have to be good reason for him to be venturing this far north in the dead of winter, and an extraordinary reason for her father to bring him into their village. Her heart was racing as she watched the clearing, her mind going to places it should not have ventured. The disappointment would crush her.

Alane walked over to join her, knowing better than to say anything. Keelia had not moved, her expression pensive.

'There,' Drust said, pointing down the hill.

A group of men emerged onto the snowy plain below. She recognised her father, and the four warriors who had travelled with him. One of the men led a horse she did not recognise. In the middle of the group walked a bearded man, hands bound behind his back. He was not a soldier, but even at that distance she could tell his clothes were distinctly Roman. Brei took a few steps forwards, hands clammy as she tried to focus harder on him. The prisoner's gaze travelled up the hill, and she felt the moment it landed on her. A warm sensation spread though her. He was too far away to see his face properly, but she knew it was Nerva.

He stopped walking, and his stance changed. She could tell he recognised her also, felt the same draw that she did. All the men stopped too, looking up the hill to see what held his attention.

'Nerva.' His name came out choked, but she felt instant relief at finally saying it aloud after months of swallowing it down.

Alane frowned. 'What?' She brought her hand to her brow, as though that would improve her vision somehow. 'Is that—'

Brei passed Adhar to her sister before she had a chance to ask the question. She needed to run, and it was not safe with a baby in her arms. She started down the hill towards him.

'Where's she going?' Drust asked his mother.

Brei's feet sank deep into the snow, slowing her down, but she did not look away from him the entire time for fear she was hallucinating. Her pace quickened, her heavy breaths sending puffs of steam into the frigid air. Nerva tried to move forwards but was abruptly stopped with a harsh jerk on his arm. They all stood watching her approach. She could feel her father's eyes on her but could not tear her gaze away from Nerva long enough to look at him.

'Nerva!' His name was out there again, the sound warming her aching ears and melting the snow between them. She was just ten feet from him, oblivious to everything else, every disapproving stare.

*Slam*.

She gasped when she hit a hard chest and looked up to see her father glaring down at her.

'What are you doing?' he asked.

She shook her head. He was blocking her view of him which panicked her. *Move*, she wanted to scream at him. 'Please.' One word that seemed to shock her father.

'Is he who he says he is?'

She tried to look around him, but he continued to block her with his body. 'It's Nerva.' She said it like his name would explain everything.

Seisyll drew a long breath and finally stepped aside. To Brei's relief, Nerva was still standing there, his face pale and lips blue from the cold. Those grey eyes watched her with the same intensity they always had.

'What are you doing here?' she asked, unsure of what else to say.

The faintest of smiles tugged at his lips, and he shook his head, searching for an answer. 'You.'

She waded towards him, the last few steps closer to leaps. Then he was in front of her. She threw herself at him, wrapping him with her arms and legs. With his hands tied, all he could do was bear the weight of her in his fatigued state and bury his face in her.

The men looked between each other, then to Seisyll.

'I love you too,' Nerva whispered into her damp hair. 'I should have told you that before you boarded.'

Brei pressed her eyes shut, holding him tighter, if that was possible. She did not care who was looking as her skin soaked up the warmth of Nerva's words.

'Untie him,' her father said, his tone resigned.

Nerva jolted as the rope was cut from his wrists. Then his hands were free and his arms went around her. The strength of his embrace made her suck in a breath.

'Geta is dead,' he whispered.

She opened her eyes but did not move.

'Caracalla ordered *damnatio memoriae*.'

She blinked. 'Damnation of his memory.'

'It will be as though he never existed.'

Brei let go of him, and he lowered her to the ground but kept his arms around her. The men continued to watch on with disapproving expressions. 'And I suppose you are part of that memory.'

He nodded. 'I was headed to Giza.'

Her mouth twitched. 'This seems a little out of the way.'

Nerva's eyes drank her in. 'You are worth the detour.'

Seisyll cleared his throat. 'Go inside.' He gestured for them to start walking. 'We will talk then.'

Nerva finally let go of her, and she took his icy hand between hers. The rest of her family stood with worried expressions on top of the hill. Nerva was about to discover that he had a daughter.

The group walked in silence. Every few paces, Nerva's thumb rubbed the back of her hand, as though reassuring her it would be all right. He should have been fearing for his life, not offering her courage. The raw joy that had surged through her a moment ago was compacting into a hard ball of fear. She was about to reveal a secret she had thought would die with her.

The walk up the hill seemed eternal. About halfway up, Brei heard Adhar's familiar squeals. She was feeling playful. Brei glanced up at Nerva. His face was serious as he took in the village, but it softened when he looked down at her. She let go of his hand as her family came forwards to meet them. Alane still had Adhar on her hip, and Keelia's hands were planted firmly on the shoulders of Drust and Lavena, holding them in place. She let go to embrace Nerva, but when Seisyll cleared his throat, she stepped back.

'It is good to see you safe and well,' Nerva said to her. His eyes went to Lavena. 'And you.'

Lavena smiled, then looked at Drust. 'He was the nice one,' she whispered.

'I see you've met my husband,' Keelia said.

Brei's father stood with his arms crossed and bushy brows pulled together in a deep scowl.

'Yes. He was kind enough to escort me here.' Nerva rubbed his wrists where the rope had scratched his skin raw.

'He's lucky it was me who found him,' Seisyll said, 'or he'd be just another Roman corpse rotting beneath the trees.'

Nerva nodded a greeting at Alane. 'Nice to see you again under *slightly* less hostile circumstances.'

Alane smiled weakly, looking nervously down at Adhar, then at Drust. She cleared her throat. 'That's my son, Drust.'

Nerva gave another nod in his direction. 'I saw you running ahead of us. You are even faster than Brei described.'

The boy pushed out his chest and grinned at Lavena.

Nerva's gaze fell to Adhar. 'Is this your little sister?'

Drust looked up at his mother, and a painful silence followed. Nerva looked around, confused by people's reaction to his question. Brei opened her mouth to speak, but nothing came out.

'Right,' Keelia said, walking over and taking her husband by the arm. 'All of you inside before you freeze. Quickly now.'

Seisyll glanced at Nerva, a warning in his eyes, before reluctantly following after his wife. The rest of the men dispersed also, their hard gazes on Nerva as they left.

'Ah, come on you two,' Alane said, grabbing Drust by the arm. 'I need your help inside.' As she went to leave, she realised she was still holding Adhar. She handed the baby to Brei, and Adhar nestled contently into her mother's shoulder.

Nerva did not take his eyes off the infant.

'This is Adhar. She's...' The words stuck for a moment, and Brei coughed. 'She's your daughter.'

Nerva continued to stare at the baby with an expression Brei did not recognise. It was difficult to read him with all that facial hair. The only sound was the hushed conversation drifting out from the huts.

Brei could not take the silence any longer. 'Please say something.'

Nerva's gaze travelled up to meet hers. 'She has your ears.'

Brei blinked with relief. 'She does.'

Nerva swallowed, his weight shifting from one foot to the other. 'Can I hold her?'

Warmth flooded her. She had expected him to be angry, but if there was one person in the world who would understand, it was him. 'Of course.' She held the baby out for him to take. He looked like he had held her every day of her life, perching her on his forearm and shifting the woollen blanket back just enough to see her face properly. They studied one another for a moment, and then Nerva's mouth widened into a grin. Just when Brei thought her heart could not get any fuller, Adhar smiled back at him.

'Look how easily Maeatae women fall for your charm.'

Nerva drew Adhar close to his chest, cradling her head in his giant hand. Brei felt the heat of tears on her cheeks and brushed them aside.

'You are not angry, then?' she asked.

He looked at her. 'I do not have the right to be angry. I told you to go. Knowing about the child would have only hardened my resolve.'

She nodded. 'I didn't know until after...' After they had broken each other's hearts. She attempted a smile. 'Now what?'

He reached out a hand and ran his finger down her cheek. 'I have no idea.'

'I can't believe you're here, and that my father didn't kill you on sight.' She smiled, but it faded quickly. 'How am I supposed to let you go? How will you walk away?'

His expression turned serious. 'I will not.' He drew a breath and pressed his lips to the blanket covering his daughter's head. 'I will not,' he said again. He pulled Brei to him, holding them both close.

'What about your family?' Brei asked, her chest heavy. 'What about Rome?'

Nerva kissed the top of her head and exhaled into her hair. 'You and Adhar are my family too.' He pulled back to look at her. 'Rome belongs to Caracalla now. I cannot return while he is alive.'

She kissed his chest repeatedly, fighting back tears. 'I promise you, the day he dies, I will take you back to Rome myself.'

Nerva looked out at the white-capped mountains, then back at his daughter. 'Adhar. What does it mean?'

Brei turned her face up to him. 'It means *sky*.'

His hand went into her hair, pulling her closer. 'As ridiculous as this love story is, as illogical, improbable, as completely inconceivable, I love you anyway. What other woman ever stood a chance against you?' He brushed his nose over hers. 'Look at this precious gift the gods have bestowed. We should take it as a sign.'

'A sign of what?'

'That the hate has passed and the war is over. I know now that I was not sent to Caledonia to destroy you. I was sent here to find you.'

Brei pushed herself up on her toes and kissed him, long and deep. He was right. Their fight was over.

'Inside,' Keelia called from the doorway of the hut. 'Let's get Nerva warmed up and fed before he falls down.'

Brei moved back but kept an arm around him. 'It wouldn't be the first time I've dragged you to safety.'

Nerva draped an arm over her shoulders, the weight of it making her feel untouchable. The three of them headed to the hut just as snow began to fall. Brei turned her face up, enjoying the sting of snowflakes on her skin. Nerva's arm tightened around her, and he brought his lips to her ear.

'How much work will it be to win your father over?'

She smiled up at him. 'He's not as easily charmed as the women.'

'I figured as much when he tied me up and marched me through the mountains on foot, despite the perfectly good horse I arrived on.'

Brei suppressed a smile. 'You're not afraid of a bit of hard work, are you?'

'Would I be here with you if I were?' His eyes shone at her.

Brei took Adhar from him. 'In you go, General.'

Nerva gave her a tired wink, then entered the hut.

# EPILOGUE

Seisyll had warned him it would not be an easy life, but Nerva found highland living far easier than the previous life he had grown to resent. He found satisfaction in the simple existence, the physical work, the routine. There were no mind games around the dinner table or constant looking over his shoulder, only honest interactions, and eventually, acceptance. For five years he lived happily among the Maeatae.

Another child came along, a boy they named Rufus in memory of his father. They both taught the children to speak, read, and write in two languages, to ride a horse, fight, hunt, fish, and love their mother as fiercely as he did.

He wrote letters to his sisters, filling pages and pages so they would not miss out on knowing his children. The letters to his mother were much shorter but frequent enough to put her mind at ease. He never told her where he was, but he knew she was smart enough to figure it out. As much as it hurt him not to hear from his family, he would not risk any harm coming to Brei, the children, or the tribe he had grown to love.

In April that year, Nerva was outside helping Rufus

make a bow when three men appeared through the clearing on horseback. One of the men was Marcus Furnia.

'Who that?' Rufus asked.

A wide grin spread across Nerva's face. 'An old friend of mine.'

Once he had assured everyone in the village that Marcus was a trusted friend, the pair went off to talk in private.

'Gods, look at you.' Marcus said. 'Please tell me you are not covered in tattoos.'

Nerva laughed, clapping him on the back before turning to him. 'You look good with a beard.'

Marcus laughed and looked around. 'As do you. Where's your lovely wife?'

'Hunting with Adhar.'

Marcus's amused gaze returned to him. 'Of course she is.'

Nerva looked him over, realising how much he had missed his friend. 'Want to tell me what you are doing here?'

Marcus's expression suggested whatever he was about to say was big news. 'I wanted to tell you this in person.'

Nerva waited, not moving.

'Caracalla is dead.' He paused, giving Nerva a chance to absorb it.

'How?'

'Killed by one of his own soldiers, on his way back from taking a piss.'

Nerva linked his hands on top of his head, exhaling. 'A fitting end.'

Marcus chuckled, then turned serious again. 'Five years I've been drifting about. Now I'm finally going home.'

'What of Cordius?'

'Emperor Macrinus wasn't a fan. Sent him to Africa. Don't think he'll be back in Rome any time soon.'

Brei had returned from hunting and stopped in front of them. A dead deer was draped over the horse's shoulders. 'Marcus?'

They both turned to look at her, and the smile fell from her face.

Brei sat in silence as they broke the news. Afterwards, Keelia took Marcus away to eat while Brei and Nerva sat processing the news.

'You have given me five years. Now it's time to return to Rome.'

'I am not going to leave you.'

'Who said anything about leaving me? We're a family. We go where you go.' She reached out and took his hand. 'I told you that the day that man died, I'd take you back there myself.'

Every day Nerva fell a little harder for her. He looked over to where Adhar and Rufus were playing with the bow. 'You think they are up for the journey?'

'Are you joking? Ever since our Adhar learned where you're from, she's talked about going to Rome to stay in the palace you were raised in.'

'It is hardly a palace.'

'Look around you. This is all they've ever known.' She squeezed his hand. 'They should know something of the world you come from.'

Nerva glanced in the direction of the hut. 'And what of your family?'

'They'll miss us, but they'll understand.'

And so the decision was made.

One month later, the family travelled to Eboracum with Marcus. Nerva no longer had to hide his identity, his past, or his wealth, which made everything simpler. While it was by no means an easy journey with children aged five and three, no one fell ill. They finally arrived in Ostia Antica at the beginning of summer.

From the port they made their way to the city on horseback—a city now ruled by Emperor Macrinus. They went straight to the house. Nerva knew his mother had returned to live there but did not know what kind of reception they would get. He entered the domus with a sense of nostalgia, panicking the servants, who had not known to expect him. They waited in the atrium, the children looking about in awe at the overpriced art and expensive furnishings.

'Are you a king?' Adhar asked.

Nerva bent and picked her up, kissing her nose. 'No, my love, just a man.'

'Your father is not *just a man*' came Aquila's voice.

Nerva turned to the doors that opened out to the garden and saw his mother standing there. While she had aged since the last time he had seen her, she still had that famous grace and wore the same superior expression.

'He is a patrician of Rome,' she continued, 'a former senator, and a celebrated legatus legionis. A man of noble birth is a king of sorts.'

'Hello, Mother.' He watched the emotion play out on her face before she caught herself.

'You came home.'

He nodded, then walked over to kiss her with Adhar still in his arms. Aquila turned her attention to the girl, her expression guarded.

'And who is this?'

'This is our daughter, Adhar.' He then turned to the others. Rufus was wrapped around Brei's leg. 'That is our son, Rufus. And you remember Brei.'

Aquila's expression was hard as she looked Brei up and down, but when her gaze fell to the boy, it softened a little. 'Of course.'

Nerva looked around, feeling as though his mother was reaching her limit so far as polite conversation was concerned. He did not want the children to be around when she turned. 'Well, we just wanted to see you on our way through.'

Aquila's gaze snapped to him. 'On your way through to where?'

Nerva cleared his throat. 'We thought we might stay in Antium.'

'Antium?' Aquila struggled to maintain her composure. 'Do not be foolish. This is your home. You will all stay here for as long as you please.' She waved in Brei's direction. 'Come along. Refreshments will be served in the garden.'

Adhar wriggled free of Nerva's arms and went to collect her brother, dragging him in the direction of the garden.

'Slowly,' Brei said.

Aquila followed them outside. 'You are not to touch any of the plants,' she called to their backs.

Nerva looked at his wife, who gave him a reassuring smile.

∼

AQUILA WOULD NEVER ADMIT IT, but Nerva could tell she enjoyed the company of the children during those weeks. She was always spending time with them, showing them things, and even had her new seamstress fit them for clothes. Brei did not object, as she knew Aquila was bonding with them the only way she knew how. As if Nerva needed more reasons to love her.

His mother wanted to throw a dinner party to announce his return, but Nerva quickly shut the idea down. He met up with a handful of friends in private.

Two weeks later, they headed to Antium. Nerva had sent word to his sisters from Eboracum announcing his return and inviting them to join his family at the villa if they were able. When they arrived at the coast in the late afternoon in the middle of June, they were greeted by the entire clan of mismatched family: Mila, Remus, and the children; Dulcia and Nero with their three daughters; Felix, Albaus, Tertia, and Nona. He hugged his sisters for the longest time, made jokes with the men, and introduced the children. By evening, they were playing together as if they had been friends their entire lives. It was a meeting of different worlds, one that should never have worked, and yet it did.

'I could get used to this,' Felix said at the end of their first meal together. He lay back and clapped two hands over his stomach.

'I would prefer you not get used to this,' Dulcia said, passing the tray of fruit tarts to her husband. 'I have enough trouble keeping you all fed.'

Nero kissed her cheek as he took the tray from her. 'We're already spoiled by your culinary skills.'

Mila looked across at her sister. 'Perhaps if you did not insist on doing all the cooking by yourself, we *could* eat like this every day.'

'We've offered to employ a cook,' Remus said, taking the tray from Nero, who stole one more tart before letting go.

Dulcia snatched the second tart from Nero's hand and took a bite. 'You will soon complain about the decline in quality if we outsource. Besides, you know I love it.'

'I hope you will all stay for the summer,' Nerva said as he took the tray from Remus, passing it to Brei.

Nona and Asha were keeping the children occupied in another room. Occasionally, their laughter drifted through the house.

'How long will you be staying?' Mila asked, settling herself against Remus.

'That is up to Brei. I am surprised she has lasted this

long.'

Brei made a face at him. 'This visit has been slightly nicer than the last.'

'I imagine *not* coming via the Graecostadium makes a difference,' Felix said.

Nero swallowed his food before speaking. 'I'm sure Gallus would have come to the rescue once more.'

Dulcia laughed. 'Oh, yes. The man is a true guardian angel.'

'I went and saw him,' Brei said.

Everyone looked at her, and Nerva just shook his head.

'Did he offer you a job?' Remus asked.

Everyone laughed, and Nerva ladled some more wine into Brei's cup before refilling his own. 'He has always had a soft spot for you.'

'Or perhaps a *hard* spot,' Felix said.

Everyone groaned, and Remus plucked a grape off the tray to throw at his head.

'Moving on to more important matters,' Mila said, turning her attention back to Nerva. 'Are you going to keep the beard?' Her nose scrunched slightly as she asked the question.

Nerva ran a hand over the trimmed growth. 'Brei likes it.'

'No I don't.'

Laughter filled the room once more.

Nero reached for his drink. 'If he shaves, he might be mistaken for one of Rome's nobility.'

'We could not have that,' Nerva said.

Dulcia watched him for a moment. 'Do you miss it? Any of it?'

Nerva let out a breath. 'The double standards, deceit, and endless dinner parties with men who could stab you in the back at any moment? No.' He shook his head. 'I do not miss any of it.'

Brei reached out and took his hand. 'I really hope you will all stay a few months. Nerva deserves to have his family around him after enduring mine for so long.'

'Only you could win over a Maeatae chief after getting his daughter pregnant,' Mila said.

Nerva nodded. 'I shall take that as a compliment.'

'I do not think it was meant as one,' Felix said, sitting up. He looked up at Albaus, who was beside him. 'What do you think? Could you bear living in this enormous villa like a king for a few months?' His hand went to his chest. 'I, for one, am prepared to make the sacrifice for the good of others.'

Albaus grunted and looked over at Mila, who smiled into her wine.

'Nowadays we can run our business from anywhere,' Remus said.

Nero reached for another tart. 'You'd better warn the cooks that Dulcia may hover in the kitchen.'

Dulcia pointed to the tart in his hand. 'There's a reason they taste so good.'

Nerva settled back to listen to the banter. He had missed it more than he realised.

Just as he got comfortable, Asha and the twins entered the room.

'They are all asleep,' Asha announced.

'Where is Nona?' Mila asked, stifling a yawn.

Asha tilted her head. 'They are *all* asleep.'

Mila straightened. 'I see. And where are you going?'

'Down to the water,' Caius replied.

'There's going to be a sea battle,' Atilius added.

Brei shot up out of her seat. 'I'm coming with you.'

Nerva laughed. 'You are as bad as the children.'

Mila and Nero stood also, then Felix. Dulcia sighed and looked at Remus, who wore a matching resigned expression. 'We might as well all go, try to walk off the food.'

Nero offered her his hand, letting out an exaggerated groan as he pulled her up. 'You could definitely do with the walk.'

Felix shoved him as he passed by. 'Do not come knocking on my door when you are banished from your room tonight. My days of sleeping with you are over.'

They descended the steps carved into the cliff face and walked down to the glistening black ocean. No one dared to enter the water under darkness. The sand was illuminated by the full moon that provided just enough light for the dramatic battle. Nerva went and sat on the grassy slope. He was content watching and letting his mind wander. He had no idea where he would be five years from then, or even one year, only that it would be a much happier path than the one his parents had carved out for him.

Having exerted herself, Brei made her way up the beach to where he was sitting with his legs up, arms resting on his knees. She collapsed in a sweaty mess beside him, and Nerva's arm went around her, drawing her close.

'You really do not mind staying here for the summer with these crazy people?'

She burrowed against him. 'In case you haven't noticed, I fit right in.'

Her breath smelled of fruit tarts. 'I feel bad keeping you from your home.'

She turned her head to kiss his chest. 'Home is not a place, it's a feeling. My home is wherever you and the children are.'

Nerva looked up at the sky, alive with a thousand stars. 'Look at that.'

Brei looked up as war raged on below them. 'That is one big and beautiful sky.'

He pressed his lips to the top of her head. 'Yes, one enormous sky.'

## AUTHOR'S NOTE

I thought it was important to point out that all the characters in this story are fictional, with the exception of Emperor Septimius Severus and his sons Caracalla and Geta. It's also worth mentioning that the third Britannia legion was made up to suit the needs of the story. That said, the challenges the soldiers faced reflect those outlined in Simon Elliott's book *Septimius Severus in Scotland*.

The death toll for Severus's campaign remains unknown. While Cassius Dio makes reference to the entire 50,000-strong army being wiped out, we know this to be an exaggeration. What historians do know is that the death toll was very high on both sides. The Caledonii and Maeatae tribes suffered severe depopulation in the region, something which took many generations to overcome.

Some modern phrases were used in instances where I felt the reader would not understand some words in a particular context. An example of this is influenza, a term that did not exist back then. The titles used to represent ranks within the army are another example. I used addresses similar to those in Hollywood depictions, such as general and commander. The last thing I wanted was readers feeling lost or coming out of the story to google terminology.

Finally, I also chose to include the Roman salute despite there being no definitive evidence that it was used by soldiers. Sometimes the best we have is an educated guess.

I truly hope you enjoyed this blend of dark history and romance.

ACKNOWLEDGMENTS

I would like to express my gratitude to the many people who contributed to this book. My biggest thanks always goes to my readers. Without you guys, I wouldn't get to do what I love. Next, a huge thank you to my rock star husband who supports and encourages me even though my writing takes time away from him. I love you to bits. A big thank you to Joanna Walsh for your ongoing support. A shout-out to my beta readers, who each brought a unique perspective, and to Steve Frost, who checked the historical components. Thank you to Kristin and the team at Hot Tree Editing for polishing the manuscript into something beautiful, and to my proofreader, Rebecca Fletcher, for catching everything I missed. A round of applause for my cover designer, Domi, from Inspired Cover Designs, for yet another gorgeous cover. And finally, a huge thank you to my Launch Team for your encouragement, honest reviews, and being the final set of eyes on my work. You guys are amazing.

ALSO BY TANYA BIRD

You can find a complete list of published works at
tanyabird.com/books

Printed in Great Britain
by Amazon